Love
IN THE
NUMBERS

S. R. MULLINS

Love in the Numbers
Copyright © 2018 S. R. Mullins. All Rights Reserved

Perfect Bound
Marketing + Press

Peoria, Arizona
www.PerfectBoundMarketing.press

Published in the United States of America

Paperback ISBN: 978-1-939614-95-7
E-book ISBN: 978-1-939614-91-9

For permissions contact: srmullinsauthor@yahoo.com

TABLE OF CONTENTS

CHAPTER ONE
Lucy

Something felt different about this morning. I can't really put my finger on it but there was something … off.

Maybe it was the changing of the seasons that bring crisp fall mornings here in the Inland Northwest. We have long left summer behind and are heading toward the long winter that will soon blanket this area with heavy snowfall. It's only late October, but the temperatures are already in the 20s at night and reach just around the 50s at the heat of the day. Halloween is at the end of next week and hopefully that won't be the first day of snow this year.

Or maybe it is just my time of the month. I do seem to get a little more emotional when mother nature plans a visit.

Or maybe it's the possible changes at work.

Today the accounting firm I work for, Murphy and Glass, is making a big announcement at our fourth-quarter meeting. They have kept all the details a secret from the staff, but the gossip around the water cooler is that our owner, Richard Glass, is retiring and we were getting a new CEO.

Normally, work doesn't seep into my personal life like this. I try to keep my work from coming home with me. My clients know I am there for them whenever they need me, but I don't bond with my coworkers. I found it was best this way after the issue I had with my last boyfriend and last job.

But I'm a typical Pisces, artsy and creative, I wear my heart on my sleeve and take everything personally. I give my whole heart to the things I do, and it became necessary for me to close my personal life off after 'He Who Shall Not Be Named.' It's just better this way, or so I tell myself.

So, on this Wednesday morning, here I stand looking into the mirror in my apartment in Coeur d'Alene, Idaho and wishing I could control the little butterflies that are shifting in my belly. I rub at my stomach absentmindedly hoping to get them to ease just a little. I took a little extra time getting ready this morning and curled my shoulder-length, dirty blonde hair, finishing it in a half-up style. My make-up is minimal as always. I don't have the talent for make-up. I have tried to watch those online tutorials to make cheeks look as razor sharp as Kim Kardashian's, but I end up looking like an overly painted clown. Not a good look.

My cell phone alarm goes off on the counter, alerting me it is time to leave for work. I take one last deep breath and gather my things.

I lucked out at the placement of my apartment. My best friend Callie's cousin, Melissa, had purchased this apartment in the Riverstone complex a few months before she met her husband Patrick. They are now living in Portland but let me rent it for way cheaper than they should. They call it an investment property, but I think they just like knowing the person who lives there and that I will take good care of the place. No drunken ragers for this lady. I prefer my nights to be filled with books rather than beers.

The Riverstone area where I live reminds me of an old downtown. There are several shop-lined streets with apartments and office spaces on the upper floors. At the bookends of the streets is a movie theatre and a stylish six-story office building. We have several great restaurants, a coffee shop, bookstore and numerous adorable little boutiques, ranging from women's clothing to local Idaho crafts. One of those boutiques is owned by Callie.

Callie and I met in college. We were assigned to be roommates freshman year at University of Texas, in Austin. We bonded the first day over a love of musicals and books, especially Harry Potter, and never looked back. She is nice enough to keep me clothed in the latest fashions. Or at least that is what she tells me. Sometimes I don't believe her.

Today I am wearing one of the outfits Callie swears looks great on me. I am a sucker for anything and everything blue. I'm wearing a simple navy-blue blazer with a flared light brown skirt and dark leather boots. We wear a lot of boots during the fall and winter in Idaho. As soon as the first leaves of the season start to fall, the boots and the leggings magically appear.

I head down the three flights of stairs toward the parking garage where my light-blue Volkswagen Jetta is waiting. It was a splurge when I bought it brand new last summer, but it had always been a dream of mine to own one and be the first person to call it theirs. My job has been good to me financially and since I work at an accounting firm, I have learned the proper way to handle my money. So, after paying off my student loans and saving enough to pay for it in full, I took the leap. Best decision I have ever made. I love my little blue bird!

I open the door to enter the garage and turn the corner to the left toward my car, and I hit a hard wall of muscular chest and the iced coffee that muscular chest was carrying. It takes me a second to realize what has happened.

The cold coffee is seeping through my clothes and I start to shiver. I drop my purse and start to unbutton and peel the jacket off hoping to get the worst of the cold wetness away from my skin.

"I'm so sorry. I was on my phone and not..." The deep voice starts but cuts off without finishing.

I look into the face of the owner of that muscular chest and I am instantly transfixed by the most beautiful icy-blue eyes. They are unlike any I have ever seen before. They seem to be changing the longer I am looking into them, becoming darker and even more alluring.

He is the most handsome man I have ever seen. He must be at least a foot taller than my 5'2", with a high-sculpted chin and wide, strong nose. His dark brown beard is thick but well trimmed. His dark hair is slicked back away from his handsome face. It's the kind of hair that is too long on the top and short on the sides, but still long enough to get your fingers tangled in.

My heart starts to go a mile a minute the longer I stare at him. His mouth starts to move, and my eyes are drawn to his lips. Holy crap, the things that man could do to me with those lips.

WAIT. His lips are moving… is he talking to me?

I shake myself out of my lustful haze and try to focus on what he is saying.

"What?" I ask.

He chuckles and says again. "I'm sorry I spilled my coffee on you. I was on my phone and rudely not paying attention to where I was going."

I clear my throat and respond trying to sound light and breezy. "That's OK. Accidents happen." I fail miserably on the breezy part, mostly sounding like someone who just ran a marathon.

He smiles down at me. "Well, thank you for your forgiveness but I insist on paying to have your clothes dry cleaned." He reaches into his pocket and pulls out a business card. "Here is my card. I'm Mason."

"Lucy." I take the card and shake his out-stretched hand. There is a spark when our hands meet, and his eyes widen a little, most likely mirroring my own.

He keeps our hands intertwined for a long moment. "Nice to meet you Lucy. I hope the next time we meet will be under better circumstances." He drops my hand and turns toward the elevator.

I watch him walk away and smile to myself at the odd encounter. I probably should have been less forgiving of someone who spilled the contents of a venti iced coffee on my chest, but I just couldn't. Damn handsome men, and their way of making women lose all focus.

I quickly return to my apartment, dump my purse, keys and the business card on the kitchen counter and run to change into a non-coffee covered outfit. It doesn't take me too long to clean myself up and change into clean clothes.

As I go to leave for the second time this morning, my curiosity gets the best of me. I reach for the card he gave me, wanting to see his name and feel even a little of our connection again.

Mason James Glass, CEO
Murphy and Glass Accounting

Oh shit!

CHAPTER TWO
Lucy

I had planned on stopping for breakfast at Bakery by the Lake before work this morning and had left a few minutes early to accommodate for the time in line. But after running into Mason, that plan is ruined. Stale bagels and tea from the breakroom it is.

The offices of Murphy and Glass are located on the fourth floor of a modern high-rise in downtown Coeur d'Alene overlooking McEwen Park. I'm lucky enough to be a vice president of accounting and get a lovely view of the park and a small section of Lake Coeur d'Alene.

Jacob Murphy and Richard Glass started their company together right after they both graduated from Gonzaga University back in the late 1970s. Sadly, Mr. Murphy died of cancer about 10 years ago, but his name and memory are still a part of the everyday operations. His widow, Marie Ann, still attends regular meetings and is very much a part of the culture of our office.

So, it looks like the rumor mill had it right. Mr. Glass will be retiring and passing the company on.

As I enter the office, Mrs. Bell our receptionist greets me with a "Good morning." I smile politely and greet her with a similar good morning. She is an older lady of about 65 with short white hair that spikes up in the back. Some people would call this a 'I need to speak to the manager' haircut. She has always been very fake-friendly toward me and is never outwardly rude. But she likes to micro-manage me. She insists on knowing every detail of my schedule including where I am going and when I will return. It can get a little suffocating at times since she is not my boss.

I gather my breakfast from the breakroom, saying hello to the few coworkers I see and head to my office. I power up my computer and sign in to my emails. I like to stay on top of emails as much as possible. I believe there are two types of people in this world … the ones with 1,000 unread emails and those with none. I am the latter. This morning I am lucky enough to be greeted with only six new emails. Three are from clients with weekly reports, two from Mrs. Bell with questions pertaining to my meetings next week and one from Mr. Glass with details on our quarterly meeting at 9 a.m. today. I skip the others and click on the one from Mr. Glass, my curiosity getting the better of me.

Dear Staff,

A reminder to please join me in the conference room at 9 a.m. for our quarterly meeting.

We will be discussing the upcoming fourth quarter, strategies for next year's upcoming tax season, and some new investment possibilities.

We will also be discussing new changes to our office staff.

Hope to see you all there.

Richard Glass

As dictated to Mrs. Candice Bell

Changes to our office staff, that is a little bit of an understatement given the business card that is currently resting in my purse. I think back to my encounter with Mason this morning and start to day dream about his icy blue eyes. Oh, and those bow shaped lips. Oh, and his strong arms. And even though I didn't get a good look at his hands, I have a feeling that they would feel amazing roaming over my body.

"Ms. Harvey… Ms. Harvey?" Candice's voice breaks me of my lusty thoughts.

I pick up the phone and respond to her page. "Yes?"

"I wanted to see if you had seen my email? You have not responded back yet."

Insert eye roll here. "Yes, I did see your emails. I am still waiting to hear back from the client on the exact specifics of those meetings. I will let you know when I have more information."

"Oh, well please reply with that information in an email." She disconnects the line before I can reply.

Okay, so it is going to be one of those days.

I have about an hour before the quarterly meeting, so I decide to put myself on Do Not Disturb and bust out some work. Candice, or as she makes us call her, Mrs. Bell, cannot IM or intercom me so I find that on days like this when she is on the war path, it is best to do this so I can get my essential tasks done. You would think that a vice president of a company would not fear the receptionist but when it comes to her, I have not been able to figure out how to get out from underneath her thumb. I have wanted to bring it up in my annual review the past three years but have never found the courage. I don't want to make waves, and complaining about a beloved employee is not the story I want going about. She has been with the company since it started and I'm sure if she really was a problem it would have been dealt with long ago. I do take most things personally.

I spend most of the time in the office with the door closed. It's not that I don't like my coworkers, I would rather keep them as just coworkers. Plus, I want my work to be the thing people talk about, not gossip and nonsense. I work very hard and I want that to be how people see me.

I turn up some '40s Jazz and get to work entering information into the multiple spreadsheets I have for each of my clients.

My role here at the firm is to be the dedicated accountant for 15 of our small to midsized clients. I handle everything from balancing books and petty cash to yearly sales goals. I also help with financial business decisions and answer their tax questions. Luckily, our tax department does all the hard work for that, but I still must know what is happening on that front to advise my clients.

The hour passes quickly and when my Outlook alert reminds me of our meeting, I am pleased with the amount of work I have accomplished. Maybe I will take an extra-long lunch and go for a drive around the lake, take a little time to clear my head, and enjoy the bit of sunshine we have been blessed with today. With the changing leaves, it makes for a beautiful drive.

I'm surprised to see the conference room is already full and I am the last to arrive. Even Mr. Glass is seated in his place at the head of the table and is chatting away with Luke Brown, our president of accounting, my actual boss and direct supervisor. Everyone must be very excited to hear the news. I shuffle quickly to my assigned seat near the other members of my team. When Mr. Glass sees that I am settled, he begins.

"Great. Everyone is here," Mr. Glass begins. Candice turns and shoots me a glare for my tardiness. "Thank you all for joining me today. Let's get started."

Mr. Glass launches into his topics and the meeting is off and running. I take notes as Mr. Glass speaks on what his goals are for the final quarter of the year and how proud he is of the work we have done in the summer months.

Next, each of the presidents of accounting, investing and tax prep give a presentation on their departments' goals and successes. Luke tells the group about a client compliment I received during his section and I blush with embarrassment. My blonde hair and freckles lend themselves easily to the shades of red that can stain my cheeks. Callie always tells me that my emotions play across my face and I can't hide anything.

The rest of the meeting is dull and seems to drag on. With

the information that I know, I want the news of the sexy new CEO to be announced. A sexy CEO who is very much off limits. I've been burned once before by dating a coworker and I will not do that again.

Clay and I worked together across the state line in Spokane, Washington. It was my first job out of college and I thought I had hit the mother load. A dream job working for a great company and an awesome boyfriend. The company did not have a rule about co-workers but thanks to Clay and all the drama he brought into the office, they had one by the time I was "asked" to leave. Clay had been too "valuable" to lose so they "suggested" I move on to a "better opportunity." I know that's a lot of quotations but as they were firing me that day, I swear I could see them aching to add those quotations to their comments. So the rule of "no dating a coworker" became necessary.

Well past the two-hour mark into the meeting, after the last presentation has been given, Mr. Glass stands and thanks everyone for coming.

We all start to leave but over the chatter Mr. Glass says, "Oh, will all the vice presidents stay for a minute?"

I sit back in my chair as the room clears out, leaving a dozen of us including Candice, in the conference room.

"Mr. Glass, would you like me to take notes for this section as well?" Candice asks from her chair at his left side.

"No, you will not be needed for this. You may return to the front desk."

I can see Candice's jaw drop and it takes her at least five seconds before she gets up and leaves. She closes the door with a little bit more force than needed.

"Some of you have heard the rumors that I will be retiring at the end of the year." My heart sinks a little at the thought of him leaving. Mr. Glass has been the best boss. "Well, I am here to say that it is true. Currently, I do not want the others to know. Some items need to be ironed out first with my replacement."

Well you shouldn't have made him business cards if it isn't final yet, I think to myself.

"What was that, Ms. Harvey?" Mr. Glass asks. Holy Crap, did I say that out loud?

"Oh, umm…" Just as I stick my foot a little further into my mouth, the door of the conference room opens and my coffee-spilling dreamboat walks through the door.

"Sorry to interrupt," Mason says with a strong and deep voice.

My face instantly flushes, and I can feel the goose bumps running up my arms. All from three little words from this handsome man. He is now wearing a dark navy-blue suit that fits him like a dream, with no tie and the top button on his crisp white shirt open showing off the tan on his chest. God, I bet he looks amazing without a shirt on.

"Not at all." Mr. Glass beams and rises from his chair. "Everyone this is my son MJ. He is the replacement I need to get ironed out." Mr. Glass laughs and throws his arm around his son's shoulder.

Mason, or MJ I guess, smiles and scans the room. When his gaze finds mine, it changes, going from business to what I can only describe as bedroom eyes in an instant. I squirm under the attention and shyly smile back. Without meaning to I bite my bottom lip and watch as those eyes change to an even darker blue.

Holy crap, I am in trouble.

He breaks our eye contact and addresses the group. "Nice to meet you all. I look forward to getting to meet each of you and learn about the strengths you bring to Murphy and Glass."

"Thank you, everyone. Have a blessed day." Mr. Glass dismisses us, and I jump out of my seat and exit the room as quickly as possible.

That man is potent and there is no way I can be anywhere near him. He would for sure make me break my rule about not dating a coworker, and he isn't just a coworker, he's the CEO.

The rest of the workday goes without another encounter with Mason and I'm so thankful for that. I skip my plans for a drive at lunch and instead close myself up in my office. I even go as far as to have my lunch delivered, just to make sure I don't run into Mason. I'm going to have to figure something out soon. I can't just hide in my office everyday hoping to avoid the new CEO and the lusty thoughts that come along with him.

I don't have plans for after work, so I decide on a lazy evening. After making a simple dinner, I curl up on my porch, with a glass of hot cocoa and settle in to read a book. I have always been a big book nerd, staring early in life. I devour as many books as I can, everything from the classics of Jane Austen and F. Scott Fitzgerald to Harry Potter to adult romance novels by authors like E.L. James and Lori Foster.

Most of the time I will read a book straight through. I hate waiting to find out the end, I must know they live happily ever after and that the bad guy is dead or in prison for a very, very long time.

I stay cuddled up on my rocking chair reading until the temperature dips low and my eyes grow heavy, but I don't sleep well that night. My dreams are filled with deep blue eyes and dark brown hair. Damn You, Mason!

CHAPTER THREE
Lucy

Thursday morning, I drag myself out of bed and head to the office, hoping for a normal day. I have an 11 a.m. meeting with one of my favorite clients, Dave and Mark McCallister. They are a father and son who own a small book printing business. They specialized in printing books for self-published authors and smaller textbooks. Their company only has about 25 employees, but most have been there for over 10 years.

My love of books may have something to do with my dedication to them. I love that they give authors a chance to publish their work themselves. They help people make their dreams come true. They were the first client I was assigned when I started here, they are my favorite and have become like family to me.

Last Thanksgiving, they were nice enough to have me over for a delicious turkey dinner when Callie had gone back home for the holiday and left me an orphan. I let it slip in a meeting that I was going to be alone and Dave would not rest until I had agreed to join them for the day.

I had never met people so kind and generous. I had only been with the company for two years at that point, but they insisted they wouldn't have it any other way. Since that day, I have been named an honorary Aunt to all the little ones and I'm not only invited but expected to attend most birthdays, holidays and children's sporting events.

Right on time, the McCallister arrive for our meeting and I go to the lobby to greet them but I stop in my tracks when I find Mr. Brown and Mason in conversation with them near the front door. I take a second to compose myself before joining them.

I put on my best smile, "Good morning, gentlemen."

"Good morning, Lucy. How are you today?" Dave asks and offers me a handshake. He is always more formal in the office and does just a handshake.

"I'm fine, thank you." I turn my attention to his son. "And you Mark, how is the new boat? Have you winterized her yet?"

Mark wraps me in a tight hug, like he normally does. "She is wonderful, Lucy. Thank you for asking. I'm sad you didn't get to join us this summer."

"Trust me, I have land legs. Not sea, or I guess lake legs. I would have been a hazard," I say, poking fun at myself.

"Well you have great legs whatever kind they are." Mark teases and gives me a wink. Mark is a shameless flirt and has my cheeks stained red for most of our meetings. But he is fiercely in love with his wife Lorna, so I know it's all in good fun

"We are just meeting your new CEO," Dave interjects, drawing Mason into the conversation.

I have been doing my best to ignore him and those eyes that kept me awake most of the night, but I meet them for the first time today and am surprised to see they are not happy. His brows are pulled together, and his lips make a hard line.

"Yes, we are very excited to have him on board. Aren't we Lucy?" Mr. Brown offers.

"We most certainly are, Mr. Brown. Can I get you two anything before we get started?" I ask hoping to pull them away and get our meeting started.

"No, I believe we are…" Dave starts to say but is interrupted.

"Do you mind if I join you?" Mason asks. My eyes fly to his face. "I would like to hear more about your business and how our services help you."

"What a great idea. I, too, will join you. See Lucy in action," Mr. Brown exclaims. "Please, lead the way."

Oh, so I guess we are all coming. I paste a big shiny smile on my face and head back to my office.

Mark places his hand on my lower back, leans in close and whispers. "New CEO, huh?" And in his best Ricky Ricardo voice he says. "Oh Lucy, you've got some 'spraining to do."

I chuckle at his silliness and give him an "I'll tell you later look" over my shoulder.

My office furniture is simple and elegant, made of dark wood and soft fabrics. My desk is near the far back wall and I have two comfortable upholstered chairs across from my desk. The walls are a light blue color, of course, with black and white photos of Lake Coeur d'Alene. There is a light gray rug on the floor, a matching cream-colored loveseat and a wide coffee table on the opposite wall of the desk for added seating and comfort.

"Please have a seat, gentlemen." I take my seat behind my desk and bring up the information I need. "Congratulations on a great third quarter. The company has done very well." I smile at my clients and show them the reports I have prepared for them.

Dave's eyes light up and he sits forward, taking the reports from my hand. "These numbers are amazing. Lucy, you have done it again. You are becoming the brains behind this company."

I smile and laugh. "Not at all. This is all you guys. Your employees really stepped up when you got those last-minute orders. The clients were very happy."

Dave hands the report to his son and turns around to address Mason and Luke, who are sitting on the loveseat behind them. "Lucy is just the best. She has really helped our little company. She was able to get us a specialized science textbook job when their other printer could not complete the job by the needed deadline.

Even showed up with coffee for the whole crew in the middle of the night to keep everyone awake and motivated. We just adore her."

I blush at his praise and meet Mason's gaze. He is smiling, and pride shows in his eyes. That look makes my heart beat a little faster. I work very hard for my clients and I want all of them to succeed.

"Please, it was nothing but a little coffee," I reply.

"No," Mark says sternly. "It was way more than that. You care, and we love that. You are our girl." He too turns to address Mason and Luke. "Sorry to break it to you gentleman but if this little lady ever leaves, we are going with her. Contract or not."

My heart glows with the praise. I don't like to be the center of attention but right now it feels good. I meet Mason's eyes and I can tell he is impressed.

Luke laughs, "Well we better keep her happy then."

The rest of the meeting goes by quickly as we discuss the financial changes to their proposed health plan, the options of bringing in a couple larger pieces of printing equipment, and how that would affect their current bottom line. They leave the meeting with optimism for the next few months and the upcoming year.

"Thank you so much for coming by today." I reach out to shake Dave's hand. "Please say hello to your wives for me and let Millie know that I will not be a Thanksgiving orphan this year."

Dave smiles and takes my hand in his. "We love having you. Please promise you will stop by for at least pie?" He gives me a pouty face. He knows that if I come for dessert I will bring his favorite orange cranberry cupcakes.

I laugh and pat his arm, "I will see what I can do."

"Later Lucy." Mark again wraps me in a tight hug and kisses my cheek. "I will see you on Saturday morning?" Mark's son plays peewee football and it's one of the events I join the family for.

"Of course." I wave one last goodbye as they leave out the front door.

I turn back to my office but stumble into a large wall of a chest and angry ice blue eyes. If there had been coffee in his hand, it would have been deja vu.

"We need to talk." He says sternly and grabs ahold of my arm, pulling me toward my office.

Oh no!

CHAPTER FOUR
Mason

For the last hour, I have watched the most beautiful woman I have ever seen flirt with another man, right in front of me. She and I need to get a few things straight.

I have never felt so possessive about a woman before. When I first saw her yesterday morning, she was covered in my iced coffee and peeling off her soggy jacket to reveal an almost see through white lace camisole. I don't think she realized how much of a view I was awarded but fuck me I was not going to ruin that. She was breath taking.

This woman is stacked. She has curves on curves and damn did I want to get my hands on them. Her face is small and delicate with full bow shaped lips that she doesn't cover in lip gloss. They are a pink rose color and just perfect for kissing. She needs to know that I was staking my claim.

Staking my claim?!? What the fuck is wrong with me?

I met this woman yesterday but for some reason she is all I can think about. I know nothing about her… is she married? Does she have a boyfriend? Hell! Does she have a girlfriend? She doesn't wear a ring and from the way she just flirted with Mark McCallister, I'm guessing she is not attached.

I take a hold of her arm and drag her back to her office,

shutting the door behind us. I was surprised by her office when I first saw it earlier. It is simple, but I would have thought it would be more decorated. Covered in girly flowers with lots of personal touches, but there are none.

"Sit," I bark out and point to her couch. I turn away from her to pace. Trying to get out some of this pent-up energy.

"No," she says in a calm yet defiant voice.

I whip around to her and press in close, our noses are less than a foot apart. Lucy brings up her head to meet my gaze. She is standing her ground and it's the sexiest thing I have ever seen. The fire in her deep brown eyes is amazing.

"Please sit down, Lucy. I would like to talk to you," I say through clenched teeth. It is taking everything in me to not kiss the defiance off her face and throw her onto her cream-colored couch.

"If you are upset at my job performance, please get Mr. Brown. He is my immediate supervisor and should be a part of any disciplinary conversations."

My chest loosens almost immediately. She thinks this is about work. Crap! Adjust Mason. You are making an ass of yourself.

I take a breath and shut my eyes for just a moment. When I open my eyes, her beautiful face has changed from defiance to concern. She looks worried about me. Damn, this woman is something else.

I set my hand on the balls of her shoulders and give her a little reassuring squeeze. "No Lucy, this is not a disciplinary conversation." I smile down at her.

She shakes her head and says in a small voice. "Then why do you seem so mad?"

Damn it Mason, you ass tart. You are fucking this whole thing up.

I guide her to the couch and this time I sit down beside her. "Listen…" I pause, trying to gather the right words.

She raises an eyebrow at me in question but doesn't say anything. She waits for me to continue.

"Lucy, seeing you flirt with that guy today pissed me off."

Her eyes widen. "I wasn't flirting with Mark. He is a client and a friend," she defends.

"You might not have meant to do it, but he was for sure flirting with you and it was driving me crazy." I pull her a little closer, wrapping my arm around her shoulder.

She doesn't push me away and I pick up her unique scent. She smells like peaches, vanilla and cupcakes. Yep, cupcakes. That is exactly what she reminds me of. She lifts her hands to my chest and for a second, I wait to see if she will push me away. When she doesn't, I take it as a good sign.

I place a kiss on her forehead and pull back to look into her eyes. "I haven't been able to stop thinking about you since we met yesterday morning. I had planned on doing whatever I needed to do to find you and meet you again. It was an awesome surprise when I saw you sitting in the conference room."

Lucy stares at me for a long moment. She is now clutching at my shirt and her breathing is shallow. I can see the pulse point in her neck is going crazy. I'm glad that I affect her as much as she affects me.

After a few seconds, she shakes her head, squares her shoulders, and drops her hands away from my chest to turn away from me. I feel the loss of those hands instantly.

"I was surprised to see you too. But you are wrong about Mark. He is like my brother and his family has been wonderful to me. Plus, I'm sure his wife Lorna would disagree too. He is devoted to her."

"Well I didn't like it." My voice has become harsh again. I can tell she is trying to bring her professional side back into this.

"I'm sorry but I'm not sure how it is any of your business. I have never crossed the line with a client and I never will." She stands, placing her hands on her hips. She is ready to fight again.

"Of course, you wouldn't. But given the chance that Mark

guy would for sure."

Her face hardens, and she stomps her cute little foot. "How dare you!" I have made her mad. And damn it, if it isn't adorable on her. "Mark is a good man and does not deserve you speaking about him like this. I think you should leave." She points to the door.

I don't leave, I just stand there smiling at this beautiful firecracker of a woman. She lets out a frustrated breath and stomps her foot again. "Please leave Mr. Glass."

OK, cupcake. If you want to play hard to get for now, I will play along.

I move into her personal space and she walks backwards, trying to move away from me. I follow her until she is stopped at the wall of her office and can't escape me any further. I bend forward and run the tip of my nose along her jaw and up to her ear, breathing in her sweet scent. I hear her breath catch at my advances.

"It's Mason, cupcake." I kiss the shell of her ear. "I can't wait to taste those beautiful lips of yours." She moans softly, and I can't stand it anymore, I move to taste her sweet lips when a loud knock sounds at the door.

"Mr. Glass. There is a phone call for you." A woman's voice comes from the other side of the door.

The spell is broken, and Lucy pushes at my chest to back me away. But I stay close, only giving her the few inches of space she is requesting.

"I will be right there," I say toward the door. "I'll be back for you, cupcake."

CHAPTER FIVE
Lucy

I stand in shock for a while… did Mason just hit on me? Is hitting on me the right word? He pretty much told me he was interested in me.

I can't wait to taste those beautiful lips of yours.

Just thinking about his words makes me shiver. I move to my desk and grab my cell phone, immediately dialing Callie's cell. We didn't talk at all yesterday and I need some time with my best friend.

She answers on the second ring. "You better have a good reason for calling me before the clock reads PM, sugar?" Callie says in her sweet southern accent.

"I need a Tubbs talk. Can you meet me with food at our spot in 30 minutes?"

I hear her groan and move about. "Make it 45 and I pick the menu."

"Deal. See you then." I hang up and try to gather my thoughts. Oh girl, are you in trouble.

I always leave a couple workout outfits in my office for just these kinds of days when I need to get away for a hike. Tubbs Hill is a nature preserve located on the south side of McEwen Park, right on the lake. There are about fifteen miles of trails crisscrossing the 165 acres.

Callie and I started the ritual of the Tubbs talks right after we moved here. Callie, being the southern belle, has always said that if you need to gossip and complain, do something productive while you do, so it balances out your life. When we ever have a hard day and need to get some stuff off our chests, we go for a loop around Tubbs Hill. Sometimes we go twice if the issue warrants it.

Callie was born in Fayette, Georgia and was a legacy at the University of Texas. The quintessential southern lady, she oozed sweetness and grace. Callie is the reason we are currently living in Idaho. Her high school sweetheart, Craig, moved up here to start a dental practice and to be closer to his extended family. Callie followed along after him and I, too, decided to take a chance on a new city. Now, six years later, they are engaged and planning a wedding for next summer.

I arrive downstairs 45 minutes later and find Callie waiting at our favorite tree and holding two green juices.

"I thought you were bringing me lunch?" I ask as I get close.

"You said I could pick lunch, sugar. And if I'm going to fit into my Vera Wang wedding dress, I need to stop letting you talk me into eating Paul Bunyan burgers and fries." She gives me a side eyed glance and we head toward the start of the trail.

"OK fine. Have it your way." I take a large drink of the juice and wince at the overwhelming grass taste.

"So, what in the world warrants a Tubbs talk in the middle of October when it is barely 50 degrees outside?"

I take a deep breath and launch into the events of the last two days. It takes about half of the two-mile hike for me to share every detail. The trail is quiet today so we are not interrupted by many people. Since Callie and Craig are both successful business owners they are known by almost everyone.

Callie listens to my story but doesn't interject the normal amount of comments. I usually get an "Oh, dear," "Heavens to Betsy," or "Bless their heart," in most of my ramblings. But today she is silent.

I end my story with "… and that is when I called you," and wait for her to give me her advice. Callie has never steered me wrong. I trust her unconditionally.

She stops in the middle of the trail, turns to look at me and one of the biggest smiles I have ever seen spreads across her beautiful face.

"He is the one!" she exclaims.

"What?" I bark in disbelief. Is she nuts?

"He is the man for you, Lucy!" She repeats in a very matter of fact tone with that big smile still on her face.

"Are you crazy?" I ask.

"No. Lucy, I have never heard you talk about a man the way you spoke about him. He has obviously made quite an impression on you. Mason sounds just like the kind of opposite you need. You hardly ever have this much spirit and fire." She starts off on the trail again and I have to jog to catch back up with her.

"But what about the fact he is my boss? Doesn't that make this a bad idea?" I ask.

"Sugar, I know that 'He Who Shall Not Be Named,'" AKA my ex-boyfriend Clay, "really did a number on your heart and it is hard for you to love again but you need to open your heart up. Give him a chance. People all over the world meet their soul mate at work. You might be surprised. Love has a way of sneaking up on you."

"How would you know?" I ask in a small and sarcastic voice. "You and Craig have been in love since the day you were born."

"Just because it happened when I was young, doesn't mean that it wasn't a surprise at the time. Or was the way I had it planned," she says softly and sweetly.

She has always been the sweet to my salty. No, I'm not an overly mean person but compared to her, I might as well be a puppy kicker.

We walk in silence for the last few minutes of the hike. She has given me a lot to think about. I hug her when we arrive at her car and say our goodbyes. "Thank you for the juice and Tubbs Talk. I'm sorry for putting down your relationship." My heart hurts a little at the possibility of hurting my best friend.

"Oh Lucy, you didn't, and you have no reason to be sorry. It is scary. But if I'm right, it will be worth it." She kisses my cold cheeks, waves and drives away.

I head back toward my office. I pass a trash can and throw the juice bottle away. As I do, my stomach growls loudly reminding me that my overly curvy body needs more than just juice for lunch. I will have to order something when I get back to my desk.

When I enter the building, I decide to take the stairs up the four flights since the bathroom is in the same hallway as the stairs and I won't have to pass by Candice to change like I would if I took the elevator.

I arrive at the top of the stairs out of breath and just a little dizzy from the effort of all those flights. After a couple of deep breaths, I'm not feeling totally better. But with my stomach running the show now, food become the number-one priority. I quickly change back into my work clothes.

I leave the bathroom and move down the hall toward my office. Just as I am about to enter my office, Mr. Glass, Luke and Mason spot me.

"Lucy," Luke greets me.

I smile. "Hey." My vision blurs a little. I really need to take the stairs more often.

"How was lunch?" Luke asks but I'm having a hard time concentrating.

"What was that?" I ask and shake my head trying to get rid of the cobwebs that have formed. Oh man that does not help.

"Lucy, are you OK?" One of the voices asks.

"Yeah, I'm fine…" I start to answer right before the world goes black.

CHAPTER SIX
Mason

I see Lucy's eyes start to roll back in her head and jump in to stop her from hitting the ground.

Luke shouts as I catch Lucy. "Candice, please call 911."

She comes around the corner and screams when she sees that Lucy has fainted.

My dad scolds the older woman. "There is no need for hysterics. Please calm down and do your job." I'm a little surprised he spoke with so much harshness in his voice. Candice had always been one of my dad's favorite employees until a few years ago when he said she had started to change. But that doesn't much matter now.

What does matter is the woman I have snuggled up against my body.

"Dad, can we lie her down on the couch in your office?" I ask. I am a very strong guy, but I don't know if I can hold her the whole time we wait for the paramedics.

A coworker in the office across the hall from us has come out and is watching the goings on. Before my dad can answer she says. "Lucy has a loveseat in her office." She rushes across the hall and opens Lucy's office door. I was hoping to get her more out of the limelight and have a larger space for her to get comfortable, but this will have to do. I need to make sure she is OK.

I lay her down on the couch and as soon as I do I miss the weight of her in my arms. I stay close, kneeling on the soft rug near her head. Her office starts to fill with other staff members who hear the commotion and are wondering what is happening. I turn my gaze on them and my dad can see in my face that I want them gone.

He starts to move the crowd from the doorway. "Alright everyone. Thank you for your concern, but please don't crowd the door. Go on back to work. I will send out a memo when we know she is OK."

The crowd dissipates but I hear a voice ask if she needs anything. It is the helpful coworker from across the hall.

I turn to her and give her a reassuring smile. "Can you please get me a glass of water?"

She straightens quickly away from the doorjamb she was leaning on. "Of course. Right away!" And she is gone.

I focus back on the woman on the couch. I can see that her pulse is racing, and her breaths are fast and shallow. With every breath, her chest lifts. She has a rack that could tempt an angel, I would love to unbutton her sweater and look my fill but now is not the time to indulge my need. But I will for sure have a semi for the next few hours.

The coworker returns with a cold bottle of water and hands it to me. I accept it gratefully. "Thank you…" I have forgotten her name.

"Kelsey," she supplies me.

"Thank you, Kelsey."

She smiles and leaves the room. I unscrew the cap and lean down to Lucy.

"Lucy, wake up. I have some water for you."

She moans but doesn't stir. I place my hand on Lucy's forehead and am not surprised to feel she is clammy. I brush the back of my hand down her soft cheek and as I do her lashes start to flutter open.

They open slowly but don't focus on anything. She smiles a sexy little smile that takes my breath away. She turns onto her side and snuggles into the couch, closing her eyes again. Like she is getting ready to enjoy a catnap.

"Hmm what a nice dream. You even smell like the real thing."

I chuckle at her sleepy flirting.

Candice enters then followed by the paramedics. "The paramedics are here, Mr. Glass." No shit, captain obvious.

"Thank you, Candice."

"It's Mrs. Bell," she says. But I of course ignore her. Not the time for that.

My dad and Luke leave the room as the paramedics enter. Dad shoots me a look of concern, I can tell he wants to stay and ensure the safety of his employee, but her office is not big enough for everyone to be in here right now.

"Well now what do we have here, Lucy?" One of the paramedics kneels in front of us and starts to reach for Lucy's arm to take her pulse. I'm surprised that he knows her name. Are they friends? Or are they more than friends? Jealousy shoots through me. Don't even think about it fucker. She is mine.

She is mine? Where did that shit come from? The jealousy from earlier is back. I never did find out if she has a boyfriend. Is this him?

"Bugger Off Caleb," she says in a sleepy voice.

All the paramedics and I laugh. I lean in and kiss her forehead not able to help myself. Man, this woman is a total surprise.

CHAPTER SEVEN
Lucy

I'm having the most wonderful dream. A tall dark and handsome stranger has me snuggled against him and is softly kissing my hair. He smells wonderful. I could stay like this forever.

But for some reason Craig's twin brother Caleb is there and is telling me that I need to wake up. Bugger Off Caleb. You are messing up my wonderful dream.

"Lucy, I need you to open your eyes. You fainted, and we need to get some sugar in your system." Caleb's word penetrates my dream world with my handsome stranger.

Oh crap! Did I faint? Where am I? Please tell me I am not at the office!

I slowly open one of my eyes before slamming it closed. Yep, I'm at work. Crap, crap, crap!

"Ha-ha. I saw that Lucy. Come on faker. You need to drink some juice," Caleb says in his commanding paramedic voice.

I groan and reluctantly open my eyes. Caleb and the other two members of the Coeur d'Alene Engine One crew are crowded into my small office. I move to sit up, and Mason helps me. He moves on the couch on my left and slings his arm around my shoulder. Caleb hands me a glass of what looks like apple juice and one of the other guys, Henry, I think, moves to my right side and starts taking my blood pressure. I take a sip of the overly sweet liquid and realize how thirsty I am. Without even trying I have the whole glass gone in a few gulps.

"Oh man, thirsty there, guppy?" he asks with a laugh.

Caleb has called me guppy since I fell off the dock a few years ago while on an afternoon spent by the lake. I was splashing around trying not to drown when he nicely pointed out that I would be fine if I stood up. Not my finest moment. And now I can add this to that list as well.

I nod my head and glance up at Mason. His face is blank, but his eyes are on fire. I can tell from those eyes, he is pissed. He must be missing a meeting to be in here with me. I look back to Caleb who hands me another glass of juice.

"When was the last time you ate?" Caleb asks and pulls out his clipboard to take notes.

"I didn't get to eat breakfast this morning. I was running late." I feel Mason stiffen a little next to me. Henry removes the cuff from my arm and reports back to Caleb. It is a little high but not concerning.

"And then Callie brought me a green juice while we were hiking Tubbs Hill. I had planned on getting something delivered once I got back to my office."

Caleb shakes his head and gives me a disappointed look.

"Did you do the full Tubbs trail?" He asks but he already knows the answer.

I nod my head and continue to sip the second glass of juice.

"Lucy, you know that isn't a good idea. That is a lot of exercise on an empty stomach for someone with hypoglycemia. You know that."

I nod again and look down at my hands. I hate being scolded and it's so embarrassing to have Mason here while it happens. I feel the tears start to form in my eyes. Oh, this is just what I need to add to the moment.

"What would the best thing for her to eat?" Mason asks. He is looking straight ahead at Caleb, but his hand rubs soothing circles on my back.

"I would say grab a turkey sandwich from downstairs. Maybe a small, side salad as well. She could use the protein."

Once he gets the order from Caleb, Mason leaves my side and moves toward my door. As soon as he is gone, I want to reach out and pull him back to me. Having him near me was so comforting.

Mason steps into the hallway and calls for Candice at the front desk.

"Please order two turkey sandwiches and two side salads from the deli downstairs." He turns to me. "Ranch dressing?" I nod and smile. "Both salads with ranch dressing. Let them know we need it right away."

I can hear that she starts to argue but he cuts her off with a curt, "Now."

I smile to myself. Serves her right.

He returns to my side, taking his position from earlier with his arm around me, letting me lean into his chest. And all those comfortable feelings are back. I sink into his side and rest my head on his shoulder.

"All your other vitals look good. I would suggest you eat and then take the rest of the day off to get some rest." He looks at Mason and asks, "Can you spare her for the day?"

"Yes, of course. I will take her home after she eats." He removes his arm from me and stands to shake Caleb's hand.

"Thank you, I'm Caleb."

"Mason." The two men shake hands.

"Nice to meet you." He turns back to me. "Alright you, go home and get some rest. You have bowling tomorrow night. Someone has to get all the gutter balls," Caleb says as he gathers his medic bag and then the team walks toward the door.

I laugh and shake my head. "Please, I'll kick your butt like always."

"Ha-ha. You wish, guppy. Take care of her." The last part of that comment was directed toward Mason and I see him nod.

I call out a thank you and try to take a couple of deep breaths to compose myself.

A few moments later, Mason re-enters the room and closes the door.

"How are you feeling, cupcake?" He asks in a low voice.

"I'm sorry." I look down at my lap and hope that he will just go away.

"Why in the world are you sorry?" His voice is hard.

I raise my eyes to his. He is tall already but now with me sitting on the couch and him standing above me, it makes me feel even smaller, I must crane my neck back to see him.

"I fainted at work. I caused the office to grind to a halt and have the paramedics come." There is a slight hysteria in my voice. I am so embarrassed, and he is not making this any easier.

He kneels in front of me and cups my cheeks in his strong hands.

"You have nothing to be sorry about." His thumbs glide over the apple of my cheek, whisking away the tears that I didn't realize had escaped. "Promise me from now on you will eat no matter how late you are. You know what…"

He stands, moves toward the door. Opening it, he calls out. "Candice. Please make a standing order for Lucy at the coffee shop across the street. I want it delivered here every morning at 8am sharp."

He doesn't wait for a reply and closes the door again. "There! Now this will never happen on my watch again." He gives me a big and wide smile. Like he just solved the whole world's problems.

And I just can't resist how sweet he is. I smile, walk over to him, and wrap my arms around his middle. I lay my cheek on his chest and listen to his strong heartbeat.

"Thank you. That is the sweetest thing anyone has ever done for me."

He is such a perfect fit. I could stand like this all day. His heartbeat is strong and steady. His scent is rich and muscular. He's all male, but so sweet and caring. He has stayed by my side since I fainted, comforting me and ensuring I was OK.

I reluctantly pull away after a minute of standing wrapped around Mason but before I can get too far away, he lifts my chin and slowly lowers his lips to mine. As our lips are less than an inch apart he whispers. "Anything for you, cupcake."

Then he gives me the best first kiss I could ever imagine. His lips are soft and warm against mine. His trimmed beard tickles my lips and chin as our lips move against each other. I sigh, sinking into his strong arms and chest. I open my lips to allow him in and his tongue explores mine, taking small licks that are driving me crazy.

One of his hands holds me close, while the other is roaming up and down my back, making me want to purr. His hands feel amazing on me. I want them on my skin, without the barrier of my shirt.

I can feel the muscles in his back flex as his arms move about my body. My hands find their way to his soft hair and my fingers tangle in the perfect length locks. He is so much taller than me, I have to stand on my tiptoes to be able to reach. It forces me to lean more into him, which he doesn't seem to mind a bit. We spend what feels like hours standing twined together, simply enjoying each other's lips while our hands explore.

We are both breathing hard when his lips leave mine, but he stays close, resting his forehead against mine. "Damn cupcake. You are addicting." I smile as he moves his lips back toward mine.

Before they reach their destination of my kiss-swollen lips, a loud knock sounds at the door. "Mr. Glass, Lucy's lunch is here, sir."

CHAPTER EIGHT
MASON

That had to be the best first kiss in history. Damn timing. All I want is to continue kissing this soft and beautiful woman. Now that I have gotten my lips on her, I want them to stay there.

"Thank you, Candice," I say to the closed door.

She tries to enter but for some reason I had the foresight to lock the door after I walked the paramedics out. Not that I was thinking any of this would happen, but I wanted some privacy with Lucy. I feel her jump in my arms and tries to pull away, but I calm her with a small squeeze. I wink and gesture for her to sit on the couch.

"Sir, the door is locked. Mr. Glass the door." She knocks and tries the knob again. Her voice is louder and more frantic when she calls out again. "It is locked. Sir, Sir?"

I whisper, "Play possum." Lucy smiles, and curls up on the couch. She closes her eyes as I requested.

I go to the door, unlock it and quickly yank it open. Candice falls a step forward, as if she had been leaning up against it trying to listen to the happenings in Lucy's office.

"Please lower your voice Candice. For heaven sakes, Ms. Harvey is trying to rest." I grab the bag of food from her hand and close the door in her face.

When I turn, Lucy is smiling from ear to ear and begins to giggle. "Shh, you are resting remember," I say and move back toward the loveseat to join her again. I set the food on the small coffee table to the side of the couch. I sit next to her and pull her back into my arms, but she doesn't melt into me like I want her too.

"I think maybe I should eat. Or my stomach is going to start clawing its way out if I don't."

I nod in understanding but lean in for a quick kiss because I can. A little moment of shock crosses her face. If she thinks I'm giving up her kisses she is dead wrong.

I pull the small coffee table toward us to eat off of, remove the food from the bag and set one of each in front of us. We eat together in a comfortable silence; she eats quickly barely breathing in between each bite. If this is how she always eats I could watch her forever. She is fascinating.

When she is done eating she turns toward me. "Thank you for lunch. It was delicious."

"Are you sure? You ate it so fast, I'm surprised you even tasted it." I smile at my joke but her face drops and she looks away. She gathers her trash and walks around to her desk to throw it away.

Fuck. "Did I say something wrong?" I ask and get up to go after her. Her walls are back up. I had them down after our amazing make-out session, but I made a major misstep somewhere.

She starts to answer but stops, being interrupted by her cell phone. "Excuse me," she softly says and turns her back to me to answer.

"Hi Callie. Yes, I'm OK. No silly it is not your fault. Yes, Caleb told me I needed to rest."

I can't make out the words but the person on the other side is obviously very upset that Lucy fainted.

"Yes, I'm taking the rest of the day off. I will be leaving soon. No, I don't think I will need anything. Of course, I will let you know if I do. Love you too."

She ends her call, sets it on the desk and turns toward me. She looks defeated and completely exhausted.

"I need to go and check out with Mr. Brown. I would like to take the rest of the day off. I have my laptop and can respond to emails from home."

She waits for my reply, seeking permission but also dismissing me. She starts to gather her things, ignoring my presence.

I should do something. I can't leave it like this. If I hurt her I need to fix it. An idea quickly forms in my head. "Don't worry about Luke. I will send an email and let him know I have taken you home. You will be taking the rest of the week off."

Her head pops up at the mention of taking more than just today off. "No, that will not be necessary."

"It is very necessary." I move toward her. She takes a step back, trying to retreat away from me but I cage her in with arms. When I'm this close to her, she can't hide her feelings from me. I can see it in her body how I affect her. "Your health is important Lucy. So, you and I are going to rest for the next couple of days."

"You and I?" She questions in a soft whisper.

I gently kiss her lips, then pull back. "Yes, you and I."

I can't resist her lips. I slowly nibble the corners of her mouth, then softly brush my lips back and forth over hers. She steps up on her tiptoes and fully plants her lips on mine. I kiss her full on as she asks and by the time I pull away we are both breathing hard and her eyes are a little glassy, full of lust.

I kiss her adorable little nose and grab her hand. "Do you have what you need?" She just nods her confirmation, not able to find words at the moment.

I smile at her, so damn cute. "OK, let's go."

Lucy and I are in my jet-black Jeep Wrangler. I am driving her back to her apartment. It took several minutes of arguing, which brought back her feisty side, for her to agree to leave her car at the office and let me drive her home. I don't know what will happen when we get there but for now just being with her is nice.

"You will want to take a left at the light." She is quietly giving me directions from the passenger seat.

I nod and squeeze the hand of hers I am holding. She hasn't said much since we set off in my car and I can almost hear the wheel turning. I decide I want to know what is going on in that head of hers.

"What are you thinking about?"

She turns her head from the view looking out her window to me. "Nothing really." She takes a breath and continues. "Well and everything too. Thinking about how stupid I was for letting myself faint at work. Thinking about the things I was supposed to do for my clients today. Thinking about our kisses…" She trails off without finishing her sentence.

"What about our kisses?"

She doesn't answer so I press just a little. "Lucy? Answer me please."

Lucy lets out a long breath and shakes her head. "I don't want to say while we are in the car. I want to see your face."

We pull into the garage and I park in my assigned spot. The condo I'm renting is in the same building as Lucy's. I had left yesterday morning to grab a coffee before I had a conference call with my former job in Seattle.

When I told them I was quitting and moving back home to take over my dad's company, my boss Kyle was not happy. He must have gone through at least three of the stages of grief within the first ten minutes because I for sure saw denial, anger and bargaining. I totally sympathize with him. I made that fucker a lot of money and he treated me very well, but I needed to come back home.

It had always been my dad and Jacob's dream to pass their business on to family. When Jacob died without children, that dream fell onto my shoulders. My sisters have no interest in accounting. My leaving for school in Seattle and not coming right back had been a fight I hated having with my dad. I wanted to make it on my own. And I had. My bank account is now in the six digits and I have the financial freedom to go and do what I want.

Coming home had been to be with my family. My parents aren't sick and dying but I want them to be a part of my life. We had always been a close family of five and being away for as long as I had I missed my time with them. I don't want to be one of those bachelors who are forever alone because they don't make the effort to be with their families. Plus, I do want a family of my own some day. Not for a few more years but I want my parents to get to be good grandparents.

As soon as the Jeep comes to a stop, Lucy is out of the car and walking to the condo entrance. I have to jog to keep up with her. I follow silently behind her, taking my cues from her. But when she tries to take the stairs I grab her arm and steer her back toward the elevator. She was falling into zombie mode; she is clearly exhausted.

The elevator ride is short and when I see her leaning her weight against the wall, I pull her to my side taking her weight. Another spot she fits perfectly in. She goes willingly, and we stay joined as we walk to her door. Right across the hall from mine, I laughed to myself. How convenient.

"What?" She asks after my chuckle.

"Oh, nothing. Just glad you live here." I lean down and place my lips on her soft blonde hair.

The inside of her condo had been exactly how I pictured it would be, and the exact opposite from her office. At work, her space is simple and plain; this is busy and colorful. The walls are a cool light blue again, with a large navy striped sectional in the center of the room covered with at least a dozen colorful and flowered throw pillows. She has a small dining table near the kitchen that appears to be set for two. But where my eye went was the large bookshelf unit that took up almost all of the wall opposite of the couch.

A small tv sat in the middle of three-section-wide book case. All the other shelves were filled with books. In front of those books were mugs, candles, and small figurines. The art she has hung on the wall seem to be quotes on top of watercolor prints. The largest one was simple and just had the word "Always" in fancy script. There was a triangle looking shape underneath the word. It looked familiar, but I have no idea what from.

"Do you mind if I change before we talk?" Her voice pulls me from my exploration of her space.

I nod. "Of course. Please get comfortable. You are here to rest."

She smiles and heads down the hallway to her bedroom. Her condo appears to be the same as mine. Down that hallway is the master bedroom with an en-suite bathroom, a smaller second bedroom and half bath across from it.

I remove my blazer and roll up my sleeves, getting comfortable myself. I decide to check out her books further while she changes. As I look there seems to be a theme with her books. She seems to like series. The first I see is Harry Potter. That seems to be the largest section, with several versions of each book and the most knickknacks.

Next, I see the Twilight series, Lord of the Rings, The Hunger Games and The Raven Circle. I continue to the other side of the shelf and the books start to change, less series I recognize and more books by single authors. The covers are also getting more and more...pink. As I read the titles I find most are romance novels. I grab one and I flip it open.

I am fucking stunned by what I find there. I opened to a page where two characters are getting ready to have sex. Sexy as fuck sex. Damn! I read for several minutes, quickly going through page after page, being sucked in by the foreplay the author is describing in detail.

"That's by one of my favorites, Kristen Proby," Lucy's voice breaks me away from the book. "It's about a Seattle Seahawks quarterback and a pediatric cancer nurse."

She walks to me and looks at the book I'm holding, seeing which page I am on. "You can borrow it if you want." She smiles sweetly at me but her eyes are a little mischievous.

I take in the woman before me. I was already semi hard from the sexy as fuck book and now Lucy is standing in front of me wearing tight black yoga pants and an over-sized, well-worn Texas longhorns' sweatshirt, showing off her shapely legs and curvy hips. Her blonde hair is up in a knot on the top of her head and she has washed off her make-up. She is the most stunning creature I have ever seen.

"Fuck, you are so beautiful."

CHAPTER NINE
Lucy

I blush at the compliment from Mason. "Thank you."

He sets the book on the shelf and motions for my hand. I give it willingly and he leads me to my couch. We sit next to each other and he pulls me close to his side as we get ourselves settled.

"So, finish what you were saying earlier," he asks looking me straight in the eyes.

"Well …" I start but an instant later he cradles me in his arms and moves me on to his lap. I shriek and wind my arms around his neck to keep from falling backwards.

I give him a puzzled look.

"You wanted to see my face and this seems like the best way to do that. We both get things we want."

I chuckle and take a breath before speaking, looking for the words I really want to say. "Well, that had to be the best first kiss or any kiss I have ever had." He smiles the biggest smile and moves to kiss me again.

I pull back, stopping him. "… But I don't think it is a good idea." And just as quickly that gorgeous smile is gone. I continue, trying to see if I can get that smile back. "After all you are my new boss and it would probably not look good if I jump into a relationship with you so quickly. My ex was a coworker and it did not end well. He messed me up a little. I think we should just be co-workers for right now."

His eyebrows are pulled down low and there are several adorable wrinkles that have formed in the middle of his forehead.

I giggle and run my finger down those wrinkles to the tip of his nose. "I'm not saying that I don't want to get to know you, because I do. I like you but I'm not ready for us to be any more than friends right now. Let's take it slow and get to know each other."

In the next instant I'm on my back with Mason above me.

Holy Crap, he is strong.

"I think we can have lots of fun not taking it slow, cupcake."

He leans down to kiss me and I meet him half way. His lips have a little bit more determination this time. Like he is trying to prove a point and I think I might just let him.

His tongue slowly licks and probes my lips and I open them, allowing him in. Our tongues tangle and I change the angle of my head to deepen the kiss. His hands are buried in my hair and I am clutching at his shoulders trying to get closer to him. His hips are not resting on mine but I can still feel how hard he is. I roll my hips up, hoping to feel him. He groans into my mouth but breaks the kiss and pulls away. I instantly miss his lips and try to follow after him. He sits up and back enough that I cannot get to his lips.

He chuckles and smiles down at me. "Slow, huh?"

I shrug my shoulder and try to look as innocent as possible. He throws back his head and lets out a loud belly laugh.

"OK, cupcake. We will do it your way. You take a nap and I will be back at 7."

He leans down to kiss my forehead, but I jump into action. I grab two hand fulls of his dress shirt and pull him forward so all of his weight lands on me. I kiss him my way and take advantage of his surprise to dominate the kiss. Sliding my tongue along his and quickly gaining entrance to lick and explore him. I decide to prove my own point. That doing this my way can be very rewarding. He seems to agree because not to long after we start he takes com-

S. R. MULLINS

mand of the kiss and sends my heart reeling. Wetness floods between my legs and I wrap my right leg around his hip, hoping to relive some of this great need that is starting to grow.

He grips the back of my neck and angles my head to suit his needs. The other moves down to my hip. I need to feel his skin, so I start to pull his shirt from the waistband of his pants. Once free, I insert my arms under his shirt and feel the warm skin of his muscular back.

He starts his own exploration. His large hand moves under my sweatshirt and start a slow journey up toward my breasts. My nipples are hard and aching for his touch. But just as it reaches its destination a loud cell phone ring sounds in my small apartment.

He pulls his lips away. "Sorry, cupcake. That is my dad's ring tone."

I want to scream but shaking off the disappointment, I nod giving him permission to answer it. He moves off the couch to where his jacket is, collecting his cell phone.

"Hey Dad. Can I call you right back? Thanks."

He hangs up quickly and crooks his finger, beckoning me to him. I leave the couch and walk toward him. He pulls me into his arms and hugs me tight.

"Be ready at 7."

"What are we doing?" I ask, not letting him go from my arms just yet.

"We are going to have a date night in at my place."

"Is it far?" I ask.

He chuckles, stepping toward the door and I reluctantly let him go. He pulls me behind him to the front door, opens it and points down the hall. "No, not really. That is me there, with the blue door."

"Oh." I remember hearing movers last weekend, but I didn't see who it was that moved in. "That's very convenient."

He chuckles again, kisses my forehead and guides me back into my apartment. "Get some rest and I will see you later. That is an order."

"So bossy," I say in a sassy voice.

"You have no idea, cupcake." He pulls the door closed and is gone.

I collapse back against it and sigh. Maybe Callie was right.

CHAPTER TEN
Lucy

It's 6:59 p.m. and I'm standing by my front door in a simple blue sundress that is a little too summery for an October night in Idaho, but I like it and wanted to feel pretty. Plus, it gives me a reason to wear my favorite periwinkle lacy strapless bra. It has a delicate silver buckle in the front with a very cute pair of matching lacy boy short. They are the perfect combo of sexy and cute.

I have a love of sexy underwear. They're my reward for being able to fit into them. I grew up never really caring about my weight. When I got to college though, the freshman 15 turned into the freshman 25. Followed by the sophomore 50. By junior year I was overweight and unhappy. I tried to lose the weight by not eating anything and starving myself, but I found myself very sick. It's when I discovered I have hypoglycemia and my eating habits were really an issue for my health.

Callie hated watching me gain the weight but did her best not to judge and make me feel bad about it. Being a great friend too, she had jumped right in with me and made a pact to work on our health together.

At first, it had been hard to workout with Callie. She is a lot more athletic than I am and made it look so easy. It was an everyday struggle for me to see even the smallest change. I didn't give up and slowly, I did start to see the difference it was making. By the time I graduated I was back down to a weight I felt comfortable with. I'll never be as small as Callie but I like my curves. I think they make the lingerie look sexier.

Right when the clock strikes seven there is a knock at the door. I leap to open it, not able to hide my excitement at seeing Mason. I find a sexy man on the other side of the door, wearing a black long sleeve t-shirt pushed up on his muscular forearms and jeans that hugged his legs in all the right places. He greets me with a big smile, but after he looks me up and down, the smile turns to a frown.

My heart sinks with disappointment. Not really the reaction I was going for.

"What's wrong?" I ask looking down at myself, feeling self-conscious.

He steps in and shuts the door. "You were supposed to be resting all afternoon," he says with an accusing tone.

"I did."

"No way. You look way too good. You must have spent hours getting ready."

I laugh a full belly laugh and throw my arms around his waist, hugging him close.

"That is the sweetest backwards compliment I have ever gotten." I stand back and smile up at him.

He smiles back, grabs me by the shoulders and turns me toward my room.

"Go put that sweatshirt and yoga pants back on. You need to be comfortable."

"But I am comfy in this," I say over my shoulder and drag my feet.

"Nope, off you go." He pushes me in that direction and playfully smacks my butt.

I roll my eyes but decide to play with him a little bit. I flip up the back of my dress for just a second and show him the panties I am wearing.

"Well I guess I will change out of these too," I say and smirk over my shoulder.

It's more brazen then I normally am with a man I hardly know, especially one I told a few hours ago that I wanted to take things slow and just be friends. He is bringing out this flirty side of me and I'm having way too much fun. Mason is so fun to flirt with.

He lets out a deep growl and I can hear him lunge toward me. I sprint to my bedroom and slam the door closed before he can get to me.

I hear him bang into the door. "You are going to pay for that, cupcake," he says.

"Promises, Promises."

"Facts cupcake. Facts!"

I quickly change out of the dress back into the outfit he requested. I leave on the sexy lingerie just in case.

When I open the door, we are both standing there with big grins on our faces. He looks past me into my room but I hit the light before he can snoop too much.

"Ready?" I ask in an overly cheery voice.

He laughs and shakes his head. "Yeah, let's go."

I lock up my apartment and move down the wide hallway to his door. We enter his apartment that is a mirror image of mine. Mason's apartment is pretty bare of furniture. His living room consists of only a large, leather sectional, coffee table and a giant TV mounted to the wall. His coffee table is covered in snacks and drinks and there are several large fluffy pillows on the couch with a soft oversized chenille throw. The pillows and throw are clearly new. Most men don't have those things unless a woman has bought them for him. He has obviously gone to a lot of trouble to make this nice for me.

"Wow... This is great." I wrap my arms around him and lean my head on his chest, hugging him to me. No one really does nice things like this for me. He plants a kiss on the top of my head and continues to hold me. He doesn't pull away or move to separate us. We just stand there together, holding each other. I like the feeling of being in his arms.

My reasons for not dating him and being just friends are crumbling by the second. The pros and cons list in my head is currently complete chaos and anarchy. Stupid dating-coworkers rule!

After a few long minutes he says, "Would you like to sit down and watch the movie?"

I pull away and smile, "Yes, please."

Mason offers me a drink, snacks, and acts as the perfect host. We settle on the big comfy couch. He sits next to me and pulls me to him, fitting me perfectly in the crook of his arm and snuggled up against his chest.

"What are we watching?" I ask, taking a sip of the cup of hot cocoa Mason made me.

"I thought you could walk me through the first couple Harry Potter movies. From your collection of the books, you seem like you might be an expert."

"Harry Potter is always a good idea. I will be happy to be your tour guide. Welcome, Mr. Glass to this evenings screening of Harry Potter and the Sorcerer's Stone. Published by J.K. Rowling in 1997 and made into a major motion picture in 2001. Starring new comers, Daniel Radcliffe, Emma Watson and Rupert Grint." I spout off my knowledge of Harry Potter facts and can feel his chest rumble with laughter.

"I picked the right tour guide, I see."

We make it through the first two movies curled up on his couch before I feel my eyes start to droop. He of course notices right away, stopping the third movie only ten minutes in.

"I think it is time for Sleeping Beauty to return to her castle."

"No, I'm fine." I lie, but yawn half way through, giving myself away.

"Nope, sorry pretty lady. The night is over." He stands and turns back to me. He lifts me effortlessly into his arms.

"Put me down. I'm too heavy and I am fully capable of walking on my own." I say in fake protest and lean my head on his shoulder.

"Hush. You are perfect." He kisses my forehead and walks me out his front door and toward mine.

I want to think of any excuse for the night not to end but my eyes are heavy, and my bed sounds just perfect to me. He lowers me to my feet in front of my door and I unlock it.

"Thank you for tonight. It was magical."

"You are welcome. Get some sleep and I will stop by to see you tomorrow afternoon."

"OK, good night." I smile at him and turn to go inside. But before I get a full step away, I hear him say, "Just one more." Grabbing my upper arm, he turns me back around and pulls me in for a passionate kiss. Holy moly, can this man kiss!

CHAPTER ELEVEN
Mason

As we kiss I can feel her melt into my arms. My tongue dives into the heaven she calls a mouth and I take everything she is willing to give me.

Knowing we are in the hallway and giving any of our neighbors who walked out a show, I push her backwards and into her apartment. I find the nearest wall and pressed her against it, for some reason having this woman up against a wall seems to be the perfect position. She is a foot shorter than me and against a wall I can boost her up and access all of her easily. My arms went under her luscious ass and wrapped those sexy legs around my hips. She lets out a throaty moan at our contact and wiggles, looking to get closer. It's the fucking sexiest thing I have ever heard.

I remove my lips from hers, kiss along her jaw and pull her earlobe in between my teeth for a small taste.

"Fuck, cupcake. Keep making noises like that and I might forget that you are needing rest."

"Fuck rest."

The shock of hearing those words from her sweet mouth has me leaning back to see her face. Her eyes are heavy with lust and her lips are red and puffy from my kisses. Seeing her this way seems to snap something inside me and all bets are off. This woman is going to be spending some time beneath me tonight.

Using my hips, I pinned her more firmly to the wall. My left hand moved from her ass to the most perfect breast I had not yet had the pleasure to see. Yet being the word of the minute.

"Well now, sounds like somebody is a naughty girl." I massaged her lush breast as my lips found the perfect spot on her neck. They are the perfect handful.

She moans and thrusts her chest out, encouraging me to continue. "Yes, please Mason."

"Damn, cupcake. I love hearing my name on your lips."

"Mason." She says again with a little more desperation.

"I got you, Lucy." It was time to find a bed, now!

My hand leaves her breasts and she grabs for them, trying to keep them where she wants them.

"Don't worry. They will be back there soon."

I lift her away from the wall and she attaches her lips to my neck, making my eyes cross as she sucks and leaves small love bites.

My legs move as fast as they can toward her room. We enter her bedroom and I decide to leave the lights off for now. Later on, I will have those lights on and take my time looking her over.

She bounces once as she hits the mattress and I follow quickly behind her, covering her curvy body with mine. Like two magnets our lips attach themselves together.

Lucy's small hands go to the bottom of my shirt working it over my head. We break apart only long enough so I could pull it over my head. We kiss and touch, exploring each other, but I want to feel her soft skin next to mine.

"You need to catch up, cupcake."

The little mink smiles a sexy smile, reaches her arms above her head and wiggles her shoulders, inviting me to do the job for her. My pleasure.

I, of course, do not hesitate and whip the oversized sweatshirt off her sexy body and over my right shoulder. Her beauty stops me for a second. I already had an idea of what I would find under that shirt but fuck she is magnificent. She isn't the slimmest girl I have ever been with but damn, on her it looks fucking delicious. My eyes take a long and slow journey down her torso. Her generous tits are trying to escape her sexy as fuck lace bra with each breath she takes. Her belly is soft with what I think they call a muffin top but fuck I don't give a shit. It means more of this sexy woman I get to explore.

She starts to cover herself while I stare at her. My eyes shoot to hers and I can see that a little shyness and insecurity has creeped into them. And I'm not having that. I want my sexy minx back.

Mine? Yes, fucking mine!

"Oh no, cupcake. No covering yourself." I moved her arms from their place covering her body and pin them above her head with my right hand. "I just unwrapped this present and I need to do some more exploring. You leave those arms there. If they move I will be force to punish you."

Her eyes flash and I can see that she wants to defy me just to see what will happen. Oh fuck, she is going to make this fun.

My lips start right below her ear and I spend several minutes exploring her long slender neck. I decide it's time to move down her chest to her hardened nipples, hidden beneath her lacy bra. I kiss the pale flesh of her cleavage and run my tongue from the valley between her tits to the outside. Lucy lets out a soft moan.

"Like that cupcake?" She doesn't answer out loud. I look up to find her eyes closed tight.

"Give me those eyes beautiful." She hasn't yet complied with my order. "Lucy! Open your eyes." I kiss back up to her lips and slowly nibble.

"Lucy?" I notice that her breathing has evened out and the moaning has lessened. I sit back and stare down at her.

Holy shit, Lucy just fell asleep on me.

CHAPTER TWELVE
Lucy

I slowly come awake, wondering what time it is. I'm surprised my alarm has not woken me up yet. Normally it is the thing that rips me from a nice dream and my warm bed. But this morning, no ripping. I roll over to my back and start to stretch my muscles from their sleepy state.

"Good morning," a deep voice says behind me, scaring me half to death. I scream and throw my arms out, hitting the voice straight in the face.

"Ouch!" I turn and see Mason clutching his face.

"Oh, Mason. I'm so sorry!" I sit up and reach for him. "Are you, OK?" I ask and try to move his hands away checking for the damage my arms just caused but I notice he is laughing.

He rolls and switches our position and I find myself beneath his strong body. I wrap my legs around his hips.

"I'm wonderful, cupcake." He leans in for a kiss and I can't think of a better way to start a morning then with a kiss from this big and sexy man.

"Mason, this is not us going slow." I giggle and loop my arms around his shoulders, ignoring my own protest.

"Mmmm hmmm but that's not what you said last night." He hums into my neck, kissing, nibbling and exploring.

I giggle again, enjoying the way his beard tickles my neck. He is just so much fun to be with.

"No, really Mason." I push on his shoulder, removing his lips from the amazing spot below my ear. "We agreed on slow."

He groans and leans his forehead onto him. "You are going to be the death of me, cupcake."

He kisses the tip of my nose, which must be the cutest thing ever, and sits back from me.

"Tell me something about you," he requests and pulls me to him.

"Like what?" I ask and cuddle in close, leaning my head on his chest.

"I don't know? Anything."

I think it over and decide to tell him a little about my past. I hate sharing this but with him I want to. "Well… Lucy isn't my real name," I say and wait.

"Oh really?" he asks. "And who might I have the pleasure of spending time with?"

"It's a bit of a long story," I say, hoping to dissuade his interest. I shouldn't have started this topic. Instant regret.

He kisses my head. "That's OK, cupcake. I like hearing your voice."

Oh man, that just melts my heart.

"Well, my parents are hippies. Not your normal "let's eat all organic" hippies, they are super hippies. I grew up in a commune in Northern Nevada." I pause waiting for a reply.

"Keep going." He slowly drags his fingers up and down my arm, making goosebumps form.

"My parents met while they were in college at Berkeley. They fell in love almost at first sight and married within two months of their first meeting. They were not really school people, so they decided to drop out and join the commune. They thought that they could do more for the world by living green and supporting a community.

"While my mom was pregnant she called me 'La Semillita' which means tiny seed in Spanish. When I was born, they went with that same theme and named me…" I pause. I hate to say it out loud. "Flower Bud. Flower Bud Harvey." I hold my breath for a second waiting on his reactions.

He begins to laugh and I can feel the rumble move through his chest. "Flower Bud? I like it."

I sit up and hit him in the chest. "Don't laugh! I hate it!"

He wraps his arms around me and pulls me back to him. "Where did Lucy come from?"

"When I was about 5, the state of Nevada came in and told everyone at the commune that the children who were school aged needed to be enrolled at the local school. I had an amazing kindergarten teacher named Ms. Kirchner. She could tell I was a shy child and asked me my name. When I said Flower Bud, she could tell that I didn't like it, she asked me what name I would rather go by. I said Lucy and she never called me anything but that.

"Even in front of my parents, she never faltered. I had it changed legally the day after I turned 18."

"I do like Lucy better," he says and kisses my forehead.

I sit up and cross my legs, looking down at him. "OK, now it is your turn. Tell me something about you."

He sits forward too and rests back against the headboard. "Well my name is Mason. No secret names here," he jokes, and I throw a pillow at his face.

He laughs and easily catches the pillow. "Sorry, I couldn't resist! Well, you already know about my family."

I shake my head. "Tell me anyway. Pretend I don't work for your dad."

"I am the oldest of 3. I have two younger sisters, Michelle and Mary Ann. My parents met while at Gonzaga but waited until they both graduated to get married. Mom is two years younger than Dad so he stayed around Spokane waiting for her. That is when he and Richard started their company.

"I, too, went to Gonzaga but moved to Seattle after graduation with a couple of friends to live in the big city and to make it on my own." He finishes.

"That was a very short version of your life," I say, wanting to know more. I love hearing his sexy deep voice.

He gives me a wolfish grin and before I know it, he has lunged at me and pushed me onto my back with my head at the foot of my bed.

I gasp in surprise. "Hey!"

"I think I have a better idea, Flower Bud!" He kisses along my neck and up to my jaw.

"Don't call me that!" I try to say in a stern voice but his lips are stealing away my resolve.

His kisses make their way up to my lips, where he nibbles at the corners. "Sorry, Lucy."

His lips fully land on mine and I tangle my fingers in his hair. It seems that as soon as our lips touch, my fingers automatically go there. Like they belong. I so enjoy kissing this man. I never thought I was a good kisser, Clay never seemed to want to get physical with me, but that is not the case with Mason. He will take every opportunity to have his lips and hands on me. His soft beard tickles my chin and upper lip. I will have to make sure the chafing marks can't be seen.

As we continue our toe curling kiss, I start to hear a ringing sound, but I don't recognize it.

I pull my lips from Mason's. "Mason, what is that noise?"

Mason ignores my question and frames my face, bringing my lips back to his.

But the noise is getting louder.

"Mason, wait. I think it is your phone."

He groans. "Damn it." He rolls away, stands next to the bed and retrieves his phone from the nightstand.

"It's my alarm. I have to go." He throws the phone on the bed and turns back to me. "Sorry, cupcake."

I stand on my knees, walking to the edge of the bed and wrap my arms around his middle. "It's all right. This is my day to rest. You go do what you need to do," I say and kiss his sternum.

I walk him to my front door and we stand together smiling like idiots and holding hands for a few minutes. "What are you doing tonight?"

"I have bowling league."

"Bowling league, huh." He brings my hand to his lips and kisses my knuckle.

"Yes, we are really badass," I say with a cocky grin.

He laughs. "Badass bowler, huh?"

"Hey now. No making fun, thank you." I pull my hand away and step away, pretending to be angry with him.

He smiles and pulls me back to him. "I'm sorry cupcake. I bet you are a total badass on the lanes."

"Yes. Yes I am." Showing him my best angry pout.

"Can I come and watch?"

I wait for a second pretending to think it over. He growls and starts to tickle my sides. I squeal and try to get away from him, but he is too strong and keeps me close, continuing to tickle me.

"Mason, stop!" I scream out, laughing and thrashing to get away. "Please, stop!"

"Not till you say you want me to come." I fall to the ground laughing so hard I am crying. He follows me down and doesn't stop.

"Come on, cupcake. Say it. Say you want me to come." He is smiling and laughing too.

"Fine. You can come." I say through my tears, trying to catch my breath.

"No, say you want me there."

"Yes, Mason. I want you there. Please come." He stops tickling me and I take several deep breaths to calm myself but continue to laugh between each breath.

Mason pulls me to my feet and I smack him a few times playfully, chastising him for doing that. He catches my arms and pulls me in for a passionate kiss.

He moves away and both of us are breathing a little heavy again. "Good bye cupcake. Have a good day!"

He walks out the door and leaves me alone. And there is a smile on my face that I'm hoping won't be going away for a while.

CHAPTER THIRTEEN
Lucy

Well, Friday did not go at all like I thought it would. It had started so well and then went to total shit and I have no idea why.

About a half hour after Mason left this morning, I realized I didn't have his phone number. So, I devised a plan to wait until around 4 p.m. and then call the office and speak to him in person. But around noon I got a text from an unknown Washington number.

Unknown Number: *Hello cupcake. I realized that I forgot to leave you with my number. So here it is, save it and make sure you use it.*

I decide I want to play a little.

Me: *New phone… who is this?*

Within seconds I see the three little dots pop up.

Mason: *Very funny. How is your day going? Are you getting some rest?*

Me: *Yes, I'm having a very nice morning. I'm catching up on some reading.*

He responds almost immediately.

Mason: *Is it one of those sexy Kristen lady's books?*

Me: *Kristen Proby? No. I'm rereading my favorite Harry Potter. You inspired me last night.*

Mason: *? That it isn't catching up on reading. You've already read it.*

Me: *Hey now buck-o. No one asked for your opinion of my reading habits.*

Mason: *LOL!*

Me: *So, bowling starts at 7 p.m. at the Post Falls Lanes.*

Mason: *Change of subject, huh? OK. I will see you there. Do you want me to take you?*

Me: *No, Callie and I usually ride together.*

Mason: *Who is Callie?*

Me: *She is my best friend; we were college roommates. She is basically my family.*

He doesn't respond right away and my immediate instinct is to say something else to keep the conversation going, but I wait and about 5 minutes later my phone chimes with his response.

Mason: *Nice.*

Me: *Yeah, you will get to meet her fiancé Craig tonight as well.*

Again, he doesn't respond right away. I wait and decide to draw him back into a new conversation.

Me: *How is work?*

I stare at my phone waiting for those three little dots to appear… but they don't. I continue to stare at my phone for several more minutes before I decide to walk away for a little while.

But for the next three hours, I am glued to my phone like a crazy person. Checking all my social media a million times, playing Disney Emoji Blast and glare at the texts from Mason, willing the three little dots to appear.

My over thinking brain starts to go into overdrive and reread over our text conversation several times trying to figure out what went wrong. Part of me knows he probably just got busy, it is a work day for him, but the other part, the single white female crazy side won't let it go.

My ex Clay would play mind games like this with me while we dated. He would make plans, then not respond several hours before those plans. After I texted him a bunch of times, he would have a reason to complain I was being dramatic and clingy. He loved having a reason to complain about my behavior. I was never in the right with him. I don't miss that type of shit and I really don't want this kind of thing with Mason.

The day ends with no more communication coming from Mason. He never texts me back and doesn't show up to watch me bowl. Callie could tell that something was wrong, but I tried to play it off that it was from the fainting on Thursday, but she knows me better than that. She gave me a knowing smile and I'm certain she will be bringing it up again

I arrive home later that night, a little tipsy and imagine Mason in the scene from "You've Got Mail." When Tom Hanks is trying to come up with excuses on why he doesn't show up to meet Meg Ryan.

I crawl into bed, feeling rejected and lonely. Looking back on this morning seems to be a little bit of a dream, like it almost wasn't real.

I woke up this morning determined to have a great day and forget about yesterday.

On Saturday mornings, Mark's 10-year-old son, Carter, has a peewee football game and he seems to think I'm a good luck charm. They won a game last season after a long losing streak and it happened to be the first one I went too. Carter has been convinced from that day on that I was his good luck charm and I was told without fail I had to be at all of them.

Luckily it is not too cold this morning and with my soft Idaho sweatshirt and hot cocoa it is just perfect. In the next month we will all be huddled under tents trying to stay out of the snow. These kids are so tough. I have never been overly athletic but the idea of running around playing football in the snow sounds just horrible. I will gladly stand on the sidelines and cheer them on, no matter the weather, but there is no way I would trade places these kids.

"Good morning!" I greet as I approach the McCallister Family and the Coeur d'Alene Vikings sideline.

"Good morning, Lucy" Mark's wife Lorna says and is the first to wrap me in a big hug.

The next few minutes are spent hugging and greeting everyone in the McCallister family. They are a very tight knit family and make everything into a family event. After all hugs have been issued, we find our way to our spots on the side of the field.

"So, Mark tells me you have a new boss," Lorna asks.

"Yep." I say with a frown into my travel cup as I take a large drink.

"Is he handsome?" She asks and wiggles her eyebrows at me.

Lorna has been trying to set me up for months, but I have declined each time. She wants me to be happy which is great but I have always thought I would find someone on my own. The old fairy tale of me walking into the room, our eyes meet from a distance and we both know instantly we are a made for each other has always seemed like what was right for me.

But so far, my fairy tale has not worked out. Maybe my prince charming got lost…?

"He is my boss, Lorna. I don't think that would be a good idea. Even if he is super handsome."

"Oh, super handsome, huh?" She laughs.

My cheeks instantly heat at the comment and I laugh, knowing I'm caught.

"OK, yes. He is super handsome and charming. But, I have been burned before trying to have a relationship with a coworker. I don't want to go down that road again."

I know it is 180° from how I left things with Mason yesterday morning, but his radio silence has changed my mind. The rule stays in place.

"Fair enough. Any other gentleman on your radar?"

"Nope. The other fish in the sea seem to be swimming away as fast as possible," I say with a little more bitterness in my voice then I mean too.

"Uh-oh. That comment sounded like it had a bit of a backstory. What happened?" She turns in her chair to face me, turning her focus from the game.

I take a deep breath and tell her the story that has unfolded with Mason in the last few days. She is the second person to hear this story and the more I talk about it, the weirder and more foreign it sounds in my head. Like it happened to someone else in a Hallmark movie and I am relaying the plot.

"… And then he never texted me back. I went to bowling alone and I have heard nothing from him." I let out a long sigh and sink down further into my chair.

"Well, he does not sound like the kind of guy you want." She gives a reassuring smile and turns her attention back to the game.

My heart aches with the pity I saw in her eyes and I do my best to hold back the tears.

The game goes well, and Carter's team wins.

"Lucy! We won! Did you see my touchdown?" Carter comes running over to me after the game.

I wrap him in a big bear hug. He is tall for his age and soon he will tower over my small 5˝2´.

"I did see. Didn't you see me on the sidelines jumping up and down and yelling 'Go CARTER?'" I reenact my goal dance for him.

"You are a terrible dancer," he snickers at me.

"WHAT?!?" I pretend to be offended. "I'm the best dancer ever." I pull him in and start to tickle his ribs.

He laughs and squirms, trying to get free. "Worst dancer ever." He gets free and runs away, still laughing.

"Take it back!" I yell and run after him. I catch him quickly and tickle him again. "Say I'm the best dancer ever!"

He falls to his knees, laughing with tears rolling down his cheeks. "Never!"

I continue my tickle assault until finally he cries uncle and admits I'm a great dancer. He stands up and wraps his arms around my waist.

He whispers. "You are my lucky charm, Lucy!"

I kiss his sweaty little head, my heart bursting with love. And just like that my whole day is turned around.

"Are you coming to lunch with us today, Lucy?" Mark asks.

Carter jumps around on his toes, bobbing his head in agreement. "Yes, please! It's Red Robin day!"

I have no idea how he has this much energy. He just played a full game. And of course, I can't say no.

"Only if you promise to share your fries with me?" I tease him.

"Lucy, their fries are bottomless. No one has to share." He runs away to catch up to his friends.

I turn to Mark and laugh. "Well then I guess I have to come."

Mark is carrying his 13-month-old, Lily, in a baby carrier on his chest as we gather our chairs and walk toward the cars. Lily is absolutely precious and is currently taking a nap without a care in the world.

"Thank you again for coming," Mark says.

"I have been told my presence is mandatory." I laugh and say casually back to him.

Mark stops and puts his hand on my arm, stopping me as well.

"No Lucy. Really, thank you. Carter adores having you at his games. And you don't have to come. It really means a lot to us that you take the time to come out here on a Saturday morning. We are so lucky to have you here and to care about our boy."

This time I can't stop the tears. "There is no place I would rather be," I say with a watery smile.

He pulls me in for a side hug and we start walking again toward the exit. Carter comes running back to us.

"Dad, can I ride with Lucy in blue bird to Red Robin?" He asks and hops around in front of us.

"I don't think she wants your dirty football gear in her nice car," Mark says.

Carter looks at me with hopeful eyes. "Please, Lucy?"

I take a second to think it over, "OK, fine. On two conditions?"

"Anything!," he says and hops a little higher.

"Your mom says it's OK and you promise to car dance with me!"

"OK!" He yells and runs away again toward his mom to get her permission.

Lorna smiles over at me and nods her head in agreement. Carter lets out a yell and jumps with his fist in the air. He is just too easy to please.

Our ride to lunch is short and Carter selects two of his favorite country songs for us to jam too. It is too cold out for us to have all the windows down, but Carter insisted. He is shivering a little when we get to the restaurant but the smile is worth it. He is going to be such a great man. Red Robin is in the Riverstone complex and right below my apartment so I park in the garage in my assigned parking spot. As we get out of my car I notice that Mason's jeep is not in its spot and I can see the remanence of the coffee spilled on me three mornings earlier.

I think we can have lots of fun not taking it slow cupcake.

Get out of my head!

"What did you say, Lucy?" Carter asks and pulls me from my thoughts of Mason.

Crap! "Oh, nothing kiddo." I grab Carter's hand and we walk out of the garage toward the restaurant.

"I see your window, Lucy." Carter points to my window. "You haven't put up your Halloween decorations yet? It's in like 6 days." He asks accusingly.

I laugh. "Sorry buddy. I will get right on that."

"You better," he says very matter-of-factly.

"What are you going to be this year?" I ask him as we enter the restaurant.

"Only the best costume ever! Adam Thielen baby! He is a wide receiver for the Vikings just like me!"

Of course he wants to be a football player. It's all this kid thinks about. Most people in Idaho are Seattle Seahawks fans but since Carter plays for the pee-wee Vikings, he is loyal to them.

"Mom got me a real jersey and I'm gonna wear my pads. It's gonna be killer."

"Sounds like it! I can't wait to see it." We join his family and are seated at a big booth. The whole extended family didn't come along, so it's just the three adults, Carter and the baby.

"What are you gonna be?" he asks as we look over the menu.

"I'm not sure. I haven't picked yet," I say.

Carter drops his menu to the table and I look over at him. His eyes are giant and a big smile is splitting his face.

"What?" I ask.

"You should be a Vikings cheerleader!" he yells out.

We all laugh and he continues on his train of thought.

"They have the best uniforms. They are purple and gold and have rhinestones all over them. Girls love rhinestones!"

"Great idea, buddy!" His mom agrees but he is looking at me for confirmation that I will do it.

"I will look into it."

"Yes!" he yells and again punches his fist in the air. What a kid!

Our lunch is delicious, and the rest of the time Carter is talking a mile a minute about all the cool things we are going to on Halloween in our matching costumes. I guess I am committed now.

Is it too much to hope that the Viking cheerleaders' costumes are long sleeved?

CHAPTER FOURTEEN
Mason

This weekend fucking sucked.

It all started on Friday around noon when I got a call from my boss back in Seattle. One of the biggest companies our firm's invested in, took a nose dive after its CEO was accused of sexual harassment. I had to drop everything in Idaho and fly to Seattle as quickly as I could to help minimize the damage.

The rest of the weekend was spent trying to come up with a plan and a very small amount of sleep. But this morning, I was able to call my former clients and insure them that their accounts were stable and no money would be lost. Those clients trusted me with their money for the eight years I was with them and I owed it to them.

It is now 8:45 p.m. and I'm just getting home from the airport. I've thought about Lucy all weekend but never got the chance to call her.

As soon as I enter my apartment I jump into action. I quickly shower and change out of my three-day old suit and head to Lucy's apartment. I knock on her door and wait for her to answer, but nothing. I decide to knock again, thinking she might have her head buried in one of her books and doesn't notice the first knock.

But again, after waiting another minute or so, there is no response.

Fuck. I needed her tonight.

I knock on her door again the next morning, but still no answer. I call her cell phone and it goes straight to voicemail. Now she has me worried.

I arrive at the Glass offices and walk to straight to her office, without greeting anyone else or checking in with my dad. Her door is shut but I don't take the time to knock. I open the door and find her sitting behind her desk on the phone.

Holy shit, she is so beautiful. She takes my breath away. Today she is wearing a black suit jacket and bright purple silky looking top. Her hair is down and wavy, the soft golden locks framing her sweet face.

She looks up from her computer and her eyes harden. She continues to listen to her phone call but doesn't take her eyes away from mine.

"Yes, of course Mr. Geoffrey. I will be happy to take care of that for you."

I take a seat in the chair across from her and settle in to wait until she is done with her phone call. She breaks eye contact when her client asks her a question and she focuses back on her computer. She is so smart. She is able to explain the information correctly and, in a way that is easy for them to understand.

My phone vibrates in my pocket with an incoming text.

Checkers: *Hey shit head. I heard you are back in CDA. Beers this week?*

Rob Lloyd or Checkers and I have been friends since middle school. He is the manager of a very successful custom auto shop in town.

Me: *Hell yeah. Tomorrow, Capones in Hayden at 6.*

Checkers: *What are you a fucking old lady? Gotta be home before Jeopardy by 7?*

Me: *Fuck off. See you then.*

"So your phone still works I see." Lucy says pulling me from my phone. Her eyes are hard and her lips are set in a thin line.

"Yes, cupcake. It still works," I say and put it in my pocket. "How was your weekend?"

She lets out a breath and looks away. "Fine, thank you. But please don't call me cupcake, Mr. Glass."

I cock my eyebrow at her. All the walls that I had broken down last week are back up. "Mr. Glass, huh? We are back to that."

She meets my gaze and her eyes are sad. "Yes," she says quickly and clipped.

"And why is that Ms. Harvey?" We can play this little game if she wants.

"Because…" She is interrupted by a voice coming over the phone system.

"Ms. Harvey, you have a call on line two. Can you please take it? Or must I take another message for you?" Candice from the front desk asks.

"Yes, Mrs. Bell. I can take it. Please excuse me, Mr. Glass."

I get up to leave but walk around to her desk. She sits stick straight in her chair as I approach her. I lean in and kiss her cheek. "Can we have lunch today, cupcake?" I whisper in her ear staying close to her. Enjoying the sweet smell of her hair.

She clears her throat and starts to move away but I set my hand on her shoulders and keep her in place. "I can't today. I have a meeting in Spokane with Luke."

"Dinner?" I ask and place a couple of kisses on her neck below her ear.

Her pulse is speeding up and I can see the goose bumps that have formed on her arms.

She swallows hard and nods her head. Smiling, I place one more kiss on the crown of her head and leave her to work.

At the door, I turn to look at her one more time. She is looking down with a small smile on her face. She is just adorable.

I spend the rest of the day in meetings, getting to know the ins and outs of my dad's company. It's a new industry for me. Investment finance is a lot different from small business finance and this company provides a lot more services than I thought they did. Or we did, I should say. This is my company now, too.

A small knock sounds at my door at a few minutes after 5 p.m.

"Come in."

The door opens, and Lucy enters.

"You had said earlier you wanted to have dinner, but no time was arranged." She is standing just inside the door. I have a feeling she is trying to keep her distance.

I crook my finger at her, beckoning her toward me.

She shakes her head and stays where she is at. I laugh out loud at her trepidation.

"Why not?"

She looks down for a second, then looks back at me and says, "We need to talk, and distance would be better now. I'm not very happy with you and when you get close I seem to forget that."

"You aren't happy with me, huh?" I come around my desk, lean against it and fold my arms over my chest.

She stomps forward, showing her annoyance with me. "Yes." She places her hands on her hips but does not continue.

"And why is that, cupcake?" Her eyes flare at my term of endearment.

"I have asked you not to call me that."

"Why not, cupcake?" It's fun to rile her up.

"Because, I don't think it is a good idea for you to have a pet name for one of your employees."

"One of my employees, huh? Is that all you are?" I ask but don't move from my spot. She takes another step toward me.

"Yes, I think that would be best if I stay just your employee."

I take a moment to search her eyes before I say, "That is not what you said the other night."

Her mouth drops, and a gasp escapes her lips. She turns and moves to leave. I jump into action stopping her before she is out the door. I cage her in, pressing myself against her back, trapped between me and the wooden door.

"Where are you going, Lucy?" I ask and run my nose along her neck.

"Home, I don't want to play anymore games with you Mason."

"This isn't a game."

"Huh, really." She turns in my arms and faces me. "It sure seems like you are playing games."

"Nope, not with you."

She pushes her hands on my chest and moves me away from her. She ducks under my arm and turns back from the door, moving deeper into my office.

"Really? So it's not a game that we have a great night together, no not sex but still a great night. And we make plans for the next day and then you not only don't show up but you give me no explanation for the missed date. And not a single word from you for the next three days." She is pacing back and forth as she gives her little speech. Making wild hand gestures and being so damn cute.

"Then you show up at work, and expect everything to be right where you left it? I don't think so." She paces back to me and gets just inches away. She points a red tipped finger in my face. "That is games Mason Glass and I will not play them."

She is completely right. We had plans for Friday night and I stood her up, and I never did text her over the weekend like I kept planning too. Time just kept getting away from me.

I grab the hand she is pointing toward me and bring it to my lips, placing a soft kiss on her knuckles.

"I'm sorry, Lucy. The weekend was crazy. I had to go to Seattle to deal with an emergency with my previous job. I spent the whole time I was away crazy busy dealing with my former clients."

"And at no time while you were there, did you have two seconds to send me a message?" Lucy asks with distain dripping from her voice.

She is right again. I should have done that. No wonder she has her walls back up today. She thinks I stood her up and don't give two shits about her.

"I'm sorry, Lucy. Really. I was so focused on everything that was going on." I go to pull her hand to my lips again, needing more physical connection with her but she removes her hand from mine and takes a step away.

"I can't do stuff like this Mason. I'm the kind of girl who takes it very personally when you stand her up. A simple text is not hard. You really hurt my feelings."

I'm such an asshole! I close the distance between us and she allows me to wrap her in a hug. We stand together for several moments, me just holding her. I lay my lips on her soft hair, taking a deep breath of the smell that will forever be Lucy to me.

"You are right and again I am sorry, Lucy. It was fucked up of me to do that. I promise it will never happen again."

"Please, don't make promises like that." She keeps her eyes trained on my chest.

I place my fingers under her chin and lift her beautiful eyes to mine. "But I do mean it. I will make sure it never happens again." I do mean it and I want her to see in my eyes that I am serious.

"Just say you will try, but don't promise," she asks.

I nod my head in agreement and smile at her. "Do you forgive me?"

She nods once and smiles her soft smile at me. And I just can't take it anymore. I lean down less than an inch and my lips meet hers in a light kiss. Her lips are so soft and they taste sweet. I want to sink deep into them but she is still a little wary of me so I keep it light. I've just gotten her forgiveness and I don't want to give her a reason to push away again.

As I start to pull away she sighs, opening her mouth just enough for my tongue to gain entrance. I take the opportunity and I change the kiss. Licking in slowly, enjoying the taste that is all Lucy. She runs her tongue along mine and her hands move from my arms to my shoulders, pulling me down and closer to her. Her passion ignites something inside of me, she wants this as much as I do. The damn is open.

I pick her up and walk over to my desk, setting her on the polished surface. She wraps her short, curvy legs around my thighs and pulls me closer to her center. Her hands are tangled in my hair, taking charge, she moves my head to the angle that she wants. Taking the kisses she wants and not apologizing for it.

My hands start their own exploration as our lips remain fused together, coming up from her hips, past her curvy waist and cup her breasts through her silky shirt they are hiding under. Her nipples are pebbled hard and I ache to see them, to take them into my mouth and lick each one until she can only remember my name. I want to see their color; will they be a light pink or a deep rose like her lips. She moans her approval and arches her back, begging for more. Fuck yeah, I will give her more.

My lips take a journey down her neck, exploring the smooth white skin there. She leans her head back, allowing me more room to explore all I find there. Her moans and gasps fill my ears and fill the space of my office. Damn, she is so responsive. I find a small tattoo at the base of her neck, where it meets she shoulder. It is a small simple red heart. I haven't noticed it before now, I wonder if there are anymore hiding beneath her clothes.

I push her suit jacket off her shoulders on to my desk while continuing to kiss and explore. I hear something fall from the desk, but I don't give a shit right now. The whole place could be burning to the ground and it would not tear me away from this woman.

She works to remove my jacket off my shoulders, but leaves it hanging from my arms, impeding my movements while she moves on to unbuttoning my shirt. I'm held captive in my own suit jacket, my arms no longer able to move and touch freely.

I remove my lips from Lucy's to try and get my jacket off but she pulls my head back to hers, wanting to continue our kissing. I try again but she's determined to keep our kiss going. I laugh at the little minx and turn my head, this time dislodging our lips.

"Cupcake, wait. My arms are caught." I'm still wrestling with the jacket. I look at her beautiful face, made even more so by her lust for me. Her little brown eyes are heavy under her long lashes and her lips are swollen and a lovely shade of dark rose.

She giggles when she sees the predicament I have found myself. She turns me by my shoulders and finally removes the jacket from me. I turn back to her and pull her into my arms again, holding her close. She feels so good in my arms, she fits.

"I think maybe we should skip dinner and go straight home," I say, hoping she will agree and we can continue.

She nods her head and smiles up at me. "Yes, please."

CHAPTER FIFTEEN
Lucy

I had every intention to ignore Mason today but the second he arrived in my office this morning, my plan was all shot to hell. He looked so damn handsome in his navy-blue suit. Men in well-fitting suits are for sure one of my weaknesses.

We are driving back to our apartments in separate cars. He tried to convince me that we should leave mine here, but I won out in the end. I don't like leaving my car at work in downtown. Plus, it gives me a few minutes without him to make sure I'm not letting my lady bits run the show.

Maybe I should torture him a little more and make him take me to dinner first. No, that would be just as awful for me as well. I need him! Back in his office, he had me poised on the edge and neither of us were anywhere close to being naked.

Mason pulls into our garage behind me and we park in our assigned spots. I turn off the ignition and gather my things, but before I can open my door, Mason is there opening it for me. His big strong arms pull me out and press my back against the Jetta, takes my lips in a hot as hell kiss. Making my toes curl and hot moisture pool between my legs. We kiss for a long few minutes and when he stops, we are both breathing heavily. His lips are a little swollen as are mine and his eyes are heavy with lust.

"You should warn a lady before you take her breath away. It's just common courtesy," I say in a sassy whisper.

He laughs and leans his forehead on mine. "I'm sorry about that, cupcake. Should I tell you now that I plan to keep taking your breath away the rest of the night?" He asks.

My heart beats a little faster at his declaration and the anticipation in my belly grows. I nod my head with excitement.

He kisses my nose and turns us from my car. We walk toward the elevator hand in hand and I'm loving the physical connection with him. We don't have to wait long for the elevator and he clutches me close for the ride to our floor.

We head down the hall toward our apartment doors. I pause at my doorway since it's the first we arrive at but Mason has other ideas.

"Oh no, cupcake. The first time I have you will be in my bed," Mason says in a commanding voice.

I'm flush with excitement just thinking of all the wonderful things Mason is about to do to me and I can't freaking wait. I haven't felt this much chemistry ever.

Chemistry? Yeah chemistry. Preach it, Sister Sarah.

He makes my body come alive every time I am near him. None of my exes or any of my fantasies have ever been anywhere close to this.

We enter his apartment, and once the door clicks closed, the clothes start to fall off. I get down to my bra and panties in a heartbeat, good thing I wore cute ones today, and Mason is down to his tight black boxer briefs. I soak in his bronzed skin and the light sprinkling of hair on his chest. He obviously works out. His muscles are defined and I can see them flex with every movement.

I reach out to touch him, but he grabs my wrist.

"No, cupcake. I can't take you touching me right now." His voice is thick and heavy with lust.

"Well, this is going to be awkward if we can't touch each other," I joke.

"Oh, I will be doing a lot of touching, but you won't."

I give him a questioning glance. He smirks, grabs my hand and walks me toward his room.

I didn't explore when I was here last week for our movie night and I take in what my brain allows, through my lustful haze. Mason's room is minimal, with just a bed and a dresser. The bed has a wide slatted headboard made of dark, almost black wood. The sheets are a dark gray color, with a thick blanket on top. With all the dark colors it makes the room feel like a cave. A sexy masculine cave, but still a cave.

"Lie down on the bed please, Lucy." He kisses my shoulder and pushes me a little toward the bed.

I take the few steps toward the bed and reach back to remove my bra.

He stops me. "That's my job, cupcake."

He finishes removing my bra, pealing it down my arms and tosses it somewhere behind me. His hands replace my bra cups and he squeezes my breasts, rolling my nipples between his thumb and index finger. I can feel myself getting wetter from the wonderful torture.

"Mason," I say in a breathy moan, begging for more.

"God, you have the greatest tits." He continues the kneading of my breasts, keeping his eyes trained on them.

"They are just like everyone else's," I say, starting to feel a little self-conscious from the amount of scrutiny.

"Oh, no. Yours are perfection. They fit my hand perfectly. And when I do this…" He pauses and rolls my nipples with more pressure. As he does, my knees weaken and change to jelly. "You respond in the best way. You are so responsive."

"Mason, please," I moan with desperation in my voice.

"Let's see if we can get you to come only touching these perfect breasts." He continues to rub and pull and torture me in the sweetest way.

I feel the fire that continues to build inside me. I have never come like this before, but he has me so primed. He kisses my ear and bites down on the lobe, and I come apart in the next instant, crying out Mason's name.

My knees buckle from the intense pleasure that has just rocketed through me. I'm breathing heavily, and I can feel my heart racing. Mason lifts me and places me on the middle of the bed.

"Mason, I need you," I say and reach out to pull him down for a kiss.

"Nope, remember baby. This is my turn to explore." He pulls my panties down my legs and off. "Wow, look how wet you are."

Normally that kind of comment would make me blush but I'm too turned on to be embarrassed right now.

"I might be just a little turned on. You already made me come once, and I haven't gotten to even touch you yet," I whine and wiggle my upper body, enticing him to let me have my way.

"Ha, ha. Oh no you don't, you little tease. This is my night to make you feel amazing." I smile at this sweet tone. "And since you are still arguing with me, it seems I have not been doing my job."

"What job?" I ask as he moves down toward my feet. He picks up right foot and places a kiss on the inside of my ankle.

"To take your breath away."

Oh, man. He is so charming! I decide to stop complaining and enjoy the pleasure this handsome man is giving me.

He kisses along my calf and up the inside of my thigh, but before he kisses my center, he moves on to the other leg.

"Your skin is so soft," he says against my skin as he leaves wet open mouth kisses along my legs.

"I didn't shave this morning." I sigh and wish my skin was hair free.

He pinches behind my knee and gives me a stern glare. "Take my compliments, Lucy. I'll tell you if there is something wrong. And so far, there is nothing wrong with the body I am discovering."

Mason moves in and settles his shoulders between my out stretched thighs. "And this is the best thing I have ever seen." He kisses my pubis and my hips shoot up off the bed. He holds my hips down and licks along my pussy lips. My eyes roll back in my head at the pure awesomeness that is Mason's tongue. It doesn't take long of him licking and eating at me for another orgasm to roll through me.

I breathe in deeply trying to catch my breath as Mason kisses his way up my body to my lips. I can taste myself on him, it's so sexy.

"Mason?" I say in a not so calm voice once we break from our kiss.

"Yes?"

"Can you get inside me now?" I beg.

He laughs and reaches into his nightstand to retrieve a condom. Mason rolls it on and positions himself at my entrance. "Are you sure about this, Lucy?"

"Yes, damn it! Please, now!"

He pushes inside, deliciously stretching me. He is bigger than anyone I have been with before, but my body happily allows him in. He pushes forward slowly until he is all the way seated inside me.

I moan at how full I feel. I love feeling the weight of him on top of me. I reach up and bring his lips down to him, kissing him with everything I am. He starts to move, quickly moving in and out of me. His pace continues to quicken as we move toward our mutual orgasms.

"Fuck, Lucy. You feel so amazing!" He says not slowing down.

"Mason, I'm gonna come," I cry out.

"Yes, baby. Come, I'm right behind you," he grunts out.

I throw my head back and come for the third time tonight. Two more thrusts and I can feel Mason find his release too. He buries his face in my neck and clings to me as our breathing starts to slow.

All too soon, he leaves me and walks to the en-suite bathroom. I hear the water run and he returns with a washcloth and without the condom. He runs the warm wet washcloth along my still sensitive pussy, making my legs jerk. His lips turn up in a self-satisfied smirk.

Mason lies down and pulls me into his side, snuggling me close. I rest my head on his chest and close my heavy eyes.

CHAPTER SIXTEEN
Mason

I wake slowly feeling warm soft skin cuddled up against my side. I look over to see Lucy's face lying on the pillow next to mine. She is a mess; her hair is in knots around her face and her black eye make-up from yesterday is smudged on her cheeks. But damn, she is beautiful. Her left arm is wrapped tightly around my chest and her legs are tangled with mine under the sheets.

I glance at my phone on the nightstand and see it is still pretty early. If I get us up now, we will have some time to get a little dirty before we get in the shower. I remember from last week, that she doesn't like to be startled when she first wakes up, so I decide to make it a slow and sexy good morning.

I lift her arm to bring it to my mouth, wanting to place kisses there and work my way to her sweet lips. But she isn't having it. She moans her displeasure and moves closer to my side. Her head leaves the pillow and moves to my shoulder, seeking more closeness. Even her legs tighten around mine.

"Baby, it's time to wake up," I say softly and lean over to kiss her forehead.

"Hmmph," she says with her head still buried in my shoulder.

"Lucy, baby. We have to wake up." I kiss down the shell of her ear and down her soft cheeks.

"No," she says quietly and kisses my shoulder.

I laugh at this silly woman lying next to me. She is such a breath of fresh air. I slowly move out from beneath her and leave her lying on her back. I take the pillow I have just abandoned and hand it to her.

"Hold on to this. And don't move," I whisper the instructions into her ear. She gives a little nod and clutches the pillow. I lay wet kisses on her shoulder, exploring her creamy white skin with my lips.

I cover myself in a condom and slowly push inside her from behind, slipping in easily. She is still wet from last night. This angle allows me to be so deep inside her. She moans her approval and I continue for the next few minutes, making slow and sweet love to this amazing woman.

We part ways to get ready in our own apartments, but I hurry so I can watch her while she does. I'm currently sitting on her bed, reading emails while she is finishing her make-up and hair.

"Tonight, after work, I have to go to Spokane to get a Halloween costume," she tells me.

"Oh, yeah? What are you going to be?" I ask still looking down at my phone.

"Mark's son Carter wants me to be a Viking's cheerleader."

She peaks my interest at the word cheerleader. "A slutty cheerleader?" I ask her and wiggle my eyebrows at her.

She laughs and turns from the mirror to face me on the bed. "No, I am hoping more for a cheerleader that wears long sleeves and pants. It is supposed to be in the 40s tomorrow night."

"Why does he want you to be a Viking's cheerleader?"

She tells me about Mark's son Carter, and his pee-wee football team. I can tell she adores him and would do anything for him. I rise from the bed and move to the door of the bathroom, leaning against the door jamb.

"What if the two of us go as Viking's super fans?"

Her eyes light up, she turns and throws her arms around my shoulders. "Really? You want to wear a matching Halloween costume with me?" she asks in a hopeful and giddy tone.

"Sure, why not? I haven't been trick-or-treating in years."

She smiles the biggest smile I have ever seen. She pulls me close and kisses my cheek. "Thank you, he will love that."

I kiss her softly, turn her back to mirror and smack her ass. "Finish getting ready, baby. I'm going to need some coffee this morning. Someone kept me up all hours of the night."

She laughs and rolls her eyes at me. I love hearing that laugh. It is my new mission in life to keep her laughing.

Lucy and I are able to find the perfect Vikings' super fans outfits. I paid a little extra and had Carter's name and number put on the back of our jerseys. We got some purple and gold face paint and we added some strips under our eyes in the bright colors. Lucy's hair is in pigtails with ribbons tied round each. She looks adorable.

Carter went insane as soon as he saw Lucy's outfit. "Lucy, you look awesome! And that's my number and MY name!" He jumps up and down for at least a full minute. He was a little wary of me at first but when Lucy gave me the thumbs up we were all good.

Mark's house is in an established neighborhood with houses fairly close together near Hayden Lake. The evening was not too cold and walking from house to house kept my blood moving. I chatted with Mark and his wife while Lucy and Carter ran from house to house collecting as much candy as possible.

By the end of the night they both have an almost full plastic pumpkin and Carter is exhausted.

"Thank you so much for coming, Lucy! You are the best!" he says in a sleepy voice.

She hugs him close and kisses his forehead. "I wouldn't have missed it for the world. You better get to bed, buddy. You have a game in the morning."

He nods this head and walks into his house. We say our goodbyes to Mark and Lorna and head back toward our building.

"How are you doing, baby?" I ask as we speed toward home.

She is leaning her head against the headrest and her eyes are closed. "Good." She turns to me and smiles. "Thank you for coming along! He had the best time."

"You are great with him. I can tell he adores you."

She smiles big. "He is such a sweet kid. I love getting to watch him grow up."

I rest my hand on her thigh and give her a little squeeze. She intertwines her hand with mine. We drive in comfortable silence for the rest of the way home.

Tonight, we are staying at her place. We take quick showers and wash off the make-up. We climb into bed and she cuddles up close to my side. I have found in the last few nights I have spent with her, she is like a clinging vine. She wraps herself around me and hardly moves once she finds the spot she is most comfortable.

"Good night, honey. Thank you again for today."

My heart jumps at the term of endearment. She hasn't called me anything but Mason. I pull her chin up and place a kiss on her lips. "You're welcome, baby. Sleep good."

CHAPTER SEVENTEEN
Lucy

So far this weekend with Mason has been great.

He joined me at Carter's football game Saturday morning and cheered just as loud as the rest of us when Carter made a break for the end zone. It wasn't the ideal day to be outside with the rain and wind. The first of November packed quite a punch this year. But Mason was very attentive, making sure I was as warm and dry as I could be. He even went and got everyone hot cocoa during half time.

Swoon!

I'm trying not to get too ahead of myself but he is getting very close to Book Boyfriend status. But I'm not reading too much into it…. OK that was a lie!

Of course I'm reading into it!

Saturday night, he took me to dinner at Crafted in downtown. We were joined by his sister, Michelle, and her best friend Jason. I have met Michelle before at the office Christmas parties and liked her a lot. She is a tall woman with dark brown hair that is long and super curly. She is one of the lucky ones whose hair is just always beautiful. Her dark features are very similar to Mason's but softened in a way that makes her a very lovely woman. Jason is almost the exact opposite of Mason and Michelle. Where they are dark, he is blonde with bright green eyes.

I could tell from their interaction that Michelle and Jason have a very close relationship. I asked Mason on the ride home if there was anything more than just friendship between them, and he said no. They have been friends since they were little and that was as far as it had gone. I'm skeptical but I didn't press the issue.

Crafted is always a good time, with a ton of beers on tap and great food. They have a large patio area that is packed all through the summer. They keep it warm with heaters and fire pits as long as they can through the fall until the snow arrives and it's too cold.

The conversation and alcohol flowed freely between the four of us, and before long we were closing the place down. I got a little bit more tipsy than I meant to and Mason made sure to punish me for being naughty!

Another swoon moment!

It's now Sunday and Mason and I are cuddling on my couch, making out like sex-crazed teenagers. We had just been sitting together on the couch, Mason watching football and I was reading. Next thing you know, his lips were starting a long exploration of my neck and I am on my back with Mason above me.

"Damn, baby. I've had you at least 15 times in the past four days, twice being last night, and I want you so bad again my teeth ache," he says in a heated groan. I can feel how hard he is.

My heart feels like it might explode in my chest from his charming words and the amount of pure lust coursing through me. "Well I think we might be able to arrange that, just once more." My sassy side always comes out when I'm flirting with this handsome man.

"Oh, really. Just once more huh?" He tightens his grasp on my hips.

"Yeah, maybe I can allow that."

"Well, aren't you very generous," he says with a smirk on his face.

I shrug my shoulders and return his smirk. He laughs and kisses my nose, which I have come to find is the best thing ever! I love when he does that.

He sits up, pulling me onto his lap and he turns his attention back to the football game. I lean my head on his shoulder and snuggle in close. Besides watching Carter and a few Longhorns games, I don't really watch sports.

"Are the Seabirds your favorite team?"

"Seahawks. And yes, for football."

"What's your favorite of all?"

"The Seattle Mariners."

"Baseball?" I take a guess.

"Yep." I tuck that little nugget of information for a later date.

"Big baseball fan, huh?"

"Yep." His answers are one word. He is really concentrating on the game.

A commercial break starts and one for the new BMW comes on, drawing my attention.

"God, I would love to have one of those some day," I sigh with dreaminess in my voice.

"A BMW?"

"Yeah, I like them."

"What kind?"

"Any of them but the 3 Series is my favorite."

He pulls back and stares at me.

"What?" I ask.

"I didn't think you knew anything about cars."

"Oh, trust me. I don't. But I know those are pretty and I like them."

He laughs and we turn our attention back to the game. We spend the rest of the game snuggled up together on the couch.

As soon as the game ends, Mason picks me up and wraps my legs around him, heading toward the bedroom. I bury my hands in his hair and pull his lips to mine. His hands squeeze my butt as we move closer to my bed.

As we draw near I hear Callie's text tone, and it pulls my attention away.

"Who is it?" he asks traveling his lips along my jaw.

"That's Callie's text tone," I say, biting my lip. Callie is really the only family I have and I always make it a priority to answer her.

He turns me back toward the coffee table and smacks my butt. "Go on, baby. Answer Callie back."

I smile back at him and jog the few steps to my phone.

Callie: *Got plans for dinner?*

"She wants to know if I have plans for dinner," I respond back quickly.

Me: *Nope, what do you have in mind?*

"I thought I would cook for you." Mason says seconds after I hit send.

"Oh. Crap. I didn't realize you had something in mind."

He frowns but doesn't say anything.

Callie: *Be at my place at 4.*

"She wants me at her place at 4." I look over at the clock and realize it is already 2:45 p.m.

He continues his silence. "Would you like to come?" I ask him in a shy voice. I want him to come but I can't read his face. Is he mad I didn't ask him first what he wanted to do?

His frown deepens, and he runs his hands through his hair. "No. I have to go." He heads to the door, slips on his shoes and walks out before I even have a chance to process what just happened.

I arrive at Callie's a little before our arranged time, feeling completely distracted. I have been replaying my interaction with Mason since it happened. We hadn't talked about having plans for the evening and I did invite him to come along. I haven't messaged him; I'm not sure what to say.

I knock and open the front door. She lives in a safe neighborhood, so she leaves her door open for me when she knows I'm on the way. She and Craig purchased the cute little cottage in Post Falls after they got engaged. It has a wide front porch and large area in the backyard for a garden, both of which sold Callie on the property. Craig was sold on the proximity to his dental practice. He rides his bike most days in the summer.

"Hello!" I call out closing the door behind me.

"In the family room, sugar," Callie returns.

I can smell Callie is making her delicious homemade chicken curry. Yum!

I find Callie in the living room perched on the couch in sweatpants with her long hair in a knot on top of her head.

"Hello, sugar! How are you?" She jumps up and wraps me in a tight hug. She pulls back and kisses my cheek making me laugh. She always gets extra affectionate after we haven't seen each other in a few days. She knows how my parents were so she over compensates.

"Hi Callie. Where's Craig?" I ask and take my designated spot in her large comfy armchair.

"He, Caleb and Mitch went out to meet up with their Uncle Joe at the hunting cabin. They've been gone all weekend! It has been blissful to be alone but I needed time with my best friend today." Mitch is one of Craig's many cousins that live over in Spokane.

"Well thanks for the invite and thank you for making curry."

"How can you tell I'm making curry?" she asks with a shocked look.

"Callie, it is my favorite meal. Of course I can smell that you're making it!" I say with a laugh.

"Well, there goes my surprise then." She stands with a huff and heads toward her kitchen.

I follow along after her, still laughing at my silly best friend.

"Tell me more about your week. I saw your pictures from Halloween. Carter seemed to have a great time." She grabs two large bowls down from her cabinets and I get us something to drink.

"He did. It was so much fun. Mason came along and Carter really liked him. Water?"

She stops what she is doing and turns to me abruptly. "I'm sorry, who came along with you?"

Oh yeah, I never told her that Mason and I had made up last Wednesday. "Mason," I say shyly.

"WHAT?!?" she shouts. "Tell me!" she demands.

"Well, I saw him at work on Wednesday and we have been spending some time together since then," I say teasing her.

"Stop it! Give me the details you brat!" she demands again a little louder.

"Curry first! Then I'll tell you everything." I go back to gathering our drinks and flatware.

"Ugh, you're killing me sugar!" She hurls herself again the counter in her best dramatic southern belle impression.

"Oh my goodness, Scarlet. Settle down!" I give her back my best southern accent.

"Man, sugar. You're getting good at that," she compliments.

Callie dishes each of us a large bowl of jasmine rice and the creamy curry. We carry everything to the table. Just as soon as I am settled in, Callie launches into questions about Mason and I.

I answer them and tell her all about our last few days together.

"I do need your advice on something."

Callie's smile widens. "Anything, you hardly ever ask me for love advice."

"That's not true."

"Yes." She draws on the word yes, giving it extra emphasis. "You tell me about your love life but never ask for my help."

I roll my eyes at her. "OK, well I need your help with this. When you messaged me earlier today, Mason and I had been making out. And I didn't ask him if he had plans for us before I responded to you that I didn't.

He seemed really upset that I didn't consult him. And after I invited him along, he stormed out of my place." I shrug my shoulders, feeling defeated again.

She gives me a perplexed look and then says, "OK, first…
you stopped making out with Mason to read my message?"

"Yeah, he said I could" He did, I think.

"Well that might be the first issue. Guys might have us be-
lieving they don't have emotions but sometimes they are more sensitive than we are."

My heart drops. I have totally fucked this up.

"Hey, its OK. We can still fix this. Let me see your phone?"

I hand over my phone; she unlocks it and pulls up my text
messages. "You haven't sent him anything since last week."

"I told you, we have been together every day since Wednesday," I remind her.

"OK, let's send him something."

"What are you going to say?" I ask and look over her
shoulder to see what she is typing.

"I think you should say that you wish he was here. Let him
know you are thinking of him."

Me: *I wish you were here.*

She hits send and we wait. My eyes are glued to the screen
hoping to get a reply soon. I'm on pins and needles for several seconds before those three little dots appear.

…

CHAPTER EIGHTEEN
Mason

I just received a text from Lucy telling me she wished I was with her.

I'm currently sitting at a bar with Checkers, four beers in. I had bailed on our plans to meet up earlier in the week when Lucy and I went to get the Halloween costumes. After I left her place this afternoon, I called Checks and made plans to meet up for beers.

"Get a text from your girl?" Checks asks and finishes his beer.

I stare hard at the phone, not really wanting to reply. "Yeah, she's with a friend."

"A guy friend?"

I turn toward him and give him a hard glare, there better not be a guy there. "No, her best girlfriend Callie." My eyes go back to the screen and I write out my reply.

Me: *Miss you too.* Fuck, no that sounds too clingy. I delete the message without sending it.

"You're upset your girl is with her best friend?" he asks with a laugh in his voice.

"No man, fuck you."

"Then what the fuck is your issue? She said she missed you."

Me: *Really? It seemed like you didn't want me to come along!* No, way too aggressive.

"Yeah, but she made plans while we were hanging out. And then when she asked me along, it was a total pity invite."

He lets out a loud laugh. "A pity invite? Come on, Mas." He slaps me on the back. "Don't be such a girl. If she didn't want you to come, then she wouldn't have invited you."

Fuck, he is right. I hate to say that I got jealous of her best friend, but I did. I had plans to spend the evening with her again tonight and as soon as Callie sent her the message, she made plans with her.

I pick up my beer and finish it off in one long drink. I pick up my phone again, deciding what I need to say.

Me: *I wish I was there too, baby! Have fun with Callie.*

As soon as the message is sent, a large weight is lifted from my shoulders. I was carrying around all this anger all afternoon. I have always been a little possessive with the women I date but when it comes to Lucy, this shit is on a whole other level.

I order another beer just as my phone chimes with another text from Lucy.

Lucy: *Will I see you later tonight?*

Me: *If you want too.*

Lucy: *:) Of course, I do.*

Me: *Then you will see me later.*

Lucy: *:)*

"Fuck, you look like an idiot man."

"Why?"

"You are grinning like one."

"Shut up, buy me another beer."

I bang on Lucy's door when I arrive home around 10:30. I ended up needing to take an Uber home. The last couple beers turned into a couple of tequila shots and that snowballed until I was stumbling around like a 16-year-old at his first house party.

Lucy answers the door, looking just adorable, in her pajama pants and college sweatshirt. Tonight's have little dragons on them. I can't wait to get them off of her, that's if I don't pass out first.

"Hi, baby," I slur and take a step forward, tripping over my feet and almost falling on my face.

She catches my shoulders and helps right me. "Hi. Did you have a good time?"

She wraps her left arm around my middle and loops my right around her shoulders, being my own personal crutch. She is more than a foot shorter than me, so it is awkward as we walk together but her help is so sweet.

"Yes, Checks says hi." She walks me back to her room and lays me down on her bed.

"Checks, huh? Who is that?"

"My friend's Checks," I say as a matter of fact. Duh!

She laughs and pull my shoes off. "Oh that Checks."

"Yep, he says, hey." Now that I am lying down I realize how tired I am. I close my eyes for just a second. Why is her bed spinning? I wonder why she would have a spinning bed.

"Mason, can you take this and drink some water?"

"When did you go and get that?" I ask, she was just taking off my shoes. She is fast.

"I just went and got it." She laughs her cute little giggle. "I have been gone for a couple minutes. Can you sit up please?" She helps me sit up and when I open my eyes, I notice she has changed clothes.

"When did you change? Where did your sweatpants go?" She is wearing a cotton nightgown that has thin straps and is tight around her beautiful breasts. I can see the outline of her nipples through the material. The longer I stare I can see them harden.

"Mason, please take these. You are going to have a hell of a headache tomorrow if you don't."

"Oh, baby. You are taking care of me." I wrap my arms around her waist and bury my face in between her breasts. I feel a splash of cold water down my back and hear Lucy gasp.

"Mason, you are going to spill this whole glass of water on my bed. Baby, can you please drink this for me?" She is combing her fingers through my hair and it feels just wonderful.

"You just called me baby." I sit back and look into her eyes. She has a sweet smile on her face.

"Yes I did." She kisses my forehead.

"I like it."

"I like it too. Could you do me a favor and drink some water?" she asks sweetly.

"Will you keep calling me baby?" I ask and take the cup of water from her hand.

"Yes, I will. Take these aspirin too, please."

I quickly throw back the aspirin and drink the full glass of water in a few gulps.

"Thank you for taking care of me." I hug her close and fall back on the bed, taking her with me. I roll with her and tuck her beneath me. "Let's go to bed."

I take up my new favorite spot cradled in her arms with my head buried in her neck.

"Sounds good, Mason. Can I go turn off the light really quick?"

I don't want her to move; she feels great right where she is. "No, we can sleep with the lights on."

She laughs and tugs on my hair. I let her slip from beneath me and she goes to turn the lights off. It doesn't take her long to complete the task and as soon as she is within my reach I pull her back to where I want her.

She laughs my favorite sweet giggle and settles in my arms. "Goodnight, Mason."

I groan my displeasure at her use of my name. "Sorry. Goodnight, baby."

I smile and fall quickly into drunk sleep.

CHAPTER NINETEEN
Lucy

Drunk Mason is hilarious and sweet. But hung-over Mason is not a happy camper. Most men don't handle being sick well and he is no exception. He woke up around 4 a.m. and ran to the bathroom to throw up. I did my best to make him comfortable as he got sick, but I couldn't take it away completely.

After the first round of getting sick, I make him some dry toast, hoping it will help soak up most of the alcohol. But not too long after, he got sick again, bringing the toast up along with it.

I run him a warm shower, hoping to ease his discomfort. I always feel better after taking a shower. He doesn't stay in the shower long and like a zombie walks straight back to bed without even drying off.

He must have had more to drink than I realized.

Mason was sleeping when I left for work. He had gotten sick two more times since his shower and I convinced him to tell his dad he wasn't going to be in this morning and get some more rest.

Around lunchtime I head home to check on him. He hasn't responded to my texts and I'm getting a little worried. When I arrive at my apartment, Mason has not moved an inch. I feel this forehead and he is burning up.

"Mason?"

He stirs a little but doesn't wake fully.

"Mason? How are you feeling?"

He turns over, and I can tell he is getting dehydrated.

"I think you have the flu."

"Yeah," he says in a small, weak voice.

Oh, the poor guy. "I'm going to call your dad and let him know. Then get you some medicine but first I need to get some fluids in you. Can you drink some water for me?"

He nods his head and sits up. I get him settled against my headboard and bring him a large glass of water. He takes it from me and drinks as much as he can.

"I should probably go home. I don't want you to get sick too," he says in a quiet voice.

"I had my flu shot. I should be OK, plus I don't think it's a good idea for you to be alone while you are this sick." No one likes to be alone while they are sick.

"Thank you, baby."

"Would you like me to get you some comfy clothes?" I ask, wanting him to be comfortable.

"Yes, please." He gives me a shy smile and it melts my heart.

"OK, I will go get you some clothes, then head to the store. Is that OK?"

He nods his head, then leans it back and closes his eyes.

I kiss his warm forehead and hurry across the hall for his clothes. It doesn't take me long to get him a couple pairs of sweats, a few t-shirts and boxer briefs. I gather his toothbrush too. I help him into the clean clothes and leave for the drug store a few minutes later.

I call his dad on the drive to the store, giving him an update on Mason. I assure him I would be back in the office soon. He thanks me for the update and tells me to take my time, that there is no rush to come back.

I'm back at my apartment within 20 minutes. I might have gone a little overboard with all the things I purchased but I have never taken care of Mason before. Most people have certain things they like to have when they are sick and I don't know him that well, so I get a little bit of everything. Actually, a lot of everything. I'm loaded down with five bags as I push through my front door. I set the items on the counter, when I hear a female voice coming from my bedroom.

What the hell? Who is in my apartment?

I hurry back toward the room and stop abruptly when I see Mason's mother sitting on the bed next to Mason.

"Lucy. Hello dear." She walks over and wraps me in a hug.

"Hello, Mrs. Glass." I hug her back, but I'm still in shock that she is here.

"Please, call me Christine. I'm sorry to invade your apartment like this. I hurried over when Mason's dad told me he was sick." She gives me a kind smile and moves back to the bed beside Mason.

I've never had a boyfriend's mom in my bedroom before. Luckily, I'm not a messy person so there is nothing that is too embarrassing.

"Not at all. I am just glad I cleaned recently," I joke with her.

I really like Christine. Just like her daughter Michelle, I have met Christine at the company Christmas parties and around the office. Michelle and Mary Ann get their dark hair from Christine, but the siblings get their height for sure from their father. She stands about the same height as me, with kind blue eyes like Mason's and a great sense of style.

She laughs and smiles back at me. "You have a very nice place here. I promise I didn't snoop." She winks at me.

"Thank you. I like it." I look around my room, proud of the space I have created for myself. "How are you doing, Mason?" I ask, bringing the focus back to the sick man behind her.

"Like fucking shit," he groans.

"Mason," his mother scolds making me giggle. He raises an eyebrow at me. Oops, I will be paying for that one.

"Let me get you some medicine and something to drink." I turn to leave the room heading toward my kitchen.

"I'll help you." I hear Christine say from behind me. "Oh, wow. Did you bring the whole pharmacy home with you?" She says seeing the number of bags I acquired at Walgreens.

"Yeah, I might have gone a little overboard," I confirm as I empty the bags and put the popsicles I got into my freezer. "I wasn't sure what he likes when he is sick so I got a little of everything."

She unloads the bag full of tissues, canned soup and blue sports drink. "That is so thoughtful of you. He doesn't like to eat a whole lot when he is sick but he will really enjoy those popsicles." I smile. Those are my favorite when I'm sick too.

We finish unpacking the bags and helps organize the supplies on the counter.

"I'm going to grab a TV tray to set the items on for him." I leave the small kitchen and get a TV tray from next to the entertainment center.

"You are a good caregiver," she says.

"My mother was sick a lot when I was growing up. I took care of her."

"Oh, your poor mother. What was wrong with her?" She gathers the box of tissues, over the counter flu medicine and cough drops.

"She was allergic to strawberries."

She laughs, "That's it?"

We arrive at the bedroom and I see Mason has fallen asleep. I don't wake him yet, I won't until we have everything ready for him. That way he doesn't have to be up for too long.

After we leave the room for the second load, I answer her questions.

"Yep, she had a theory that she could force her body to get over the allergy. It did not work." I grab three glasses and fill them with water, blue sports drink and ginger ale.

"No, I don't see that working," Christine laughs.

"Do you think he would like some tea too?" I ask.

"No, he is not a tea drinker. And he won't eat those crackers either." I stop unpacking the sleeve of Ritz crackers. "He prefers saltines."

"Oh. I've got those, too."

She smiles at me. "You really did think of everything."

"I tried. I feel so bad for him. No one likes to have the flu. I just want to take care of him."

"You really like him." It's a statement, not a question.

I look into her eyes, and I can't understate my feelings to her. "Yes. Yes I do."

She pulls me into a tight hug and holds me for a long moment. When she pulls away, she gives me a soft kiss on the cheek.

"Let's get that boy some medicine and I will get out of your hair. You aren't going back to work today, are you?"

"Yes, I'm going back in a little bit. I'm only on my lunch break."

She stops and turns back to me a little shocked. "No, I will call my husband. You stay here and get some rest too. We don't need both of you getting sick."

"Oh I got a flu shot a few weeks ago," assuring her I would be fine.

"No, you are staying here. If you must, do some work from home, but stay here. You might not be getting sick but those germs will spread through the office like wildfire."

"I didn't even think of that. That would be awful." Yeah there is no way I can go back to the office and get everyone else sick.

"Yes, it would. The flu is awful already this year. Don't want it spreading."

We walk back to the bedroom and I go straight to Mason's side. I run my fingers through his hair and quietly say his name. He opens his eyes and he gives me a sweet smile.

"Hi baby."

"Hi. I have some medicine for you. Can you sit up and take it for me?" I continue to run my fingers through his hair, loving the softness.

"You are always trying to get me to take things and drink things. You aren't poisoning me, are you?" He says but moves to bury his head in my lap and wraps his arms around me.

I chuckle and lean down to kiss the top of his head. "The medicine isn't down there. And no, I'm not poisoning you. I'm doing the opposite."

"But something that will make me feel better is." I gasp in shock and my head whips around to his mother.

She is standing there laughing. "Such like a man to still think like that even when they are sick."

"Baby, is my mother here?" he asks but doesn't move.

"Yes. She is, you let her in while I was at the store."

"Oh, yeah. Hi Momma." This time he sits up against the headboard and looks toward him mom. It looks like he is having flu amnesia. She chuckles but doesn't say anything. Just watches our interaction with a wide smile on her face.

"I brought you some medicine and something to drink. Can you take this for me, please?"

"Please what?"

"Huh?"

"You know what I want you to say."

I roll my eyes. "Please, baby?" I ask sweetly and lean forward to kiss his forehead.

He hums his approval and nods his head. I smile at this surprising and sweet man. He sure does love that term of endearment.

I hand him the medicine and give him the option of the three drinks we have carried in. He chooses the sports drink and uses about half of the glass to take the medicine. When he is done, I settle him back under the covers and he falls right back to sleep.

His mother and I leave the room and I walk her to the front door.

She hugs me close again as we stand at the door.

"Take care of our boy, and if you need anything, do not hesitate to call me."

"Will do." She gives me a look and I say. "I promise."

She pats my arm and leaves.

I head back to my room and change from my work clothes into something that is more comfortable. Minutes later I hear my phone go off in the kitchen and head out to check it.

It is a text message from my boss Luke, telling me to stay at home and away from the office for the next few days. He asks to please set up an outgoing message and to reschedule any in office meetings for the following week. Then he ends the message telling me to feel better.

That seems odd. I'm not the one who is sick but I don't push it. I respond with a quick thank you.

My second bedroom is set up as an office so I head there to get some work done and set my out of office message. Since I had gone in earlier, I had a pretty good idea of the things that are on my plate for the week, so I settle in and get some work done.

I spend the next few hours in my office and take a few breaks to check on Mason. He sleeps most of the day and only wakes to take more medicine and use the bathroom. Callie came over around dinner time to bring me food, when she found out I had stayed home to take care of Mason.

"I brought you Mexican food," she says with two large bags of food.

"Are you feeding the whole building?" I laugh at the amount she has brought with her.

"I thought you might be trapped here for a few days, so I wanted to keep you fed." She hugs me close and unpacks the food. "You do have to share some of your dinner with me."

"Of course."

We sit at the table and eat, talking about random things like best friends do.

"Have you heard from your parents lately?"

"No, not since the summer."

"Have you thought anymore about going there for Christmas?"

"No, I don't want to. The last was such a disaster. I don't want to relive it."

"Sugar, that was five years ago. Maybe it is time to try again."

I let out a long breath. "I just don't know if I want them to be apart of this new life I have made. They always make it clear I'm doing everything wrong and that I'm not the woman they raised me to be."

"And I don't want to be like them at all. I like this new life that I have made for myself. Commune life is not for me."

"No, I don't think you would do well there," she laughs, and her smile is contagious.

"And plus I have you for family. That is enough for me."

"But I'm not your blood family. And it's important to have those connections too."

"I know but they just don't get me. We are the complete opposite."

"I get that. But how are you going to feel in a few years when you have your own kids? Won't you want them to be in their life?"

She has this same argument with me every time we talk about this. She wants me to reconnect with them. She seems to think it will be movie perfect; that we will run into each other's arms and forget everything in the past. And I don't think we can do that.

No, my parents didn't beat me or starve me, but they didn't treat me like they ever wanted me. I was treated like an outsider since the day I was born. I think I was just an accessory for them. Just another thing to have to show the commune they were a part of their way of life. They were selfish parents and still are.

"Oh, sugar. Let's not talk about them anymore. Let's talk about my wedding…" She pulls up her Pinterest page and all other worries are gone.

She stays for another hour or so and we browse through the internet oohing and aahing over everything wedding. After she leaves, I settle on the couch to chill. I watch tv most of the evening and when it's bedtime I make myself a bed on the couch, leaving Mason to have the bed. Around midnight, I wake being carried toward my room by Mason.

"Mason, what are you doing? You have the flu. You should be resting," I say and try to get him to put me down.

"I have been in bed all day without you. I need you."

Swoon!

I ended up spending the whole week home with Mason. The flu really hit him hard. Thanks to my flu shot, I never caught it and stayed healthy.

We had lots of visitors over the week, including both of his sisters and his parents on Friday night. The four of them stayed with Mason while I went bowling. It felt a little weird to leave my boyfriend's family in the apartment we don't share, but they insisted that after being Mason's caretaker all week, I deserved a little time for myself.

When I got home, they had cleaned both the kitchen and my bathroom for me, changed out the sheets on the bed, and stocked my fridge with a whole weeks' worth of food.

Yes, you heard me right, I said boyfriend. Mason and I have made it official that we are dating with my friends and his family, but we are still hush-hush at the office. He doesn't like it but I assured him it was only temporary, so he went along with it.

CHAPTER TWENTY
Mason

Tonight we are at Lucy's bowling league. There are only a few more weeks before the wrap up right before Thanksgiving, so I made it a priority to be here for her tonight. She plays in an eight-pin, no-tap league which apparently means if they hit eight pins in the first half of the frame, they get a strike and don't have to hit the other two down.

I like to tease her and say that no-tap is cheating and that bowling is not a team sport. It is so hot to get her all riled up.

She looks so adorable in her team's bowling shirt. Her hair is in a ponytail and her eyes are shining with happiness. She is currently sitting down on the benches with her teammate, laughing and having a good time, while I enjoy a beer behind her at the high-top tables.

Most of the other teams are sitting around not talking but Lucy's team isn't. They are drinking, talking and laughing with each other, cheering each other on.

Lucy isn't a bad little bowler. She isn't getting 300 each time but it looks like she averages four or five strikes per game. She is having a great time and that is what matters.

"Mason, right?" I turn my head to find the EMT from Lucy's fainting spell last month. He sticks out his hand in greeting.

"Yes, Caleb?" I take his hand and give him a firm handshake.

"Yeah, good to see you man. Are you here with guppy?"

I throw him a questioning look. "Lucy, sorry I have been calling her that for years."

I take a long swig of my beer and try not to deck this guy in the face. Damn, she brings out my jealous streak. "Yeah, we are dating."

He slaps my shoulder. "That's great! Lucy is an awesome girl. We all think so."

"Yeah she is amazing." I take another long swig of beer, trying not to sound sarcastic but his is pissing me off. Stop talking about my girl.

"Caleb, it's your turn," one of the other ladies calls out from the lanes. I don't remember her name.

Lucy introduced me to everyone earlier, including her best friend Callie. I was instantly impressed with her. Lucy had told me a lot about Callie's successful business before we met, but I could tell right away that she was a very smart and accomplished woman just like Lucy. Her fiancé, Craig, was also a very cool guy. She had told me all about how they ended up in Idaho, and after moving home to be with my family, I have a lot of respect for him.

They are great guys and I don't mind if we spend time together in the future.

Her team lets out a cheer and I look down to see Lucy has gotten a third strike in a row. She is jumping up and down celebrating her great frames. She runs toward me and leaps on to my lap.

"Did you see that?" She asks and kisses me before I can answer. She tastes like cinnamon from the fireball shot they all took at the start of the game.

"I did, that was great! You are totally a bad ass bowler, baby." I pull her in close and kiss her again.

"Thank you for coming."

"You are welcome. Are you hungry? Do you need another drink?"

"You are so sweet! I would love something to eat. I don't care what, you pick!"

"And a drink?"

"Yes, please. I will take a beer, whatever you are drinking."

"You are very easy going tonight."

"It's because I'm happy."

"I make you happy, huh?"

"Yes," she kisses my nose and continues, "yes you do."

"Lucy, sugar. It's your turn again." Callie calls from the lanes.

"Coming." She gives me one last quick kiss before she leaves my lap.

I watch her bowl an eight before I head to the bar to order her a beer and some food.

"MJ?" A leggy red head comes up to my side while I wait for our drinks.

"Hello." It's Tiffany Sanders. She was my high school girl friend. I haven't seen her since.

"How are you doing, handsome?" She wraps me in a hug and I return it.

"I'm good, Tiff. How are you?"

"I'm really good. Pregnant with my second baby." She points down and I see the start of a baby bump.

"That is so great." I wrap her in a second hug. "Who is the lucky guy?"

"Joe Finley." I remember him, guy was a prick.

"Awesome, good for you guys."

I see movement out of the corner of my eye and see Lucy turn and start to leave the bar area. "Lucy!" I call out her name, stopping her. She takes a second before turning around with a bit of a forced smile on her face. I walk over to her, pull her close to my side and lead her back to the bar.

"Lucy, this is Tiffany. We went to high school together. Her and her husband are about to have a second child." I can feel the change in her the second I say 'her husband'. I guess my little cupcake has her own jealous side.

"Tiffany, this is my girlfriend, Lucy."

Tiffany extends her hand, and Lucy takes it right away.

"It is so nice to meet you. Congratulations on your baby."

Tiffany places her hands on her belly. "Thank you. We are very excited. Joe is hoping for a boy. Oh, excuse me. It's my turn to bowl. Nice to meet you Lucy, and good to see you again MJ."

Tiff leaves and I wrap my arm around Lucy's waist, pulling her close and whisper in her ear, "Were you jealous, cupcake?"

Lucy shakes her head and tries to pull away, but I keep my firm grip on her. "Yes, I think you were." I kiss her up her neck and playfully tug at her ear lobe. "Tell me the truth."

"Yes, a little bit. She is very pretty." She whispers back to me.

"Oh, cupcake. She is just a girl I knew in high school. You are all I see." I pull back and tell her while holding her gaze. Her eyes flare and a lovely pink color floods her cheeks. She rises up on her tiptoes and lightly touches her lips to mine.

"I have to get back to bowling," she says staying pressed close to me.

"OK, I will be back over in just a minute." I kiss her lips chastely and turn her toward the door to the lanes.

She turns and gives me a sexy smile over her shoulder, her hips sway as she walks making my eyes zero in on that fine ass. Damn, she is beautiful.

I gather our food and drinks and head back to the lanes. They are almost done with the first game. Man, that goes by quickly. Lucy is standing near the table where I was sitting before. She has her phone in her hand and she is concentrating hard at whatever she is looking at. I set our food and drinks down at the table and watch her for a minute. She is typing away furiously on the keys.

"Work." Callie says, breaking me from my staring at Lucy. "She does that a lot. Her clients are very important to her. She loves her job. Sometimes I think she does it more for the people she meets than the numbers."

"How much is a lot? She isn't burning herself out, is she?" I ask, concerned she isn't taking the time she is at home to rest and recharge. I know she is a super hard worker, her work ethic shows. While I had the flu, she stayed up on all of her work at home without even breaking a sweat.

Callie smiles a knowing smile at me. "Those are great questions and the right ones. She is very dedicated, and I think sometimes she works too hard but I try not to nag her. She can be very sensitive to criticism."

I nod my head, taking in this new information. I haven't found that to be true yet, but coming from Callie, I will take it as fact. I look back over to Lucy, and she is still in the same spot, still typing away.

I step over to Lucy and wrap my arms around her middle. "Food is here, baby." I look down at the screen to see if I can see what she is working on. It seems to be a status report email to Candice the receptionist. Why would she need to update her with information?

She turns in my arms and I keep her close. "Sorry, I was just answering a quick email that I got after we left today."

"You know, you aren't expected to answer those on your off time."

She breaks eye contact and looks down at my chest, suddenly fascinated by the buttons there. "I know, but I feel bad. I don't want a client to be sitting there for days waiting for an answer."

I place my finger under her chin and lift her eyes back to mine. "I thank you for your amazing dedication, but don't let it take over your life. Promise?"

She nods her head in agreement and I give her a quick sweet kiss. "Now come and eat before the next game starts."

She sits on my lap as she eats her nachos, laughing and talking with her team. I can tell why she likes them and the more time I spend with them, the more I like them, too. I watch her carefully, learning her different smiles and facial expressions. Her face is so expressive, you can tell almost instantly what she is thinking and feeling. It is amazing to watch.

The next two games go quickly. I have a great time with her and the teams. Joe Finley comes by and says hello during one of the games, along with a bunch of people I knew in high school and from around town. I didn't realize how many people had stayed in town after high school and college. It's cool, like a mini reunion.

When we get home, I take extra special care of my girl. After what Callie shared with me about how hard she works at home and how well she took care of me when I was sick, she needs to have someone take care of her for a little while.

I run her a hot bubble bath filled with all sorts of sweet smelly things she had in her bathroom. She sinks into the warm water and I climb in behind her. I pull her back to lean onto my chest and force her to relax. I rub her shoulders and take my time washing her soft skin.

"You're good at this," she says in a sleepy whisper.

"Good at what?" I ask.

"Baths," she says in a matter of fact tone.

"Baby, I think they just took my man card away for that comment." I laugh.

"Well, I'm pretty sure you can get it back by taking me into the bedroom and fucking me into the mattress." She winks over her shoulder

I'm instantly hard. "Damn, baby. All you have to do is ask."

I stand from the bath with her in my arms. I wrap us in her soft fluffy towels and then just as she asked me too, I take her into the bedroom and for the next several hours fuck her into the mattress.

CHAPTER TWENTY-ONE
Lucy

It's the night before Thanksgiving and we are making cupcakes to take with us tomorrow. Mason pretty much has moved in with me since the week of the flu and I have really loved having him here. We are going to three dinners tomorrow, Craig's extended family in Spokane with Callie and Craig, Mason's family here in Coeur d'Alene, and I promised the McCallisters I would come by with Mason for dessert.

We are in the kitchen and I am frosting the orange cranberry cupcakes I made earlier. Mason comes up behind me and sticks his finger in the bowl of frosting.

"Hey, don't stick your fingers in my frosting." I slap his hand but he still is able to steal a second finger full.

"Hmm, tastes good, cupcake," he says and then kisses my neck.

"Thank you, but if you keep eating all the frosting I won't have enough for the cupcakes."

He moves his hands underneath my shirt and to my breast. "I can think of something that taste much sweeter than that frosting." He whispers into my ear.

I moan and lean my head back on his shoulder, enjoying his touch. I love feeling his hands on me. He rolls my hardened nipples between his fingers. "What's that?" I ask, not sure how words are actually forming in my brain.

"Your lips, baby." He kisses along the back of my neck at my hairline and to the other side, while still messaging and squeezing my breasts. My heart races when he calls me baby, it happens every time he calls me that.

He unhooks the front claps of my bra and cups my breasts fully in his hands, making my knees weak and moisture gather between my legs. I grip on to the counter to stop myself from falling to the floor.

"God, Lucy. I love your body," he says in between the kisses he is peppering on my skin. "Are you ready for me?"

"Yes, I want you. Always." I moan as the fire builds inside of me. Every time I'm with Mason, it seems to get better.

"Fuck, yes!" His left hand leaves my breast and dives into my panties. He pushes two fingers inside of me and uses his thumb to tease my swollen clit. "You are so wet. I can't wait to push inside this hot pussy. I want you to come for me, baby." With just two more strokes, I come hard.

I call out Mason's name as the powerful orgasm rips through me. My knees and elbows give out, I almost fall to the floor but Mason wraps me in his strong arms and keeps me up right. It takes several moments for me to get the strength back. I turn in Mason's arms and pull his lips down to mine and kiss him. I drop to my knees in front of Mason, needing to make him feel as good as he makes me feel. I unzip his jeans and reach inside and pull out his rock-hard cock.

"Baby, you don't have to do that," Mason says as I run my hand along his length.

"Oh yes, I do baby. You make me feel good and it's mine turn to make you feel good."

"Being inside you makes me feel good." The last word is a groan as I lick from balls to tip, enjoying the saltiness of his skin. I lap at the bead of liquid that forms there.

Mason tangles his fingers in my hair but doesn't try to control my movement. I take as much of him into my mouth as I can, but he is too big for me to fit the whole thing. I suck hard, hallowing my checks and moving up and down at a fast rhythm.

"Fuck," he calls out as I remove him from my mouth with a pop. "Christ, your mouth was made for this."

I come alive at his praise. Loving that I can bring this much pleasure to him. I continue to suck him off for several minutes until his legs are starting to shake.

He taps my shoulders. "Baby, stop. I'm so close!"

I hum my acknowledgement around him but continue lapping at his hard cock. I want him to come in my mouth; I want to taste him.

"No, baby." He reaches down and picks me up. I wrap my arms around his neck and my legs around his waist. "I only come inside you."

I pout, wanting to continue. "But I wanted to taste it when you came."

He carries me toward the bedroom. "Fuck Lucy, don't say things like that. I'm hard enough as it is. This is going to be quick."

He sets me down next to the bed and we get to work taking off our clothes at a fevered pace. As soon as we are both naked, we lunge at each other. Not wanting to be apart for another second.

I back up and crawl back onto the bed, Mason following, not allowing even an inch between us. He grabs a condom from my nightstand, rolls it on and pushes inside of me in record time. My back bows off the bed from the wonderful pleasure that I feel every time he is inside of me.

He rests his forehead on mine once he is fully seated inside me. "Do you feel that baby? I fit so perfectly inside of you. It's like you were made for me."

My heart starts to beat even harder at his sweet declaration. The words "I love you" starts to bubble up inside of me but I stop them. I know it is how I feel but I don't think I'm ready for him to hear them yet. It's only been a month since we started dating and in all the movies I have seen, it is relationship suicide to say it too early. I don't want to ruin this.

He starts to move, setting a fast pace. I throw my head back and close my eyes, totally taken over by this pleasure with him.

"Yes, Mason," I moan.

We both quickly rise to our climax and come together. Falling over the edge with Mason is becoming the best thing that I have ever experienced.

CHAPTER TWENTY-TWO
MASON

We have plans to go to three Thanksgiving Day dinners together today. It's not that I don't want to go and spend time with all these people, but I really don't want to share Lucy.

She looks so beautiful today. She is wearing a simple navy-blue dress that makes her eyes pop and her hair looks angelic. I swear to God, she is fucking glowing.

"Ready to go?" she asks me from the kitchen.

I enter the kitchen and stare at her for a long minute. She is moving around her kitchen with such purpose. Lucy is a great cook, everything she has made for me has been delicious and most of it has been from scratch. You can really tell she loves to do it.

She told me once that all the meals at the commune were cooked in a family meal style. All the families would bring different parts of the meal and everyone sat around one table and ate together. Nothing processed or pre-made was used; everything was fresh. Lucy learned everything she knows from making those big family style meals.

"Do we have to go?" I murmur and hug her close to me.

She giggles, turns in my arms and leans her head on my chest. With our height difference, she fits perfectly right at my heart. Hmm, how fitting.

"You don't want to go and spend all day stuffing our faces with food?" she asks still buried in my chest.

I lie my lips on her soft hair. "I would rather stuff you all day."

She pulls back from me with a large smile on her face and continues to finish things up in the kitchen. "Naughty boy."

She might be telling me off, but I can tell she likes it. I have found that my little Miss Flower Bud has a dirty mind. She enjoys sex just as much as I do, and will get things started as many times as I have. And I fucking love it. There is nothing sexier than a woman taking what she wants and not being shy about it.

"Can you help me carry the cupcakes down to the car?"

"Of course." I walk over and pick her up, throwing her over my shoulder like a sack of potatoes and I head toward the door.

She screams and beats at my back. "Let me down, you big butthead." She is laughing as she does, so I know she doesn't mean it.

"I have the cupcake I want right here." I smack her ass, making her shout again.

"Mason! Come on. Let me down. We have to be at your parents' house in fifteen minutes." She is giggling loudly and continues her assault on my back, but her hits aren't hard.

"OK fine." I set her down on her feet. Her hair is wild and her face is red and flushed.

"You are too ridiculous." She hits my chest, smooths her hair and walks back to the kitchen.

We gather the three boxes of cupcakes and head for my parents' house. They live on the other side of the Spokane River a few miles away, but you have to go a few miles out of the way to get there. They purchased this place on the lake after all us kids had moved out. It sits right on the river and has a personal boat slip that we all use during the summer, but it's way too cold for water sports today.

"Who all will be there today?" she asks as we head over the 95 bridge. I see Cedars off in the distance and make a mental note to take her there for dinner soon.

"Should be a small group. My parents, us, my sisters, Jason and Grandma. Maybe a couple of Mary Ann's friends from school."

"Oh, do I get to meet your grandparents today?"

"Only my mom's mother. My dad's parents live in Michigan and we don't see them very often."

She interrupts my thoughts singing, "How I wish I was in Michigan, Yes I wish and wish and wish again. That I was in Michigan." She seems to know a million random songs.

I smile and shake my head at her. "Grams has been around for most everything. She even lived with us for a while after Pops died about ten years ago."

"I hope she likes me," she says in a small voice while looking out the window.

"I know she will, baby." I bring the hand I am holding to my lips.

"I never knew any of my grandparents." She pauses for a long minute. "My parents said we were better without them."

She is sitting in her seat with a look on her face I have never seen before and never want to see again. She looks so sad and almost haunted. How the fuck could her parents treat her like that? Taking that love away from their only child.

She is quiet the rest of the journey and I am unsure what to say. We arrive at the house and I leave the car in a flash, walking to her side. I pull her from the car and hug her tightly to me.

"I'm sorry, I didn't mean to be a bummer," her voice is thick with emotion.

"You have nothing to be sorry for baby. If you decided this is too much for you, let me know and I will take you straight home for our own stuffing."

She gives me a shy smile and a tight squeeze. "Stop it. No more talking of stuffing around your parents."

I lean down to her and kiss her sweet lips. But like most of the times I kiss her, it quickly escalates, with lots of roaming hands and tangling of tongues.

"Gross, you two. Get a room." I hear from behind me.

I pull back and we are both breathing hard. Michelle and Jason are getting out of Jason's truck that is parked right behind my Jeep. I didn't even hear them arrive.

"Shut up, brat," I yell toward Michelle.

Lucy's cheeks are stained red and she is hiding her face in my chest.

"Hi Lucy. Ignore these two, they are the worst," Jason says and pulls her from my arms and he hooks his arm around her shoulder, leading her into my parent's house.

"No, Mason is sweet. I think I will keep him." She looks over her shoulder and gives me a wink.

Michelle walks up next to me and winds her arm through mine. "I'm glad you brought her, MJ. Grams will really like her."

I smile down at my little sister. "I'm glad too. I see Jason is with us again this year."

She rolls her eyes and laughs. "Yeah, we are going to his family's house later."

"You know that is not what I meant. Are you ever going to make your move on Jason? Make an honest man out of him."

She punches me in the side. "Stop it, you know our relationship isn't like that. He is just my best friend. Plus, I think he is dating a girl on the south hill."

We enter the house and I drop the conversation. They have been best friends since middle school and they would do anything for each other. I can see in the way Jason looks at her he wants more, but I don't know what it is that holds him back from being with my sister. In my opinion, they would be perfect for each other, but anytime I bring it up Michelle gets very defensive.

I can hear my parents greeting Lucy and Jason in the living room as I slip off my coat to be hung on the coat rack. "Thank you so much for bring the cupcakes, darling. That is so sweet. They look delicious."

Lucy smiles proudly. "Thank you for allowing me to join your family."

My dad doesn't say anything just nods his head. That is strange. Lucy is someone he knows, and I thought someone he liked.

"Come in and get comfortable. Dinner is almost ready and my mother should be here soon."

"Your mother is here," we hear from the entry way. Gram has arrived with Mary Ann.

My Gram is one of my favorite people. She is one of the strongest women I know. She has lived through two rounds of breast cancer with a double mastectomy, a hip replacement and losing her husband. But through all of that, she never complained. She just took what was given to her and made the best of it. Grams loves us all fiercely.

She is a small woman, just a little over five feet, with short white hair and large framed glasses. Her nails are always polished bright red, matching her lipstick. Today she is wearing a black pantsuit that I have seen almost every Thanksgiving.

"Is this the Lucy I have heard so much about?" she asks looking Lucy up and down. Lucy smiles shyly and looks to me with worried eyes.

After a few long moments of scrutiny, she asks, "Where is your family from Lucy?"

"A small town in Northern Nevada." Lucy confirms after clearing her throat.

"And when did you move here?"

"Three years ago, after I graduated from the University of Texas."

"Not too long then. And you work with the boys?"

"Yes, I'm a vice president of accounting."

She pauses for a minute, pretending to scrutinize Lucy. I know she is just giving her a hard time. She is too nice to be judging anyone. "Wonderful. Well you seem like a lovely woman. Now someone get me a dirty martini."

We all laugh and I can see the stress leave Lucy's shoulders. Michelle, Mary Ann and Mom head to the kitchen while Jason leads Grams to the couch offering to bring her the martini she requested.

I pull Lucy close and kiss her forehead and I whisper in her ear, "I told you she likes you."

"Lucy, can you help me in the kitchen for a second?" my mom asks from the kitchen door way.

"Of course." She leaves my arms and heads in her direction.

I walk over to the bar and join my dad who is fixing Gram her drink.

"Would you like something to drink?" my dad asks, without looking me in the eye.

"Sure, will you grab Lucy and I a beer, please."

"OK." He hands me the beers, not saying a lot.

Dad and my relationship has always been a good one. We were always fishing, camping, being outside together or watching baseball together. We were very close and he taught me a lot growing up but after I moved to Seattle, our relationship took a turn. He wanted to have me at the business years ago. Me coming back was supposed to help our relationship, bring us close together again.

I hear giggles come from the kitchen. Lucy is such a good fit with my family. "The girls seem to like Lucy" he says but with a bit of sarcasm in his voice.

"What's the attitude for Dad?"

He shakes his head not answering my question.

"Seriously, Dad. What is the issue? I thought you liked Lucy?" I ask again, but again no answer.

I go to push again but Mom comes out the kitchen carrying the turkey. "OK, everyone. We are ready."

I grab Lucy and my beers from the bar top and head to the dining room, but my mind is still spinning a mile a minute, trying to figure out why my dad is acting so weird.

I hold out the chair for Lucy and she gives me a grateful smile.

"Thank you. Is that beer for me? Or are you double fisting tonight?" she asks when I take the seat next to her.

"Speaking of fisting," I whisper into her ear suggestively and hand over the unconsumed drink.

"Stop it." She giggles and smacks my arm. I lean down and give her a quick kiss.

"Knock it off you two, people are trying to eat," Michelle jokes from the other side of the table.

"Yaah! Knock it off," Mary Ann adds in.

"Don't you start too, Mary Ann." I groan

Lucy smiles wide and gives me another loud kiss before doing the silliest thing I have ever seen her do, she sticks her tongue out at my sisters. And that earns her another much longer kiss.

Gram and Lucy are currently sitting on the living room couch with their heads together, talking softly and smiling at each other. I'm not sure if I should be terrified or not.

Don't get me wrong; I'm really glad that they are getting along. Lucy is the first woman I have brought to meet the family, and none of them batted an eye when I said she was coming, which I am very glad for. I want them to like her, she will be around for a long time. But it looks like the two of them are plotting something and that is what has me worried. An awful thought of having to take the two of them to the ballet or some crap like that pops into my head. Hell no!

I decide to talk to my dad again, trying to figure out what is going on with him and Lucy.

"Dad, can we talk for a second?"

He is sitting in the family room with the Cowboys game on.

"Sure, MJ. What can I do for you?" He replies but in a very business-like voice.

"I want to know why you don't like Lucy."

"Who said I don't like Lucy?" he says but his eyes never leave the game. I know he is lying.

"You haven't said more than two words to her all day."

He mutes the television, turns to me and takes a deep breath.

"MJ, it is not that I don't like her. I'm just afraid she is not being honest with her intention for you."

"What intentions? We are dating."

"Yes, but it all happened so quickly. She sees you at work one day and then the next thing I know you are taking her home, then you spend a week at her home with the flu, and now she is here for Thanksgiving.

"You are a very important part of Murphy and Glass. I'm just worried she is using you to climb the corporate ladder."

What the fuck? "Dad, what are you talking about?"

"I'm just worried she is using you. I noticed you did give her a couple of new clients. Was that her idea or yours?"

"Do you not know Lucy at all? How can you say such a thing about her? She would never do anything like that! Lucy is a very hard worker and I thought she would be the best fit for those clients. She had nothing to do with that decision." My voice is raised and my blood is starting to boil in my veins.

"OK, settle down. You are my son MJ. I want to make sure that you are not being used."

"Damn it, Dad! No, she isn't like that." I run my hands through my hair in frustration.

How could he think that about Lucy? She isn't trying to use me for work. We hardly ever talk about work. And when we do, she doesn't ask for favors or help. Well that one time she did but that was a tricky situation.

Plus, I was the one who spilled my coffee on her that first morning. I was the one who asked her out in her office the next day. I have been the instigator of all of this. She wanted to take things slow, she had the rule about not dating a coworker. Was that all just a ploy to make me want her more? Was she playing hard to get?

Fuck! I hate that he is making me doubt my relationship with her.

"Mason?" Lucy's voice pulls me from my thoughts. "It's time to go." She gives her sweet smile.

"OK, Lucy. Let me say good bye." I stand from the couch and walk to her, searching her eyes to see what I see in their blue depths. Looking for something that could be hidden in them.

Damn it! He has gotten in my head.

CHAPTER TWENTY-THREE
Lucy

I just had the greatest time with Mason's family. They are so fun and welcoming. And his mom, Christine, is a great cook. You could tell that everything was home made with lots of love. His grandmother is a delight; we warmed right up to each other.

I did notice a little tension between Mason and his dad, I will have to ask him about it later.

We decide to stop by and drop off the dessert for the McCallisters before heading to Spokane. Sometimes the dinner with Craig's family can go a little late. They are a party family, so I suggested we stop off first.

We are on the highway and heading toward Spokane, the sun sets early in the winter here so at 4 p.m. the sun is already setting. We are headed west into the Spokane Valley and the clouds are framing the sun making a beautiful sunset. I look over at the man driving and I feel so happy.

"Thank you for coming with me today."

"You have already thanked me once today, cupcake," he replies.

"I know but it means a lot that you are coming along and that you invited me to your family's house."

Damn, I need to kiss the crap out of him.

"Can you pull over for a second?" I ask.

His eyes fly to mine. "Are you, OK?"

"Yes, I just need to do something."

"What?" he asks, his voice laced with concern.

"Please, just exit here."

He does as I ask and as soon as we are parked he turns to me, "OK, what is…"

I stop him mid-sentence by climbing over the console and laying my lips on his. I tangle my fingers in his hair and hold him close, kissing him with as much passion as I can.

He grips my ass in his hands and settles me over his lap. I grind down, loving the feel of him on my center. I reach down to unbuckle his pants, deciding that I need him now and I don't care who in this Wendy's parking lot see us.

"Baby, stop." He moves his lips from mine and tries to stop my hands.

"No, I need you," I say in a desperate tone.

"No." He moves my hands to his shoulders and frames my face with large his hands. "I'm not going to have you in my car in front of a bunch of strangers."

I pout. "But I'm all turned on."

"You are the one that started this all. Why did you start this?"

"You just looked so sexy over there I decided I needed you," I say matter of factly, climbing back into my own seat.

He shakes his head and starts the car back down the road.

"Now the rest of the night I will be horny and wet with need for you."

"Damn it, Lucy. You can't say things like that." He hits the steering wheel with the heel of his hand.

I giggle at him, but his face is so serious, and my giggles turns into a full out belly laugh.

He turns to me, his eyes still serious, "What?"

"Oh, I just adore you." I link my arm with his and lay my head on his shoulder.

He doesn't say anything back like I expected him too and that has me a little concerned. He seems to be a little bit more upset than I realized. I lift my head and look at his profile. His brows are pulled down and his lips are set in a thin line. The conversation with his dad must really be bothering him. I decide I will ask him about it later, once he has calmed down a little.

The rest of the drive to Craig's family's house doesn't take too much longer. It turns out that Mason knows some of Craig's cousins from high school and baseball. I learned that Mason played baseball in high school and was pretty good. I wish I could have gotten to see him in those sexy, tight baseball pants. Yum!

They are currently drinking beers, talking about sports and joking around like no time has passed since the last time they saw each other. He seems to be in a better mood than he was on the car ride.

Callie and I are sitting on their porch around the fire, drinking a fireball drink that is 90% fireball and 10% apple juice, but it is going down super smooth. You can almost not taste the large amount of alcohol.

"I really like Mason, sugar. You two fit well together," she says, her southern accent is a little thicker from the alcohol.

"I really like him too, Callie." I pause and take a large swig from my drink. I need to admit something to her. "I think I more than like him actually."

She smiles knowingly and wiggles around in her seat, doing a mini happy dance. "Have you told him yet?"

"No, it's too soon. We have only known each other for a little over a month."

"Well don't wait too long. We can't have double weddings if you don't hurry up," she jokes.

"Oh yes, we must get the flowers ordered. Can't have a double wedding without twice the number of flowers." I joke along with her.

"Do you think we can get Craig and Mason to wear matching outfits?" she says, full out laughing now.

"Yes, bright pink bow ties with matching cummerbunds!" Oh that would be awful!

"No, floral print, they can match all the flowers." She falls into a fit of laughter and clutches her stomach.

I roll my eyes at her and take another long drink. I look over at Mason and he meets my gaze. I smile at him but he doesn't return my smile. Hmm that's odd.

"Gather round folks," Craig's aunt Cindy calls us all into the large dining room. We head inside and I stand next to Mason and take his hand, giving him a squeeze and a smile.

"Let's thank the Lord for this meal and this time together."

We bow our heads and Cindy says a lovely prayer blessing the food and the family. Noise erupts as soon as the prayer is over. We gather plates and fill them with all the wonderful food. This meal is different than Mason's family. Theirs was a little fancier, with side dishes displayed in crystal bowls. Craig's family is so large everything is in mis-matched bowls, coming from lots of different households. But they food is just as good.

I dig in and load up my plate. I notice Mason is hanging back, drinking his second beer and doesn't move to eat. My heart sinks, something is wrong and I have no idea what.

"I'm going to have to go out of town for a few days," he says in the car on the way home.

"Oh really, when?" I'm checking my Instagram feed, looking at all the pictures of my friends with their families.

"Tomorrow," he murmurs.

"I thought you were coming to the bowling party on Saturday?"

"Something came up." He is being very vague and quiet.

"Where are you going?"

"What is with the twenty questions, Lucy? I said I was going out of town." His voice is clipped and a little louder than needed in the car.

I set my phone in my purse and turn in my seat toward him. "I asked you two questions."

"I said I had to go out of town and that is all you need to know."

"OK, sorry," I say in a small voice and turn away from him, staring out the window.

The rest of the car ride is silent. He walks me to my door, gives me a chaste kiss and turns away.

"Mason, wait?" He stops but doesn't turn around. "Is something wrong?"

He turns with a hard look on his face. "Great, more questions."

"Wow, seriously! What the hell?" I stand my ground and plant my hands on my hips.

He runs this hand through his hair. He has been doing it all night and the long locks are falling over his forehead and into his eyes. "I just don't like all the questions, Lucy. If I tell you I have to do something, I don't want to have to spend an hour explaining myself to you." The last part of the sentence is almost spit at me.

He is being a jerk and I don't want anything to do with him right now. Tears start to form in my eyes and I take a shaky breath before I speak. "Fine. Have a safe trip."

I turn and enter my apartment, slamming the door in his face. Dick!

CHAPTER TWENTY-FOUR
MASON

I feel like an asshole for hurting Lucy's feelings, but I need some space. When Craig's cousin, Kyle Butler told me that Lucy was over with Callie planning our dual weddings, I went into panic mode. After the conversation my dad and I had about Lucy, the news from Kyle sent me into a fucking tailspin.

Could my dad have been right? We have only been dating a fucking month. There is no way we are ready for marriage. Hell, I really, really like Lucy, but I'm not ready to be her husband.

Now I'm standing next to my best friend Braxton in some shitty Seattle bar, kicking myself for being a dick and leaving things the way I did.

"Dude, finish your beer. Those two girls are heading to another bar and want us to come along." He points to the two blonde chicks that he has been chatting up most of the night.

"Fine, whatever." I chug down my beer and throw a twenty on the bar.

"I'm taking the one on the left."

"You can take them both for all I care."

Brax slaps me on the back and we head for the door, following his soon to be conquest.

My phone vibrates in my pocket as we are walking towards the next bar. I'm surprised to see its from Lucy since she hasn't said anything in two days.

Lucy: *Duck you!!!!!*

Huh? What is she talking about?

Me: *What?*

It doesn't take long for another response.

Lucy: *You sleard me, duck you!*

She must mean fuck you, I think she is drunk texting me.

I don't know what to say back to her. Any apology I send her won't be heard right now, she is drunk and obviously pissed.

Lucy: *You hurt me and I don't like that and now I don't like you.*

Crap!

Me: *I needed some space. It sucks but it's the best I could think of in the moment.*

We arrive at the bar but I stay outside, glued to my phone.

"You coming?" Brax asks near the door, one arm slung around each of the girls.

"I will be there in a minute." I shout towards him without looking away from my phone.

Lucy: *Duck that!!!*

I take a seat on a bench and answer her back.

Me: *Can we talk about this when I get back into town?*

Lucy: *No. I don't want to talk about this with you anymore.*

Before I can respond she sends me another message.

Lucy: *I cried and I hate when my heart makes me cry. It's hurt.*

Fuck, I just wanted to slow us down a little.

Me: *I needed some space.*

I repeat myself, not sure what else to say.

Lucy: *you already said that*

The words are in all small type, no missed spelled and no punctuation. Normally all her texts are large and bold with lots of exclamation points and emojis. This one is the complete opposite.

Me: *I'm sorry.*

It isn't what I want to say, I want to say it in person when I can look her in the face.

Lucy: *too late*

Crap! I walked straight inside and to the bar. I order two shots of tequila and shoot them back. Not enough

I order two more. This isn't fixing it. I knew it wouldn't, but I was hoping for a miracle.

A busty redhead comes up on my side. She pushes her large tits onto my arm. Her perfume smells like cheap air freshener. "Hey there sexy. Wanna buy a gal a drink?"

"Not tonight." I remove her from my arm. "Sorry."

"Come on big boy, just one. I'm feeling awful thirsty." She runs her fingers down my face. She has those long awful nails that come to a point.

"I said no. Take the hint. I'm not interested."

"You are such a jerk. I just wanted a drink." She huffs away but leaves a lot of her perfume behind.

The smell makes me long for Lucy, the simple peach and vanilla scent that is all her. I order another tequila and it's starts to finally set in. I throw down some cash and then go in search of Brax.

I have to get out of here, the music is way too loud, the smoke is thick and toxic and there is a fuck ton of people bumping into me.

I find him in a back booth enjoying bottle service with the two blondes from the other bar.

"Hey, I'm gonna get out of here," I yell over the awful music.

"Why man? What's up?" Brax asks but doesn't leave his seat.

A hand clasps my shoulder and turns me around. I find myself staring at a hipster about 4 inches shorter than my 6'4". He is wearing a beanie low over his forehead and jeans at least 4 sizes too small. He looks like the kind of shithead that works on an organic beet farm, where they give the beets a choice on whether they want to grow or not.

"Hey, are you the fucker that wouldn't buy my girl a drink?" He points to the red head from earlier.

"Yeah man. I'm not interested." I move to turn away but the asshole puts his hands on me again.

"What is she not hot enough for you?"

"Are you fucking serious man?"

"Yeah, buy my girl a drink." He pushes me, the little fucker just actually pushed me.

"You want me to buy your girl a drink?"

He gets in my face, his breath smells of old socks and vodka. "Yeah, are you fucking deaf? Buy my girl a drink." Ending his statement with another push.

"Fuck off man. I'm not buying her a drink."

The asshole pushes me for the third time and I snap. I pull my arm back and punch the guy right in the nose. I can hear the pop of his nose breaking and then blood rushes down his face.

Out of nowhere one of his friends sucker punches me in the eye. Fuck that hurts! Braxton jumps in and pulls me away toward the back exit. I can hear the yells of the bouncers telling us to get the fuck out and never come back.

We push out the door and into the night air. I can feel my head starting to spin from the alcohol and blood rushing to my face.

"What the fuck is wrong with you, Mason?" Braxton asks once we are away from the door. "You have been acting like a nut ever since you got to town."

I run my hands through my hair, trying to fucking clear my head. This is all so fucking stupid.

"Fuck man. I have no fucking clue."

"You finally going to tell me why you came to Seattle all of a sudden?"

"I've been seeing this girl and I think she might be using me."

"No, you aren't that stupid."

"What?" My head whips up to see my friends face.

"Do you really think you are stupid enough to get with a girl who would use you? You are fucking smarter than that Mason."

"How do you know that?"

"Mason you know how to read people. You can see a fake coming from a fucking mile away. Always been able to. Remember that guy that came in to the firm a few years ago, within minutes you knew the fucker has a scam and made sure everyone knew about it. No female could get the jump on you, no matter how hot."

Damn it, he's right. Lucy has never ever been fake with me. It's one of the things that drew me too her.

"As much as I don't want to hear all the details, tell me about her. Maybe saying it out loud will get your head right."

We sit in the cab of his truck in the dark bar parking lot and I tell him all about the last few months with Lucy. By the end of the conversation I realize that I am a real fucker and don't deserve to have her in my life. I defended her to my dad but I didn't defend her to my own damn demons. She isn't the girl I have just treated her like. I have to get home. She is mine and I love her. I need to get back to her, now!

I make Brax drive me straight to the airport after I wised up. It's still the middle of the night but I want to be there when the first plane for Spokane leaves. I will sleep on a bench if I need to. Brax promised to send me the few things I had at his place. I decide to go straight to her from the plane and beg on my hands and knees.

CHAPTER TWENTY-FIVE
Lucy

I think my head is about to explode.

I'm pretty sure I tried to drink my weight in rum. I wake slowly, not wanting to open my eyes right away. I can already feel the needles of the pain coming through my eyelids.

"Callie," I moan from my spot on her couch.

"Yes, sugar." I hear her whisper, she is close but I'm not sure where she is at this point.

"I think I'm dying."

"Don't yell, sugar," she groans. I'm pretty sure she is lying on the couch opposite of me.

I giggle but my stomach turns at the movement. "Oh my god. I can't believe how much we drank last night." I slowly start to sit up but don't open my eyes. "I need water."

I peek one eye open and notice the room is still dark. Someone had the foresight to draw all the blinds so we wouldn't be woken up by the sun. Even with the darkness, I'm able to get to the kitchen for water and ibuprofen without dying. I carry the water back to the couch and sit down with a thud. I get Callie some water too and set hers on the side table near her head.

The front door opens and Craig sneaks quietly in. He is carrying a bag of bagels and three very large coffees. He is being extra careful to not make any noise as he makes his way to the living room.

"Good morning," he whispers to me.

"Morning," I whisper and smile back.

He walks over to Callie and kneels before her. He brushes her bangs off of her forehead and peppers her face with light, sweet kisses. "Good morning love," he says in between kisses.

Callie finally opens her eyes and I can see the love she has for Craig. She wraps her arms around his neck and pulls him close. "Hi muffin. God you smell good this morning. Where have you been?" she asks.

"I had to go and get my favorite girls their favorite hang over cure." His voice is still quiet.

"Oh, you drove all the way to get us bagels and coffee?"

"Of course Callie. I have to take care of my beautiful fiancé and her best friend."

"You are the best future husband ever." He helps her sit up and I pass over the water I got her earlier.

"Thank you, Luc. Here, are you hungry?" He passes me the bag of bagels and cream cheese.

Our tried and true hangover cure is a chain bagel place that we had in Austin. The closest location is all the way in downtown Spokane. Craig got up early and took the time to drive almost thirty minutes into Spokane just to bring it back for us.

I look in the bag and see he has gotten several of my favorite blueberry bagels. There are also a handful of Callie's favorites and three tubs of whipped cream cheese. God, he is a saint.

I pull out one of mine and bite right into it, not taking the time to toast it or add cream cheese. The second bagel can be doctored up but this first one just needs to get in my stomach to soak up the alcohol.

Callie and Craig are snuggling up on the couch across from me and he is feeding her little bites of bagel. She doesn't handle hangovers very well, she never has. But, Craig is so great at taking care of her. You can tell he loves her very much by the nice little things that he does for her.

"What hangover movie shall we watch today, ladies?" he asks.

"You pick, sugar. I can't think right now." Callie moans from her spot.

"I think we need some Judy Garland. The Pirate please monsieur."

"You got it." He kisses Callie's head and puts on the movie for us.

Callie and I each spent a paycheck once on only movies, so now we both have an extensive collection of classic movies and musicals. They snuggle back together and we enjoy watching Judy get put under the spell of Gene Kelly. I wish Mason was here to snuggle up with me and my heart breaks a new… Ugh!

The drive home from Callie's house feels extra-long and lonely today. The sky is dark and grey which matches my mood perfectly. I didn't share with Callie what had happened with Mason on Thursday night or the drunk text I sent yesterday. I must have read his response twenty times but now even sober they still don't make sense to me.

How could he need space? I have never been the one to initiate us spending time together. I guess I should have said no more. Damn it. I guess I'm damned if I do and damned if I don't when it comes to men.

I stop and get some soup knowing that my poor stomach can't survive a heavy meal. I'm planning on an early night. Tomorrow is going to be a busy day at the office after a four-day weekend and I'm still exhausted from the hangover from last night.

Getting to my apartment door, I send a look toward Mason's, wondering if he is home yet from Seattle.

I open the door, turn on the light and almost die from fright when I see Mason sleeping on my loveseat. My scream startles him awake.

"What the hell are you doing here, Mason?" I walk to the kitchen, not overly interested in his answer.

"I came to see you. What time is it?" He is still sitting on the loveseat, scrubbing his hands over his face.

"It's sometime after four." I unpack my soup and busy myself in the kitchen, needing the distance. He was the one who wanted space, so I will give him space.

"I've been sleeping since eleven. I caught the first flight back this morning." He is coming toward the kitchen but I turn my back to him, running water in the sink as a distraction.

I hear him let out a deep breathe. "Listen, Lucy…"

"No, you listen, Mason." I stop him and spin around ready to give him the tongue-lashing he deserves when I see the state of the side of his face. A large dark purple bruise is taking up most of his left cheek; his eye is swollen and blood shot.

I move quickly to him, frame his face with my hands and turn it so I can get a closer look. "Oh my god, Mason. What happened to your face?" The skin isn't broken but looks like it hurts.

"It's nothing."

"Have you put any ice on this?"

"Lucy, it's fine."

"No, it's not. Go sit down and I will get you some ice." I push him toward the kitchen chair.

I find the frozen peas I have in my freezer and rush back to Mason's side. I stand in front of him and move in between his spread legs.

"OK, here. Put this on the bruise." I gently place the peas on the face and I see him wince. "I'm sorry, this should help though."

He places his hands on my hips while I hold the bag on his swollen face, keeping me close.

"Am I allowed to ask what happened? Or is that too many questions?" There is quite a lot of sass in that sentence.

"Yeah, I'm sorry about that Lucy. It happened last night at a bar."

I wait, hoping there will be more to the story. "Some hipster got mad that I wouldn't buy his girlfriend a drink and he kept pushing me. I punched him in the nose, and one of his friends got in a lucky punch. Braxton and I got out of there after that."

"You punched a hipster?" I adjust the bag of peas. He doesn't wince this time and the swelling is already going down.

"Not my finest moment." He moves his hands up my back exploring.

I step back out of his reach. "Here, leave this on your face for a little bit longer." I have to get away from him. His hands feel too good on my back and I know the longer I let him touch me, the heat between us will continue to grow and all of my reason for being mad at him will be forgotten.

"Lucy, wait."

He wraps his arms around my waist pulling me into his chest and leans his chin on my shoulder. "I'm sorry Lucy. My dad and I had a weird conversation about you at dinner, then Kyle told me you and Callie here talking about us getting married and I freaked out. I needed to get away for a little while and think…"

I quickly spin around, dislodging his arms from around me. "Marriage? Callie and I weren't talk about us getting married."

"Kyle said he heard you two talking about having a double wedding."

I roll my eyes in disgust and irritation. "It was a joke. Callie always jokes that she wants us to have a double wedding, she has been saying that for years. Is that seriously what started that whole thing?"

He shrugs one shoulder, looking uncertain.

"Oh my god, Mason. You can't be serious! Why didn't you just ask me?" I pace away from him and into the living room.

"I don't know."

"Really Mason?!? This right here is the whole reason I didn't want to date someone. I can't do the drama."

"Lucy, I'm sorry. I don't want drama either."

I ignore his comment. "What is going to happen the next time you get upset with me? Will you get mad and you freak out at work? I'm not going to lose my job over your misunderstanding."

"Lucy, stop. It was a little misunderstanding." He walks to me and tries to take me in his arms again.

But I pull away and pace again. "No, it's not a 'little' misunderstanding. You really hurt me, Mason." This time I can't stop the tears, I can feel them sliding down my cheeks. I stop pacing, and my shoulders sink forward, letting all the emotion that has been weighing so heavily the last few days leave my body.

"Oh, baby. Don't cry." He cradles my face in his hands, tipping my head up wiping the tears from my cheeks with his thumbs.

"I don't want a relationship like this Mason." My heart is beating so hard thinking of the possibility of saying goodbye to him for good but after I realized how much he could hurt me this weekend, I don't know if I can live through another heart break with him.

"Baby, I'm sorry. I was a complete idiot. I treated you terribly and I need to make up for that but Lucy, I don't want to lose you. Please forgive me." He softly kisses each of my cheeks, then works his way to my lips for a sweet slow kiss.

His sweet words make my heart both ache and soar at the same time. I want more than anything for him to be sincere. I want to launch myself into his arms and have him make love to me right here on the floor of my living room. I'm just not sure. I'm so scared. Mason has this huge potential to really hurt me and I don't think I can take the leap right now.

I back away from him and his arms fall to his sides. He stands in front of me not moving, just staring at me. He is waiting for me to speak first.

"I think you were right, Mason. I think some space would be good for a little while." I gesture toward the door, silently asking him to leave.

"Baby…," he starts but I stop him with a simple raise of my hand.

"OK, Lucy. I will leave for now but I'm not giving up. We are not over. You are stuck with me. You are mine."

In the blink of an eye, I am in his arms and he is giving me a toe-curling kiss. I let myself sink into the kiss. This man knows exactly how to kiss me.

He steps back after a few minutes, and we are both breathing heavy. Without another word, he walks out my apartment locking the door behind him.

You are mine.

Chapter Twenty-six
MASON

Operation—Win Lucy Back, is in full force. This morning I let myself in to her apartment before she would be up to leave her a coffee and breakfast sandwich. I made sure to leave her a note telling her good morning and how beautiful she looked this morning. I didn't have to see her to know this was true. Lucy looks beautiful every morning.

I then made sure that a second coffee was left on her desk at work a little later. Again, with another note wishing her a great day. Candice saw me coming out of her office and tried to nose her way into the situation. I told her I was leaving Lucy a note. She insisted that going forward, I leave all notes with her. HA! Not on your life lady. You are not getting in the way of me and my girl.

It's lunchtime and I'm carrying a bag of Lucy's favorite Italian food toward her office. I knock once on her door but don't wait for an answer before I enter.

"Mason," she says in a startled voice.

"Hi, baby. I brought you lunch." I set the food on her coffee table and start to unpack the bag.

"Mason, you didn't have to bring me lunch." She hasn't left her chair yet. I walk over and cage her in with my arms on her armrests.

"It's my pleasure, baby." I give her nose a quick chaste kiss. "What would you like to drink with your lunch?"

"Umm ... Iced tea I guess."

"OK, I'll be right back." I kiss her lips this time and leave to retrieve our drinks.

When I return, she is on her couch already digging into the breadsticks and dipping sauce. I smile at the adorable guilty look on her face when I catch her already eating.

"Sorry, it smelled too good to wait." She says with a mouth full of food.

"That's OK baby. Eat up." I sit down next to her and kiss her forehead. I know she really enjoys when I kiss her, so part of my plan is kissing her as much as possible.

"Have you had a good day so far?"

Her mouth is full with another large bite of food, so it takes her a few seconds to respond. "Yes, it's been good. Busy Monday, but good." As soon as she finishes her sentence, she is stuffing another fork full of pasta into her mouth.

I love how she eats. She doesn't do the normal girl thing and only eats salad. She eats whatever she wants and as much as she wants. Sometimes it is salads but not because she thinks she has to.

"Good. Anything big you are working on?"

"Not really. Just helping a bunch of clients get ready for open enrollment next week. Oh, do you know Rob Lloyd from Miller's Diesel Shop?"

"Checkers? Yeah, he and I are friends. We went out the night that I came over drunk. Remember I told you I went out with Checks."

"Oh, that makes a lot more sense now. Well he and I are working on getting them a bigger merchandise producer. They have had a giant spike in orders and they keep running out. Their printer can't keep up. We are looking for a new one that can keep up with their demand. I'm really excited for them."

"That is great. He told me that business has been picking up lately."

"Yeah, their inventory system needs updating too, but their receptionist has been there for years and the owner, Jeff, isn't ready to take that away from her."

"Well let me know if you need my help pressing the issue with him. I don't want him to lose money over something silly."

She laughs and rolls her eyes in the cute way she does. "Mason, I don't need your help."

"I know, baby. I'm just offering." I kick myself mentally for all the shit last weekend. Even when I'm offering, she won't take my help. Idiot!

"OK."

"How are things going with Candice? Has she been bothering you anymore recently?" Lucy confided in me a few weeks ago about the issues she has had with the receptionist. I told my dad and he said he would take care of it.

"Yeah, she has been fine. But I noticed something weird today."

"What was that?"

"I noticed that someone had gone in and opened a few of my files over the weekend. The last opened date was Saturday and I was not here working on them."

"Was anything changed?"

"Not that I could see, but it was still strange to me."

"OK, I will look into it and see what I can find out. Not sure why someone would be going through your files or be here on a holiday weekend."

"Thank you, Mason." She lays her hands on my arm and gives me a little squeeze.

"Hey, why don't you have a nickname for me? You have called me baby a few times before."

"What do you mean?"

"I call you cupcake and baby, but you call me Mason most of the time."

"What would you like me to call you?

"I don't know, maybe Sex God, Best Sex of Your Life?"

She lets out a long belly laugh, hugging her middle and falling back on to the couch. "No way. I'm not calling you either of those things."

"Well, then you think of something." I sit back next to her and pull her into my side. She snuggles in and leans her head on my shoulder.

"Hmm… I could call you Perry, for Perry Mason."

I laugh. "No."

"OK, how about Mr. Mason, from Downton Abbey?" I shake my head.

"But this is supposed to be my nickname for you, shouldn't I get to choose?"

"Keep thinking, baby." I run the tip of my tongue along the shell of her ear. "Come on, baby. Keep going." She is wiggling and trying to get closer.

"Umm… what about?" Her breath is coming out in little puffs.

"Keep thinking of ideas baby, or I will stop." I pull my lips back from my exploration of her neck.

"No, OK. I'm thinking. How about hunk-cules?"

I sit back to look at her face. Her eyes are closed and her cheeks are flushed. "Hunk-cules?"

She opens her eyes, and I can see both lust and humor in them. "Yeah. You are a hunk and super strong. It's from Hercules."

"The Disney cartoon?"

She nods and bites her lower lip. Fuck, that is sexy.

I run my thumb along her lips and remove it from between her teeth. "No I think we can do better than that." I lean down and take her lips. I run my tongue along her lower lip, exploring and licking every inch of her luscious lips.

"Mason," she moans and pulls me closer.

"See, this would be a perfect time to use my special nickname," I say against her lips.

"Snow ball?"

"Nope."

"Boo bear?"

"Nope."

"PAC?"

I sit back and look down at her face. "Why Pac?"

"I don't know. Sometimes when I look into your eyes, my heart skips a beat. And that is called premature atrial contractions or PAC."

I smile. "That is very scientific of you." I kiss her nose. "Pac, I kind of like that one. It's manly and it means something."

"Hey Pac." She says in a sassy voice. "Get back over here and make out with me please."

"Anything for you, cupcake!"

I pull her close and kiss the shit out of her. Her hands move right to my hair and pull me closer. She arches herself closer to me. I wrap my arms around her and reposition us on the loveseat, so she is lying down and I am on top of her.

We stay like this for a long time, just enjoying each other's lips and our fingers clutching each other close. We separate, and I know my hair is a riot from her fingers. Her lips are puffy and red from my kisses. I sit up and bring her with me.

"Damn, baby. I could do that all-day long."

"Me too, Mason." I pin her with a hard glare. "Pac."

"That's better. What are your plans for tonight?" I gather up the trash from lunch and place it back in the bag it came in.

"We are supposed to be getting some space. It hasn't even been a day."

"You wanted the space, I didn't."

Again she rolls her eyes at me. "How about one night of space and we can do something tomorrow?"

"Fine, Taco Tuesday?"

"Yes, please."

"OK, we can go over right after work and have happy hour, too. Should we invite Callie and Craig?"

Her eyes light up at the suggestion and she nods enthusiastically.

"Sounds like a plan. Have a great rest of your day, baby."

"Bye, Pac." And it's my turn to have my heart skip a beat at my new nickname. It's more appropriate than she knows.

It's 12:01 a.m. and I can't take it anymore. I've slept without Lucy in my arms for the past four nights and I don't want to go a minute longer. I let myself into her apartment making as little noise as I can. I go straight back to her room, strip out of the sweats I wore across the hall and get in bed with her. She is lying on her side clutching a pillow, my pillow.

She wakes as I pull her into my arms. "Mason, what are you doing? What time is it?"

"You said I had to wait till tomorrow to spend time with 'you again. Well it's after midnight and I didn't want to wait any longer."

"Oh, that is so sweet." She leans up and kisses me.

I want to kiss her the rest of the night but we need our sleep for work in the morning. "Go to bed, baby. Let me hold you while you sleep."

"I'd love that. It's been cold without you here."

If I had my way, she would never sleep alone again.

CHAPTER TWENTY-SEVEN
Lucy

I am such a push over. All Mason had to do was show me how he felt about me for 24 hours and I cave and forget everything.

But he was so sweet. Waking up Monday morning to a coffee with a lovely note was just the start. Then, the second coffee at work again with an adorable note wishing me a good day. Then, of course, our lunch date. And then to top it all off, he crawled into bed with me last night telling me it didn't want to be without me any longer.

Swoon times a thousand!

His book-boyfriend status is now for sure cemented in my brain. Yes, he was a jerk and said some stupid things, but he did apologize and made it up to me. There is only so much I can hold against him.

You must forgive and forget.

We woke up together this morning, and we had the best morning sex ever. Companies need to stop selling energy drinks and start bottling morning sex, best way to get your day started.

Oh, gross! That sounded so wrong. Yeah don't ever repeat that idea again to anyone.

Back to the point … after our morning of "waking up" together, Mason drove us to work. It was a super busy day since we are now only a few days from December and that is when everything really ramps up for the fourth quarter. Most people think that retailers are the only ones who see a boost in revenue around Christmas time, but a lot of businesses see a bump. Our clients want to make sure they won't lose what they just earned in the last quarter, so we work very hard for them.

Callie jumped at the chance to have dinner with us tonight and I am so glad. I want Mason to get along with them. Not that the few times we have been with them were awkward or anything, but I want them to bond. They are the closest thing I have to family.

I'm finishing up for the day when there is a knock at my office door.

"Come in." I know it's not Mason, he doesn't wait for me to invite him in.

Mrs. Bell walks through the door and quickly shuts it behind her. "Lucy, I must speak with you right away." She says in a very quick and clipped tone.

"What is it Mrs. Bell?" She has me a little curious but I'm sure it will be something about the recycle bin in the kitchen.

"It has come to my attention that our new CEO Mr. Glass is dating someone at the company." She says with shock, but her tone makes me believe it is all an act.

I want to laugh at her flat out. If she had been paying attention at all, she would know exactly who was dating Mason. It isn't like we have done a great job at hiding it. We arrive and leave together almost every day.

"Mrs. Bell, we don't have a no-fraternization policy. There is nothing wrong with coworkers being in a relationship. Plus if you have an issue you should go to HR not come in here to gossip."

Her face reddens with annoyance. "It is not gossip. I was coming to ask you to please be aware and let me know if you see anything."

I roll my eyes and decide to placate her, so she will leave my office. "OK, if I hear something I will let you know right away."

"Good, thank you. Have a nice evening." She nods and leaves through the door.

I shake my head at the ridiculous woman. Of course it is gossip. There is no reason for her to know about anyone's personal life. I'm going to have to tell Mason about this. It looks like Mrs. Bell is on a bit of a witch-hunt. She is something that rhymes with hunt for sure.

A few minutes later there is another quick knock at the door and Mason makes his entrance.

"Hey, baby. Are you almost ready to go? The tacos are calling, and we must go," he quotes my favorite set of beer glasses.

"Yes, please! I have been dreaming of tacos all day." I gather my purse and join him near the door.

"You have been dreaming of only tacos?" He asks in his sexy deep voice and pulls me into his arms.

"Yep, only tacos." I say in a teasing voice and squeeze him around the middle.

"Did tacos give you two screaming orgasms this morning?"

I throw my head back and laugh. "I remember the orgasms part but not the screaming part."

"The way I remember it, you had the wall shaking with your screams." He starts to kiss down my neck with his sexy lips, moving from the spot behind my ear, down to where my shoulder and neck meet and over my heart tattoo. He gives that spot a little extra attention.

"No…" My voice is breathy and full of lust.

"I think maybe, I need to remind you." His hands work down the back of my suit pants and he grabs a hand full of my ass.

"Yes, please. But not here, Pac. I don't want to come in my office."

He groans and leans his forehead against mine. "You are right, baby. Let's go and get tacos so I can get you home and have my way with you."

"Tacos, margaritas and orgasms from Mason. That sounds like the perfect night."

Tacos are the most perfect food in the world and they are by far my favorite. I didn't have them for the first time until I was in Texas for college but once I became aware of what I was missing, I had them whenever possible.

The four of us are sitting at a booth at the back of our favorite Mexican place. Callie and I are both drinking fruity margaritas while our manly men are drinking beers. We haven't ordered yet. We decided to enjoy a few drinks and talk before we ordered. Callie is currently telling us about an order she received from a company that misspelled Idaho.

"And the man on the phone could not understand why it mattered how Idaho was spelled. Well of course I told him that no self-respecting person who lives in Idaho would buy a shirt with Idaho spelled I-D-I-H-O-E."

We all laugh. "Idiot." Craig says finishing his beer and gesturing for another.

"How is your practice going, Craig?" I ask. Craig runs a friendly and pain free approach to dentistry that people really like. He is for sure not one of those scary dentists from our childhood.

"It's been good. Busy but good. We are adding an orthodontist the beginning of next year so there are a lot of things we need to get set up for that."

"Craig is being modest." Callie proudly states. "The new doctor is one of the best in Seattle and he is moving his family here. The word is out that the practice is really making a name for itself."

The waitress arrives with another round of drinks and I happily take my fresh drink. I like listening to them talk about the success of their businesses. They both hard working and deserve everything that comes to them.

"Callie, have you thought anymore about having Glass and Murphy take over your accounting?" Mason asks and totally surprises me. I have never hit up Callie to be a client. My jaw drops and I stare at Mason.

"Actually yes. I made an appointment to come in next week and talk about switching over." Now my jaw drops at Callie.

"Wait a second… what is going on?"

"Mason and I were talking at Thanksgiving and I told him how unhappy I am with Shelly and QuickBooks. He said that you guys would be able to help me out. I'm making enough money now that I can afford some professional help."

"Callie that is amazing! Of course I will help you!"

"Good! Cause I am your 3 o'clock on Monday."

"Yay!" I do a little happy dance in my seat.

"We also talked about maybe expanding to a second store," she says in a totally nonchalant voice and takes a sip of her drink, like that isn't the best news since sliced bread.

I can't contain my excitement and I scream out in the middle of the restaurant. "CALLIE!!!"

"Stop you crazy girl!" She laughs.

"I'm so excited for you! Have you thought about where yet?" I grab my phone and start to search storefront space. "What is our budget? Oh, here is a cute space in downtown Spokane. It's a little expensive but I think we can totally get it down."

My mind is going a mile a minute. Callie reaches across the table and stops my hands from their frenzied pace typing away.

"Sugar, stop. Tonight is not about business. Drink your margarita and we will talk about it on Monday."

"OK, fine. Callie I am so excited for you! This is going to be amazing!"

"Should we order dinner now?" Mason offers.

"I don't know if I can eat anymore." Callie moans while rubbing her stomach. "I think I ate two baskets of chips by myself."

"What?!? Of course we are eating. I must have tacos," I say a little too loudly.

Mason shushes me. "Don't shush me. Tacos are very important."

Craig chuckles at me. "Sorry, Lucy. We will not leave here without eating tacos."

"Good! You had me worried there for a minute."

The waitress comes over and takes our order. I'm not even embarrassed when I order the biggest plate with four tacos, rice and beans. I have a feeling I will pay for it tomorrow, but I can't help it.

"Callie, remember the taco place in Austin with the amazing breakfast tacos?"

"Of course, I do. I still dream about those tacos. I think we need another Texas adventure trip."

"Yes! You still owe me a trip to the Silos! Chip and Jo made that place especially for us to visit. I just know it." I finish off my third drink just as food is delivered and switch to water for my meal at the suggestion of Mason. I think he wants to have his way with me and a drunk me is not a good lay.

I moan at the first bite of taco. Mason squeezes my upper thigh, warning me to behave in the silent way he does. I devour my meal quickly, hardly stopping to breathe.

God, I love Mexican food.

"Oh man, I am so full." I am practically waddling back to the apartment. "Why did you let me eat that much," I say and smack Mason in the shoulder.

"Hey, I might have lost a hand if I tried to stop you," he says with a laugh in his voice.

"Hey." I playfully hit his arm and chest. He twists away and I continue my assault on his back.

"OK, I'm sorry! Uncle, Uncle!" He turns and scoops me into his arms, and brings me up to his eye level. With our height difference, my feet are dangling about a foot off the ground. I wrap my arms around his neck and hold on tight. I have a giant smile across my face that completely matches the one on his face.

"You are very violent tonight. I think we need to do something about that." He kisses me soft and sweet. I close my eyes and sink into the kiss. Tangling my fingers in his hair and wrapping my legs around his waist.

I can feel my passion for him growing and I need to get us to a bed.

"Mason, take me upstairs."

"Nope, not until you say it." He might have said no but I can feel him walking us toward the elevator.

"Say what?" I say and suck on a spot on his neck.

"You know what, baby. Say it." He groans and smacks my ass.

"Now, who is violent?" I giggle and nibble my way to his ear lobe.

"Say it!" We arrive at the elevator and he leans me up against the wall while he hits the elevator call button.

"Pac, take me upstairs."

"Fuck, yes!"

The elevator arrives, and he walks in still carrying me. "I think you should put me down. You will need your energy for what I have planned for you."

"Trust me, baby. I will have plenty of energy to make you scream my name."

"You keep talking about me screaming your name, and I don't remember ever doing anything close to that."

"Well there is always a first time for anything."

We arrive at our floor and as soon as we are behind the door of my apartment, he has me pinned up against it and he is tearing my clothes from me. His pelvis is anchoring me to the door, I can feel how hard he is and my need for him is getting to the point of radicalness. As all my favorite romance characters would say, if he isn't inside me in the next five seconds, I won't be held responsible for my actions.

I have gotten his shirt off of him and my hands move to his fly. I unzip it and reach my hand inside it, loving the feel of him in my hand. He is big and smooth and silky soft, but so hard underneath. And he fits me just perfectly. Or do I fit him. Either way we fit perfectly together.

"Baby, I don't want to take you against the door. But I can't walk with you holding me in your hands."

"Can you walk while inside me?"

He laughs. "No." He lifts my hands from his penis and guides them to his shoulder. He kisses me and I bury my hands in his hair, pulling his face closer. My fingers always seem to end up in this gorgeous brown hair of his. It is soft and just long enough that it feels just about perfect.

My apartment seems so much smaller when he is in it. It seems like only a few steps and we are in my bedroom and I am falling backwards on to my bed, with him following right behind. The weight of him feels wonderful atop me.

He kicked off his pants while he walked us to the bedroom but is still wearing his boxer briefs. "You are wearing too many clothes. You need to catch up." My sassy voice comes out breathy with lust. I reach down and try to work them off for him, but since he is on top of me and so much taller, it doesn't work too well.

He sits up and back on his knees and finally joins me in my full state of undress. God, he is so hot.

"Why thank you, baby!"

"Oops, did I say that out loud?"

"Yes, but I'm glad you did. I like knowing that you want me." He slips inside of me and my eyes roll back in my head from the pleasure.

"Oh man. That feels so amazing. You are always so wet and ready for me." He groans as he starts to move inside of me.

He rocks his hips back and forth and with each movement he rubs against my clit, sending little sparks of fire through me.

He leans down, kissing me while he moves inside of me. He threads his arm underneath my shoulder and cradles my head in his big hands. I clutch at his shoulders moving along with him.

"Baby, I'm not gonna last. I love being inside of you," he moans in between thrusts.

"Mason! Oh my god, yes. I love you." Shit, did I just say that out loud.

Mason goes completely still above me. My heart stops.

Oh god, that can't be good.

I keep my eyes closed tight.

"Say it again," he says in a voice thick with emotions.

My eyes fly open, and Mason's face is split with a wide radiant smile.

My heartbeat returns and starts to beat quickly in my chest. I feel tears start to form at the corners my eyes. "I love you," I say in a small whisper.

"Louder," he commands.

I obey his request and repeat my feelings.

His smile gets even bigger and my heart wants to burst from my chest. He kisses me hard and picks his pace back up. It doesn't take long before I am shouting my release and Mason is not too far behind me with his own release.

We are both breathing heavy coming down from our release when I realize that Mason still has not said it back. He didn't seem to be upset when I said it, but I really want him to say it back. We have only really known each other for a month and a half but we have shared so much. This can't be one sided, can it?

"I can hear you thinking," Mason mumbles but hasn't moved from his spot inside of me and with his face buried in my neck.

I clear the emotions from my throat and reply. "You didn't say it back."

A second after the words leave my lips, Mason is sitting up and pulling me with him. He crosses his legs and has me straddling his lap.

"Do you believe I don't feel the same way baby?" He asks. His face just inches from mine.

I can't find the words so I just nod.

"Oh, my love." My heart leaps at the word love. "Of course, I love you."

I can feel the tears rolling down my cheeks. He loves me!

"Don't cry baby. Me loving you isn't anything to cry about is it?"

I shake my head and can't stand it anymore; I have to kiss the man who loves me.

As we kiss, I can feel him harden beneath me. I reach down, position him at my entrance and sink down on to him, taking him deeper than he ever has been before. I ride him slowly, enjoying our connection. But soon we are both moving franticly and come apart together.

He loves me!

CHAPTER TWENTY-EIGHT
MASON

I swear to God, the last few weeks have been insane. Every night for the past two weeks I have had a client meeting or an event or now Christmas parties. Who has a Christmas party on December 10th? We still have two more weeks till Christmas.

My calendar is so full that I have had hardly anytime to spend time with Lucy but even with my busy schedule, thankfully I have been able to slip into Lucy's bed every night and hold her in my arms.

I have learned that my little beauty snores like a lumberjack when she is overly tired. It's adorable. The first night I stared at her for at least an hour trying to figure out where that noise was coming from. By the second night, it was like a white noise that soothed me to sleep.

So far our relationship has still been hush-hush at the office and Lucy seems to want to keep it that way. I don't love the idea of our relationship being a secret but since it seems to make her happy, and I will go along with it for now. I would do almost anything to see a smile on that woman's beautiful face.

Damn, I'm getting sappy. But I can't help it, and I don't want to. Lucy is awesome. She is sweet, incredibly smart and super sexy. She makes me laugh all the time with the random and ridiculous things she says. And fuck, her mouth and hands are sinful. She could tempt the devil to give up his devilish ways. She is unbelievably caring; she is continuously taking care of me. She makes sure there is food when I come home from my evening meetings, even when she has already gone to bed when I get there.

I really like calling her home. I have a plan to get her to move in with me after the first of the year. I don't think it will be hard to convince her; we are together all the time lately. There are some new condos down on the river that I think she would look amazing in. I can see her sitting outside by the water, by a fire pit, drinking a hot cocoa. God, she is so beautiful.

My dad and I haven't talked about our conversation at Thanksgiving, but now every time someone mentions Lucy at work, he gives me a knowing look. He has been watching her very closely. I have tried to step in several times to make sure she was never thrown under the bus but every time she has been found to have done great work. She is fantastic at her job and I couldn't be more proud of her. She doesn't need me to defend her, but I will anyway.

I have something in the works for the two of us this weekend. There is an awesome lake cabin up north and it will be the perfect place to get some time away with her. I have been teasing her all week, dropping little hints, and playing silly pranks on her. It's been driving her nuts.

Oh, I can't wait to spend the weekend alone with her and no one else!

It's Thursday night and I can finally tell her my big plan. We are sitting on her couch, eating Thai take out. I had this big plan to take her out for dinner, but she requested a night in.

"Are you sure you asked for the five? This isn't very spicy!" Lucy comments as she quickly eats her curry.

"No, I got you the three. I didn't want you to get a stomach ache."

"Pac, you know I can handle the spice."

"You think you can babe, but your stomach does not agree with you a few hours later."

"OK, fine."

She sets down her food and moves to sit on her knees closer to me. She is bouncing with energy. "So… when are you going to tell me where we are going this weekend? The things you call hints have been in no way helpful."

I do my best to pretend ignore her. "Luc, I'm not done eating yet."

She shakes my arm. "Mason, please!" She whines and pouts out her bottom lip.

"Babe, you are going to make me spill my dinner." I say in a falsely annoyed tone.

She drops back on the couch in a very dramatic fashion, covering her face with her arm. "You are killing me! You know I don't deal with surprises well."

"Actually, I didn't know that, but now that I do, I will not be surprising you ever again."

"Oh, that is the worst news ever." She says in a sad, small voice.

She is so adorable when she is being dramatic. I set my food down and decide it is time to put her out of her misery.

"OK, cupcake. Go and check the freezer."

She doesn't leave her spot, but a little smile appears on her lips. "Why?"

"Dessert." I reply.

"I don't want any."

"Lucy, just go look." I roll my eyes.

A second later, she has jumped from the couch and is running to the kitchen. She oohs and aahs at finding the gift bag I hid there. She quickly runs back over and hops onto my lap.

"You got me jewelry?" She looks half surprised and half overwhelmed.

"Maybe."

She reaches in the bag to find a small envelope. "Should I read the card first?"

"Yes, please."

Dear Lucy,

Please join me for a weekend away in Hope.

In Hope of adventure, in Hope of making love and in Hope of a special time together.

Love, Your PAC

She looks up and I can see the tears in her eyes. "Oh Mason. Thank you. I can't wait."

She wraps her arms around my shoulders and pulls me in for a long kiss. She nibbles at my lips. I let her set the pace and enjoy the sweet kisses she is lavishing upon me. I wrap my arms around her and squeeze her ass in my hand. She moans and grinds herself down on me. I decide to take the kiss to the next level, but just when I move us to pull her beneath me, she jumps from the couch and runs to her bedroom.

"Oh, goodness! I have to pack!"

I laugh when I realize she hasn't even opened the diamond necklace that is waiting in the discarded bag. I think I'm going to need to follow her and distract her from packing.

CHAPTER TWENTY-NINE
Lucy

Mason and I headed up north for the weekend. Hope, ID is about an hour and a half north of Coeur d'Alene on Lake Pend Orielle. Mason found a cabin right on the lake and we are spending the weekend there. It will be our first trip away together. There are only two more weekends until Christmas, so this was the only time for us to slip away. He made us leave work early, just after noon so we could still see the view of the lake from the cottage before the sun went down.

Part of Mason's planning had him making arrangements for me to leave early with Luke, but I had to be the one to tell Mrs. Bell. I was trying to be coy and not give too many details but I might have let slip that I was going somewhere with Mason. But I don't have time to worry about that now.

I'm going away with the man I love! We have been spending every day and night together and Mason has basically moved most of his clothes into my place, but he assures me it is going to be special. He is like a little kid as he talks about all the secret plans he has for us.

Now as we are driving north, I am the one who is bouncing in my seat.

There is still no snow on the ground in Coeur d'Alene yet, but the forecast calls for snow up in Hope for the weekend. I adore the snow!

It is so beautiful frosting the tips of the tree branches and covering the ground like a big puffy white blanket.

Man, I am feeling so poetic about the snow this year.

I can't think of anything better than cuddling up on the couch in front of the fire and watching the large white flakes slowly floating down. Normally there is a little snow on the ground before this late into December, but I guess Mr. Frost is on an extra-long vacation.

"Are we there yet?"

"Babe, you asked that five minutes ago. No not yet." He smiles over to me from the driver's seat.

I wait for a few seconds, then ask again. "Are we there yet?"

"Lucy, stop."

"Well I'm so excited! I have never been up to Hope," I whine.

"Have you been to Sandpoint?"

"Yes, but I'm not a skier so I never went past the lodge at Schweitzer."

"It's beautiful in the summer too. We will have to take another trip." He kisses my knuckles.

"That sounds heavenly. Now you have me dreaming of summer and I haven't gotten my white Christmas yet."

"Sorry, cupcake. Don't worry, you will get snow this weekend."

"Is that a guarantee?"

"Yes, look." He points out of the window as we are crossing the long bridge going into Sandpoint across Lake Pend Oreille. The mountains surrounding the lake are covered in white wonderfulness. Just about half way across the bridge, a slow flurry of flakes start falling from the sky.

"Mason! Look!! It's snowing!"

I'm tempted to roll down and stick my head out the window like a puppy, just so I can feel the snow on my face.

He laughs at me and pulls my arm up for another kiss. He is being so sweet. I love that he planned this whole weekend for us.

Twenty more minutes of oohs and aahs and we pull on to a long, winding driveway that leads to an adorable cabin overlooking the lake.

"Mason, it is so beautiful!" I jump out of the car as soon as it comes to a stop. I take two steps from the car and my foot catches a patch of ice. I flail my arms to try and catch my balance, but I don't and fall on my back in the snow. I lay on the ground for a long second before busting out laughing.

"Lucy, where are you?" he asks from the other side of the car.

"I'm over here, by the tire," I say still laughing hysterically.

"Lucy? Are you OK?" He runs around the car, crouches next to me and pulls me into his arms.

"Yes, Mason. I'm fine." I cup his cheek in my hand and run my fingers through his soft beard. "You are so handsome. Have I told you that lately?"

He leans downs and kisses my lips. We are lying in the snow in the middle of this driveway, making out like teenagers and it is the most wonderful feeling ever.

"Mason, will you take me inside now?" I give him a sexy smile.

"Anything for you, baby." He lifts me in his arms and I wrap my legs around his waist. Looking over his shoulder I can see the beautiful view of the lake. It sure is breathtaking but there is plenty of time to look out at the water later. I need Mason!

Mountain sex is now at the top of my list!

We are lying in the master bedroom looking out at the lake. The sun is setting behind the house and the light is shining just perfectly on the lake. You can see the snow falling making the view even more magical.

The cottage is a simple A frame structure. The kitchen is below the bedroom and bathroom on the bottom floor. The living room is open to the master bedroom in sort of a loft fashion. The whole front of the house is windows. I have a feeling tomorrow morning is going to be beautiful with the sunrise.

"Tell me a story about your childhood," he asks as we lounge on the bed, with our backs against the headboard.

"What kind of story?" I reply.

"How did you pick accounting?" He kisses the crown of my head.

"Well, we all had jobs at the commune."

"It's still crazy to me that you lived at a commune."

I elbow him in the ribs in gest. "Hush, you wanted a story so listen. Like I said, we all had jobs. There was a man named Gary Ackerman. He was the one who kept all the books for the group. Most of the people gave their funds to the commune and it was up to Gary to keep track of it all.

One day I was wandering around, reading a weathered copy of Moby Dick when Gary asked me in to his office. He knew I was a lonely child so he reached out and engaged me in a conversation. We would spend hours sitting and talking. He would tell me stories about his life growing up in Connecticut and his time in the Navy. He told me the best stories!

Over the years he saw that I showed promise in math and started teaching me about real world accounting. By the time I left for college, I was doing most of the finances for the commune. Looking back, I spent more time with Gary than I did with my own family."

"He sounds like a great guy. Have you talked to him recently?"

"Yes, we write letters back and forth."

He laughs. "Letters, huh? You should invite him to come up for a visit."

"I think he would like that, but my parents might be upset if they knew."

"Why?"

"Well, you know that I have cut out most contact with them. And if he comes up to visit they would find out and be upset."

"What if we go visit?" he asks.

I turn around and face him, a little uncertain of why he is asking. "Mason, no. I love that you want to help me fix my relationship with my parents, but you can't. And for now, I don't want to even try."

"But..."

I interrupt his thought. "Nope, don't go there. I'm hungry! You need to feed me."

I hop from the bed and start to dress in his shirt. I turn, and Mason is still in the same spot smiling brightly at me. "Come on lazy! I need food." I throw a discarded pillow at him, hitting him in the chest.

He leaves the bed and I take a second to ogle him. He catches me staring and sends me a little wink. "Fine but this conversation isn't over."

"Sure." I roll my eyes at him.

It turns out there is only one year-round restaurant in Hope. It is an adorable pizza place and bakery in an old ice house on the tiny main street. When we arrive, there is only one other group in the small restaurant. It is a group of five older women who are obviously locals and regulars. They are enjoying glasses of wine and chatting away.

We find a small table over to the side and look over the menu. A woman about my age comes over to the table to take our order.

"Hi there folks, I'm Teresa. What can I get you?"

Teresa takes our drink order and when she returns I ask her more about the restaurant. It turns out she is the owner and tells us a little bit of the history of the building. I make a note on my phone to Google them later and read more about it.

The place doesn't disappoint. The pizza is amazing. The in-house-made dough is soft and flavorful, the toppings are fresh, and she put on the perfect amount of cheese. I dig into the pizza and take a giant bite of the cheesy goodness. I moan at the amazing flavor.

"This is the best pizza ever. Teresa is now my favorite person."

"Wow, how quickly I am forgotten about," he says sarcastically.

"Oh sorry Pac, but this is really good pizza."

Mason leans over and whispers in my ear. "Don't worry, later tonight you will forget everything but my name."

I'm instantly wet and my cheeks flush with heat. Swoon!

Although the view of the lake is gone from the sun setting, I can tell I will want to spend a lot of time here in the future. We finish our pizza and thank Teresa for the great time, promising to be back in the future.

We head to the cabin, and when we walk inside my breath leaves me from the wonderful surprise waiting for me. "Oh Pac!"

CHAPTER THIRTY
MASON

I called and made arrangements to have a little bit of romance added to the cabin while we were gone for dinner. The lady with the rental company was a little taken aback at my request until I told her I would pay an extra $500, then she was very accommodating.

We arrive back at the cabin to find candlelight filling the entire place.

"Mason. Did you do this?" She has a look of awe on her beautiful face.

"Come on inside, baby." I grab her hand and lead her into the cabin.

The rental company did an amazing job. Almost all the surfaces are covered in white candles. The fire is roaring in the fireplace, making the place warm and cozy. Soft romantic music is playing over the sound system, champagne and chocolate covered strawberries are laid out on the coffee table. There is a pile of soft pillows near the fire and several large throw blankets.

I wrap my arms around Lucy from the back and settle them on her hips, pulling her back to my chest. I lean my head over her shoulder and kiss her neck. She turns her head, giving me more access to the soft white column of her neck. I leave open-mouth kisses, and enjoying the time nibbling on her soft skin. She reaches up and threads her fingers into my hair, pulling me closer.

My hands take a slow journey across her stomach under her shirt, loving the feel of her soft skin. She is wearing too many clothes. I disconnect my lips from her neck; I pull her puffy coat and my oversized flannel shirt down her arms. Once the items are free from her, she turns and works the button open on my shirt. Her movements are a little fevered and she is shaking, making the process take a little longer than her liking. She lets out a sigh of frustration.

"Here, let me help you." I reach up and take a hand full of the back of my shirt and pull it over my head.

Lucy takes a step back and stares at me for a long moment. I can see her breaths are labored and the flush on her cheeks. "Damn, Mason. You are so fucking hot!"

I laugh and move to bring her back into my arms. She takes a step back and holds up her hand. "Wait. I have a little surprise for you and if I don't do it now, I won't get the chance."

Before I can replay, she runs up the small staircase to the bedroom. "Should I stay down here?"

"Yes, sit on the couch and get comfortable."

Hmm, I wonder what she has planned for me. I walk over and pour two glasses of champagne before I take my assigned spot on the couch.

After a few minutes of waiting and I see Lucy standing at the top of the stairs and I almost swallow my tongue. She is wearing a black nightie that shows off her ample cleavage. Her legs are in silky stockings attached to garter belts. She has messed up her hair, giving it that wild and sexy look. Her lips are shiny from lip gloss and she is wearing the diamond necklace I gave her yesterday.

"Holy fuck, Lucy. You are the most beautiful woman I have ever seen."

She gives me a sassy smile and walks down the stair, swaying her hips. I have never been so hard in my life. I'm pretty sure I could pound in a nail with my dick right now. And the second she touches me, I might explode.

I jump from the couch when she reaches the bottom and she is in my arms in two steps, kissing the fuck out of her. I lay her on the pile of blankets and pillows in front of the fire place and cover her with my large frame. I pull up the edge of the nightie and find that she isn't wearing any panties.

"Do you like the outfit? I'm sorry, I forgot to pack the panties," she says in a husky, lust filled voice.

"Of course I fucking ... I like it a lot baby. You might have to wear this every day but then we would never leave our bed." I run my hands along her thighs, opening her wide. Her pussy is wet with want and I can't wait to sink inside her wet heat.

I run my finger along the lips, spreading around the moisture but not going inside yet. I lean down and take a long lick. Her back arches off the bed and she lets out a long moan. I take her pebbled clit between my lips and suck, loving her reaction. Her hands are now buried in my hair and she is pulling me closer.

"Oh god, Mason."

"Place your hands above your head, baby."

"But I need to touch you."

"Trust me baby." She complies with my orders and grips the pillow behind her.

I set back a little and insert one finger inside her. I begin a slow rhythm, moving my finger in and out of her. Her moans spur me on and I add another finger to the first, picking up the speed.

"You like that, baby?"

She nods her head, squeezing her eyes shut and bites her lip. She has pleasure written all over her beautiful face.

"Tell me, Lucy."

"Yes, Mason. It feels so good."

I add my thumb, rubbing her clit and bringing her closer to her orgasm.

"Oh Mason, I'm going to come." Her back bows and her hands knot in the soft blankets.

"Yes come, baby." I quicken my pace. I can feel her getting closer, her pussy is squeezing my fingers.

After two more strokes she comes, crying out my name as she does. Her head is flown back and her eyes are closed tight.

I kiss my way up her torso and settle my hips between her open thighs. I pull the cups of her nighty down and expose her supple breasts. I spend time lavishing kisses on each breast before taking the hardened nipples into my mouth.

"Mason, please. I need you inside of me," she begs in between breaths.

"Sorry, there is no Mason here right now." I bite her left breast and sooth the bite with a long lick from my tongue.

"Mason, please," she begs.

"Nope." I'm now at the pulse point on her neck, it is moving quickly.

I reach down and rid myself of my pants and slide on a condom, protecting us.

"PAC!" She lets out on a moan as I slide inside of her.

I push in as far as I can and just wait for a moment, loving the feel of her wet heat wrapped around me.

"I love you, Lucy," I say and nibble on her lips.

"I love you too, Mason. But I really need you to move."

"Anything for you baby." I push up on my elbows and start a fast pace as I bring us to release.

It doesn't take long before Lucy goes over, screaming out my name again. Only a few more strokes and I follow after her.

"Dear God, Mason. Will it really always be like this?"

"Fuck, I hope so."

I wake up to the smell of coffee and I think bacon. I reach over and find Lucy's spot on the bed empty and cold.

We made love three more times before falling into bed around 3 a.m. I have no idea how she has the energy to be out of bed yet. Even though it is 11 a.m., I feel like I could sleep for another eight hours. I should march down stairs, throw her over my shoulder and bring her back upstairs to sleep. Well I might take her once more before that.

After I throw on a pair of boxer briefs, I head downstairs. I find Lucy in the kitchen, dancing around with her ear buds in. I lean up against the door frame and watch for a little while she shakes her ass around the little kitchen.

She turns and screams when she sees me standing there. "How long have you been standing there?" She wraps her arms around my waist and takes up her favorite spot, lying her head on my chest.

"Long enough to see you shaking your booty around the kitchen. How are you this morning?" I lean down and give her a chaste kiss.

"I'm wonderful. How are you, handsome?"

"Great, but I would have been better if I hadn't woken up alone." I cup her face in my hands and run my thumbs along the apples of her cheeks. I love when she isn't wearing make-up. Not that she wears a lot but her clean face is my favorite.

"Sorry, I came down to watch the sunrise, but it's too cloudy. So I decided to surprise you with breakfast."

"And the dancing?" I ask.

She turns from me and goes back to finishing breakfast. "I was feeling happy, so I wanted to dance a little." She pours a cup of coffee and brings it over to me.

"Well, it was fucking hot."

She laughs and squeezes me tight again. "Are you hungry? I made breakfast!"

"Sure, what did you make?" I walk over to the stove and find bacon, scrambled eggs and French toast. "Wow, you went all out."

"I did. Will you help me take this stuff over to the table?"

"Of course." I help her grab the food and head for the small table.

We settle at the table with her delicious smelling food and I scoop food onto a plate for her.

"OK, your turn to tell me a story." She says after stuffing half a piece of French toast in her mouth.

"Well, I was born and raised in west Philadelphia. On the playground is where I spent most of my days, shooting some b-ball outside of school."

She lets out a full belly laugh. "Stop it fresh prince! I didn't live in a cave! I want a real story."

"Damn, I was hoping you wouldn't know that one. OK, so one day my uncle gave me this ring. One ring to rule them all."

She hits me in the arm and laughs again. "Really Frodo? Come on Mason, a real story. Tell me about Braxton."

"Well we were assigned to be partners, but we had totally opposite styles. He was the uptight by the books one and I was more of a free spirit."

"Oh my gosh, really? Starsky and Hutch! I'm about to take your breakfast away from you."

She reaches for my plate, but I move it away. "No way. You can't take a man's food away."

"Then tell me a real story."

"Fine, Braxton and I met when we both started at the investment firm. We were both junior producers and he was a cool guy and we started hanging out. About a year after we started working together, we moved in together. He is my best friend."

Her jaw drops and she stares at me, dumbfounded. "That's it. That's the whole story on how you met and became best friends."

"Yeah." I continue eating my breakfast knowing that it is driving her crazy.

"You are the worst story teller ever." She grabs her empty plate and mine as well, even though it is not empty.

"Hey! What the heck! I wasn't done."

"No! No story, no food."

I chase after her, grabbing her from behind and picking her up. She drops the plates onto the counter and squeals.

"Let me down!"

"No you stole my food and now you must pay the price."

"You withheld information, Officer Hutch. You don't deserve my delicious breakfast."

She wrestles herself away from me but I tackle her onto the couch before she can get too far away from me. She is smiling ear to ear and I have to kiss her. I'm going to make love to her right here on this couch.

CHAPTER THIRTY-ONE
Lucy

I wake up from my post caudal nap, to find myself alone and covered in a soft blanket. I stretch and can feel the soft blanket move down my overly sensitive skin. It brings up all the wonderful memories from this morning with Mason. Holy Moly that man knows how to make love to me.

Speaking of Mason, I wonder where he is. I throw on the pajamas I had on earlier and go in search. The cabin isn't big so it doesn't take long to search the inside, that is when I hear a sound coming from outside.

I slip on my winter boots and coat, heading into the snow. I turn the corner toward the back of the property. Mason is bending at the waist, showing off his ass in tight jeans and is shoveling the back patio. He has taken off his jacket and wearing only his long-sleeved Henley shirt. I can see sweat is collecting on his neck and down the center of his back.

The muscles in his back are stretching and straining as he goes about the task of removing the snow from the patio. I watch him work for several minutes, marveling at his strength and endurance.

"Damn, Pac. You sure do live up to your name."

He spins around, startled. "I didn't hear you come out." He abandons the shovel and walks toward me. Actually, stalks toward me is more accurate.

He looks so incredibly handsome. My heart picks up speed as he moves closer to me. Loving him seems to come so easily for me. It feels natural, like I was meant to love him.

He wraps me in his arm and pulls me in for a long kiss. I can taste the sweat on his lips, loving the saltiness of his hard work. His beard scratches against my cheeks as he deepens our kiss.

I pull back, "Take me inside, Mason."

Without another word he picks me up and I wrap my legs around his slim waist. He carries me inside and straight upstairs. I'm astonished by his strength. I'm not the smallest of women but Mason moves me around like I'm basically a feather. And it makes me feel so delicate and girly.

He walks us into the bathroom, turning on the shower. Slowly and silently he strips me from my clothes. He undresses himself without ever taking his eyes off of me. I adore those bright blue eyes, his strong jaw, his wide nose, and those adorable like freckles he claims aren't there.

I reach up and caress his face with my fingers, a face that means so much to me.

"Mason," I say softly, not taking my eyes from his. "I love you so much."

"I love you too, Flower Bud."

I roll my eyes at him. "I thought you weren't going to call me that."

He leans forward and kisses my left eyelid, my left check and the left corner of my mouth. He pulls back and smiles, then takes the same journey on the right side. He stays close and nibbles across my lips then takes me in a hard and fast kiss.

The steam from the shower is filling the room, making it hot and humid. The heat is inside of me too. I can feel how wet I am. I can feel the need building inside of me. Mason's hands are roaming up my naked back sending goose bumps across my skin.

I take a step away, pull him into the shower and under the hot spray of the shower. Although it is a small cabin, they have not held back on the shower. It is large, with a rain shower head, hanging high from the center of the ceiling. There are several more jets come from the three sides of the shower. The tile is classic white subway tile, done in a vertical pattern, making it modern and expensive looking.

Mason and I are standing under the spray, still staring into each other's eyes. He seems so serious today and I can't take my eyes away from him. Mason reaches over and picks up the body wash, squeezing a small amount into the palms of his hands. He runs those soapy hands up my arms, over my shoulder and down my chest to my breasts.

"Turn around and put your hands on the wall." His voice is low and hard.

I slowly turn away from him and say over my shoulder, "Why so serious?"

He slaps my ass, making me jump. "Do it, Lucy."

His seriousness would scare me if I didn't know him as well as I do. I rest my hands on the wall before me away from the warm water. Mason steps behind me and continues washing my back and down to my butt.

"Mason," I moan as his hands squeeze my ample butt.

"God, I love your body, Lucy. Every inch I touch makes me want to touch more."

"When do I get my turn to touch?" I ask on a whimper.

He slaps my ass again and bites my shoulder. "Hush."

He steps back and the warm water runs down my back, washing away the soap. I lift my head to the spray and let the water warm me back up. Mason steps into me again and lifts his right foot from the ground and places it on the edge of the shower seat.

He slips inside me, filling me to the hilt. My breath catches, and my head falls back to Mason's shoulder. He wraps his arms around me and pulls my hips back, keeping me steady as he moves in and out of me at a fast pace.

We move together and in minutes I'm close to coming. Mason reaches up and rolls my hardened nipples between his fingers, making my legs almost give out.

"Oh god, Mason. I'm gonna come."

"Do it, baby! Come! I'm right behind you." He says into my ear.

I come at his command and scream out his name. He quickens his pace, racing for his own release. He comes hard, holding me close.

"I love you, Lucy," he says quietly. The only sound left in the small bathroom is our breathing and the water.

I turn in his arms, unseating him from inside of me. I pull his face down and stare into his beautiful icy blue eyes. "Mason, I love you more than I ever thought possible." I kiss him fiercely and melt again into his arms. He is still hard and pressed between us. I can feel him harden even more as our kisses continue.

He lifts me in his arms and I wrap my legs around his hips. I cling to him like a vine. He pulls back and stares into my eyes, I reach down and place him at my entrance again.

"I don't think I can come again but I still need you inside me, Pac."

He gives me a cocky smirk, "Challenge accepted."

Mason takes me hard and fast again, up against the tile wall of the showers. And true to his word he has me calling out his name as I fall over the edge again.

His hands are halfway up my shirt a few hours later when my phone starts to ring. I ignore it, hoping it will just go away. We have been snuggling on the couch since our shower earlier. We have tried to leave each other's arms multiple times for food but as soon as we break apart and take more than two steps away, the others pulls us back.

A few minutes later, the phone starts to ring again taking my concentration away from Mason and the kisses he is laying on me. I know it's his dad's ringtone. He wouldn't be calling him if it wasn't important.

He pull his lips away from me. "I'm sorry Lucy. Let me answer that really quick."

I give him a sexy smile and say, "Hurry back."
He gives me a quick chaste kiss and answer the phone.
"Hey, Dad. What's up." And then shit hit the fan…

CHAPTER THIRTY-TWO
Lucy

"What the hell happened with Miller's Diesel Shop?" Mason roars as he hangs up his cell phone, walking back toward the couch.

"What do you mean?" I ask. What the hell is he talking about?

"They are freaking out. Their quarterly paperwork is all messed up and they were expecting an email back from you yesterday. I can't believe this. How can you have dropped the ball?"

"Excuse me! I did not drop the ball! Everything was perfect when I left the office yesterday."

"Well obviously it was not. Jesus, Lucy. They are a good client and we have to keep them happy! Plus, Checkers is a friend! I can't let him down."

"Don't yell at me Mason!"

"Pack your shit. We have to leave now and figure this out." He dismisses me with a way of his hand.

"What did you just say?"

"Lucy, fuck. I don't have time for this. Pack your shit. We are leaving."

I stomp up the staircase toward the bedroom to pack "my shit" as Mason put it. I'm so furious I can hardly see straight. How dare he speak to me like this. Everything that happened the last two days between us just went up in flames. He is such a dick.

I work my ass off for Murphy and Glass and everything was perfect for Miller's when I left. I wouldn't have gone to Hope on Friday if there was any items that needed attention.

Well… I was excited about leaving, could I have left something undone? NO! Damn it! Now he is making me question myself. I did my job and I did a good job. Something else is going on.

As I'm packing, Mason enters the room, still on his phone. I can't even stand to be in the same room with him at this moment. As quickly as possible, I throw my stuff into the overnight bag and stomp into the bathroom to grab my toiletries.

"…OK Dad. We will be back in town in a few hours." Mason joins me in the bathroom and I avoid eye contact with him.

"Damn, this is all messed up," he says as he gathers his own stuff.

I throw the last of my things in the bag and go back to the bedroom. "Yep."

I hear Mason from the bathroom. "What the hell, Lucy? You know this is a crap situation. My dad is pissed."

"Yep. I'm ready. Let's go." My voice is clipped as I carry my bag out through the small kitchen and to his car. He joins me a few minutes later after locking up the cabin and gather the last of our items.

"What's with the silent treatment?" Mason asks as he settles into the car.

"Not now, Mason. I just want to get home and get this figured out."

"Not now? God, damn it Lucy. Talk to me."

I can't meet his gaze. I look out the window so he doesn't see the tears forming in my eyes. "No, Mason. Let's just go."

We leave the beautiful cabin and head through the small downtown. As we pull on to the freeway to head south, I pull out my phone and send a text to Callie.

This weekend is ruined!!!

She quickly replies. What happened?!?

Work has messed with my personal life again!

Oh no! I'm sorry to hear that, darlin'. Are you coming back tomorrow as planned?

NO, we are coming back right now. I'll call you in the morning.

OK, if you need me for anything, please please, please call!

Will do.

We ride in silence for several miles. I can feel my emotions starting to get the better of me.

"I brought you a bottle of water for the ride." He gestures to the water sitting in the center console and I feel a tear roll down my cheek.

How can he be such an ass twenty minutes ago and now he is so thoughtful?

I clear my throat to answer. "Thank you." I take a small sip of the water but can't bring myself to drink much more. There are too many emotions running through me right now.

The rest of the ride back to CDA is exhausting. Although we did not speak the entire way, my mind was replaying the last two days. From waking up on Friday morning together, to the excitement of leaving work that afternoon, our wonderful night last night, and of course our time today. It had all been so perfect. But this crap always seems to happen to me.

One minute I think the guy I am with is perfect and I give him my heart. And the next he is running me over with a dump truck. I get that Mason wants to make this right for our clients, I do too. But treating me the way he did was un acceptable.

As we enter the outskirts of CDA, Mason finally breaks the silence. "Would you like to go home before we head in to the office?"

"No, thank you. I want to get this over with."

My car is still sitting in its parking spot from Friday morning when we arrive at the office. It is joined by Mason's dad's car, and the little red sports car that I think belongs to Candice. Oh great, that is just what will make this whole situation better.

As soon as we come to a stop, I jump from the car and quickly make my way upstairs. The devil on my shoulders tells me to let the elevators doors shut on Mason, but the angel wins out and I wait for him. He places his hand on my back as we arrive at our floor but I flinch away as if I have been scolded.

"Lucy," Mason says in a low voice. But I choose to ignore him and head straight to his dad's office to find out what is going on.

I knock on the door but don't wait for an answer. "What seems to be going on Mr. Glass?" I ask in a clipped tone.

"Lucy." He pauses as Mason enters the office behind me. "Rob from Miller's Diesel Shop called here this morning. He told Mrs. Bell that he was waiting on an email from you and that some of the reports were not complete. He was not too happy, so Mrs. Bell called me and I came right over."

I hear Mason swear under his breath. That doesn't sound like the emergency that we were led to believe.

"Thank you for letting me know. I will log in right now and see what information was missing." I smile politely and head toward my office.

Mason follows close behind me and as I pull out my office chair, he pulls another chair around to sit next to me.

"I don't need you looking over my shoulder for this." I glare at him, no longer able to hide my anger with him.

He stares into my eyes for a few seconds, reading the hurt and anger that are lurking there. Mason backs away a little and gives me some distance.

"OK. While you get it pulled up, I'm going to call Rob."

I roll my eyes. Yes, please try to fix this for me.

I get everything loaded, but as I pull the reports up, nothing is amiss. All the information entered is correct. I pull up my email and confirm this was the version of the report that was sent. And it is. What the hell?

Mason places his call and puts it on speaker while it is ring-ing.

"Checkers." The other side of the call says.

"Checks, its Mas. How ya doing, brother?"

"Hey, Mason. I'm good. What can I do for you?"

"My Dad said you had called the office today and had some concerns what your finance reports? I have Lucy here with me and I wanted to clarify somethings."

"Hello Rob."

"Hi Lucy. Wait weren't you two supposed to be out in Hope this weekend."

My eyes meet Mason's and I can feel myself starting to get emotional again.

"Yeah, Mr. Glass asked us to come back after you called. He was concerned you were upset."

"Upset? Fuck no. I called to make sure the numbers were right but I wasn't concerned. Lucy, did we really make that much money?"

I smile at the shock in his voice. "Yep, you boys had a great few months. With all the publicity you and Jeff had after the car show you attended, there was a big spike in online merchandise sales and just traffic to your website in general."

"That is fucking amazing! You hear that, Jeff? Looks like we will make a success at of this shit hole after all."

I laugh out loud and look up to meet Mason's face. He too is smiling and laughing at his friend.

"Hey, I'm sorry guys. I didn't mean to ruin your weekend. I told that lady that answered the phone it wasn't urgent. I had just planned on leaving a message. I was surprised someone was there on a Saturday."

Why was she here on a Saturday? And why was she answer-ing the phones? White hot anger crushes down on me. My eyes fly back to Mason's and his too have changed to anger.

Who does something like that. She knew I had gone away for the weekend.

"No worries, man. Just do me a favor and only call or email Lucy and I. That way we can be the ones that ignore your stupid ass."

"Whatever fucker. Go back to your weekend, I'm sorry for all of this Lucy."

"It's fine, Rob… Checkers. Let me know if you have any other questions."

"Will do. Later." The call disconnects. And I feel a rush of stress leave my body. I slump back in my chair and breathe a sigh of relief. But just as quickly as the stress leaves me, rage and anger replace it.

"The STUPID BITCH!" I roar!

CHAPTER THIRTY-THREE
MASON

Today has taken a terrible fucking turn. One minute I have the most beautiful girl laying with me in bed, our arms and legs tangled. And now she is standing in front of me with her eyes on fire. Some of that fire is directed toward me.

"Lucy," I start but she interrupts me.

She leaps from her chair and starts quickly pacing behind her desk.

"AH! I can't believe the nerve of that woman. To lie about this whole situation. She knew I had gone away for the weekend and how excited I was. She did this all on purpose. That old and interfering bitch. UGH!"

I laugh out loud at her, starting to feel the weight lift from my shoulders. But the sound of my laughter seems to bring her back to reality and she stops pacing.

I see the fire that was so fiercely burning a few seconds ago slowly fade from her eyes and hurt creeps in. Fuck!

She squares her shoulders and says, "I'm going to go talk to Mr. Glass. Let him know that there is nothing to be concerned about."

"Wait." I move to stop her touching her arm, but like in the elevator she flinches away.

"No, Mason. I don't want to talk right now," Lucy says in a small voice. She walks away and I let her but follow close behind.

God, damn it. I really fucked up.

I know that I didn't react the way I should have when my dad called, but fuck. He is trusting me to take over his business. This is something he has spent his whole life building. And when he said there was an issue I freaked out. Not my finest moment. But now she won't even look at me.

I know she cried most of the ride from Hope, and it took everything in me to not stop and pull her into my arms.

Fuck, I shouldn't have ever let it get this bad.

We arrive at my dad's office and enter without the formally knocking that I know he enjoys.

"Mrs. Bell," I start. "Will you please, step out for a minute? We would like to speak to my dad alone."

"I don't think that is a good idea. I should really stay and take notes. For disciplinary reasons." She says smugly with an evil smirk on her face. Stupid bitch.

"That won't be necessary. Lucy will not have any disciplinary items added to her file. Plus, it is extremely inappropriate for you to be involved in any HR issue since you are in fact not HR."

Her eyes widen and she looks toward my dad. I'm sick of her bullshit. There have been several complaints against her in the last few months since I started here.

"OUT!" I yell. It's time I start defending the woman I love.

She jumps from her seat and scurries out the door.

"Mason, it is not proper to yell at the staff," My dad says in a stern voice.

"Well, Dad, it is also not OK to tell lies to the CEO of the company in the hopes of getting another coworker in trouble."

"What?" he asks.

"Please Mason, I can handle this for myself," Lucy says and touches my arm.

She steps closer to my dad. "Mr. Glass, did you happen to speak with Rob from Miller's before you called us?"

"No, Mrs. Bell said he was very upset and that the work he requested had not been completed. I know that Miller's isn't one of our biggest clients, but they deserve to have their work completed when requested."

Lucy takes a breath to compose herself before she continues, I can tell there are words running through her brain that are not the most appropriate to use right now. God, I love her fire.

"Unfortunately, Mrs. Bell over stated the situation entirely. Rob was not unhappy with the reports that were sent to him. He was surprised at their earnings and wanted to make sure it was correct." My dad's eyes widen but before he can say anything, Lucy continues. "No email was missed being sent. I will take blame for this, I did not mark that it was sent on the client's flow chart. That was my error, but the email was sent.

The only person who would have checked for that was Mrs. Bell. She is in charge of making sure the items on the flow charts are being completed. It seems that she was trying to get me in trouble and have you jump to conclusion, which unfortunately sir, you did."

She is holding her own. Fucking, badass. That's my woman. And she is mistaken if she is going to get away from me. I will fucking marry her tomorrow if she agrees.

My dad sits in silence for a few moments. Before shaking his head and pressing the intercom. "Mrs. Bell, please come back in here."

As if she was standing right outside the door, Mrs. Bell enters. She walks straight past both of us and to my dad's side of the desk.

"You don't believe them, do you Richard?"

What the fuck?

In a low voice, my dad calmly says "Candice. I think it is a good idea for you to go home."

Candice reels back as if she has been slapped, turns and stomps to Lucy. "Clay was right about you. You are no more than a dramatic little slut, who is only looking to further her career by sleeping with important members of the staff." Lucy's head whips back as if she has been slapped. I rush forwards and put myself in the middle of them, protecting Lucy from his awful woman.

"Candice, that is enough," my dad roars. "How dare you speak to another employee like that! On Monday we will be having a serious decision about your behavior."

She stomps from the room and slams the office door.

Dad takes a second then replies, "I'm very sorry you had to come in. But I thank you for the time."

"Dad, what the hell? That is all you have to say. You knew we had gone away for a romantic weekend."

"Mason, I apologized once. This is a bad situation and we need to look into things a little further." His voice is calm and business like and it makes me even madder.

"No, you have been weird about Lucy since Thanksgiving and now this has gone too far. You are too busy trying to find fault in her that you are missing out on what an amazing woman she is.

"She is incredibly smart and a real asset to this company. You need to forget this shit and move on. I love Lucy and she is going to be in my life for a very long time."

I grab Lucy's arm and pull her from the office. I slam the door closed then slam my lips down on hers. She resists a little at first but soon she is melting into me and tangling her fingers in my hair, pulling me close. I grab on to her ass and lift her legs to wrap around my waist.

"I'm taking you home, baby. And I am going to spend the rest of the night apologizing for being a complete ass."

She smiles at me and a tear slips from her sweet eyes. I wipe the tear away with my thump and kiss the apples of her cheeks.

"Mason...," she starts but I interrupt her. Not wanting to let her finish that thought.

"Don't, baby. Let's just go home and we can forget all about this.

"Pac." That is a good sign. "I think we need to talk first."

"Yes, we can talk at home, while we are naked in bed and not a second before that."

I keep her in my arms and run to the elevator then toward the car. I really need to stop having to make things up to her.

CHAPTER THIRTY-FOUR
Lucy

Our weekend had a bit of a kink in the middle, but Mason is working on making it up to me. Instead of going home, we drove to downtown Spokane and rented a beautiful suite at The Davenport Hotel. The room is lush and very fancy, with soft white sheets and fluffy towels. We woke up Sunday morning to a view of snow over the Spokane River. Mason had coffee and hot cocoa delivered and we sat in robes for most of the morning just watching the snowfall.

"I wish we had been able to stay at the cabin," I muse as I sit wrapped in his arms, staring out the window.

He kisses my forehead. "I know, baby. I'm sorry about the way everything went down."

I nod my head, still not able to articulate the words. "Will you tell me more about your conversation with your dad at Thanksgiving?"

He takes a deep breath and tells me the story I missed at Thanksgiving. It all starts to make a lot more sense now, I didn't think he could have gotten that upset about a silly comment about us getting married, but on top of this I can now understand his freak out.

I turn in his arms and look at his serious face. "Mason, you should have told me. If I had known that I was under extra scrutiny, I would have prepared myself. Taken extra time to ensure everything was perfect. I could have stood up for myself if need be."

"But, baby. I didn't want you to know. I didn't want to add any more to your plate. I wanted your work to stand on its own without any added pressure."

I lean over and give my man a sweet kiss. "Thank you, Pac. But from now on, let's give each other all the information. We are better as a team, doing things together than apart. Can we do that?"

He hugs me close and I think for the first time that the future for us is more than just a pipe dream, more than just the fairy tale stories I read as a little girl. This is an adult relationship and we are working to better it together.

Monday afternoon following our weekend away, there is a knock on my office door.

"Come in," I call out to the closed door.

"Lucy, can I have a word with you?" Richard asks as he enters.

"Yes, of course."

He sits at the chair across from me at my desk. I can tell from his face that he has something on his mind. His face is so much like Mason's. I can always tell when Mason has something he wants to say. His forehead crinkles a little near his hairline and his eyebrows are pulled down low.

"I owe you an apology," he starts with a serious tone.

"For what?"

"I made a terrible assumption about you, my dear. And I unfortunately did not keep that opinion to myself. Because of that, you were not treated properly. Your work was overly scrutinized by several members of the staff. Including Mrs. Bell, who over stepped, causing you and Mason's weekend to be ruined."

He takes a second before he continues, "I thought that you were only dating Mason to get ahead here at the company and that is unforgiveable."

"Thank you for saying that. I want you to know that I would never do something like that. I actually told Mason I didn't want to date someone at work."

"He mentioned that to me," He chuckles. "I want you to know Lucy, that I think you are great at your job and a valuable member of this company. Every time your work was checked, it was extremely well done, I was extremely impressed. Mrs. Bell had to lie and over state for anything to be seen as an issue.

"I promise going forward you will not receive any special treatment." He leans in close and winks. "The good kind or the bad."

I chuckle at him. "I appreciate that."

"Also, I would like to talk about the situation with Mrs. Bell and the things this Clay person said about you."

"Well Clay is my ex-boyfriend. We were coworkers at my last job. He was the reason I was let go. I'm not sure how she knows him."

His face takes a hard glare. "I believe I have heard her mention a Clay being her nephew. I had asked Mrs. Bell to keep an eye on your work but like I said she majorly crossed a line. Mason said this is not new behavior for her?"

"No, she has been bullying me and micromanaging me since I started here. I haven't had the guts to say anything before now."

Richard's eyes flare at the word bullying and my heart sinks. I hate that I'm making this an issue. "I wish you would have said something before, but I understand why. She does attempt to rule this office with an iron fist. My guess is Clay told her about you back when you first started, and she has had it out for you from the very beginning. And I gave more fuel to the fire.

"I don't believe in discussing disciplinary measures with other employees but know that things will be changing."

"Thank you, Mr. Glass. I appreciate that."

He hugs me and says, "I'm very glad MJ has found you."

I smile brightly, "I'm very glad I found him too. I love him very much."

He returns my bright smile and leaves out my door. So much weight was just lifted off my shoulders and I slump back into my seat. I text Mason to let him know about my conversation. Seconds after the text is sent, my door opens, and Mason comes striding in, making a beeline right for me.

"What happened? Are you OK?" He is so adorable when he is trying to look out for me.

I wrap my arms around his waist and tell him everything that happened with his dad. He stays quiet until I finish the story.

"I'm glad he apologized. And I will push to have Mrs. Bell fired. She has gotten out of control."

"No, I don't want that. She thought she was doing as she was asked. Not the greatest way of doing it, but still not entirely her fault. Let's let things settle down for a few weeks and see what happens from there."

He kisses my nose the way I love and nods his head in agreement. "OK, baby. If that is what you want."

"And I think we should make it official here at work. I know most people already know but I think it would be a good idea to put it all out there in the open. No more secrets."

Mason's face lights up in an instant. He takes me in his arms, picking me up and twirling around. I yell out in surprise and begin to laugh at how wonderful it feels to make him happy.

He sets me down and kisses the shit out of me! He pulls away and has to keep his arms around me so I don't become a puddle on the floor. "This is the best news I have had all day. I will get with my dad and see what's the best way to make the announcement professionally."

"I thought we could just put up a sign in the breakroom." I say and give him a sassy wink.

"Very funny, silly girl. You know they will see us together on Friday night at the holiday party. I plan to not let you more than five feet from me all night."

"You've got a date."

"What are you doing tonight, baby?"

"No big plans, you?"

"I have another corporate holiday party in Spokane."

"OK, come over when you're done?"

"Of course, I don't sleep without you, cupcake."

I decide to take a drive after work. I leave a little early so I can watch the sunset over the water before it sets super early. There is an amazing turn out at the south end of the lake that is a perfect view of everything. The city is hidden by the bend in the lake, so it doesn't distract from the beauty of nature. We had a big snowfall last night, but not a lot is on the ground in the city. Out here though, the snow is covering all the branches of the trees making everything magical.

I'm sitting in my car, watching the sunset and listening to my favorite Rascal Flats CD. Coming out here helps to center me. I love spending time with Mason, but the alone time is good for me. I had so much alone time as a child, it is my solace. It is where I can recharge my battery.

After about the sixteenth time of them singing about blessing the broken road, I decide to head back toward town. The temperature dips once the sun goes down. My thin Nevada blood makes me wince at the 27 degrees blinking on the dashboard.

As I pull on to the road, I see a set of headlights coming toward me. As we get closer to each other, I can see the cars lights starting to veer into my lane. Seconds later they barrel into me. The noise of our two cars crunching together is deafening and the impact shoves me what feels like half way into the passenger seat.

My car comes to a stop against the right guardrail and I sit for a second stunned, before the world goes black.

CHAPTER THIRTY-FIVE
MASON

The party in Spokane, was totally fucking boring. As soon as we got there, all I could think about was getting home. When I finally do, I am surprised that Lucy isn't there.

It's now almost ten thirty and she still has not come home yet. She hasn't answered my texts or phone calls, and that worries me too. She always has her phone near her and is checking it constantly. I should have gotten Callie's number for just this such occasion. I made a few phone calls and was able track down Craig's number but he didn't answer either.

The panic is starting to set in and I'm going crazy here in her apartment without her. I set the phone down on the coffee table and take a break from my calls and worrying to get a drink.

After I down two shots of whiskey, I hear the best sound in the world, Lucy's ring tone. I sprint to the coffee table and quickly pound on the green accept button.

"Lucy, where are you?"

"Mason, it's Callie."

"What's wrong?"

"Lucy was in a car accident out on the lake road. She is here at the hospital. They are going to keep her overnight."

"Is she OK?" Car accident? Shit! My mind starts to spin with all the possibilities.

"Yes, but she has a severe concussion and some bruised ribs. She keeps asking for you. Can you come?"

"Yes, I will be right there. Tell her I'm on my way." I'm out the door and running to the garage before I hang up.

The hospital is at the top of the hill across from the apartments and it takes me five minutes to get there. I might have gone through a light that was more red than yellow, but I needed to get to my girl.

I park and run into the emergency room entrance. The first nurses' station I find is empty, so I go straight to the second.

"Can you please tell me what room Lucy Harvey is in?"

"And your relationship to her is?"

"I'm her boyfriend." The nurse gives me a questioning look but still tells me the number. "Visiting hours are only for another fifteen minutes. Please make your visit quick."

"Thank you." I run toward the set of elevators she directed me to. There is no way this will be a short visit. I will be staying the night with her, holding her hand and making sure she has everything she needs.

I rush from the elevator at the third floor. I see Craig sitting in the waiting room and I go straight to him.

"Hey, man. Where is she?" I greet him but my eyes are searching down the wall for her.

"Hey, I'm sorry I didn't call you back right away. I just got here myself."

"Not a problem. I have to go find her."

"Yeah, go. Down there, fourth room on the right." He points and I take off again.

My heart is beating so fast and feels like it is in my throat.

I throw her door open and she is lying in the bed. It's the most beautiful and horrible thing I have ever seen. Her eyes are closed but there is a bruise on the left side of her face and wide white bandaid is up near her hairline. She has an IV connected to her right arm.

I take a few slow steps toward the bed. Callie is sitting in the chair near the window and stands when I enter the room.

"Hi Mason. I'm sorry it took me so long to call you. I didn't get the call until almost three hours after the accident."

I wrap my arm around her shoulder, she is shaking with concern. "I'm glad you did call me. Why did it take so long for them to contact you?"

"Since I'm not her blood family, she still has her parents as the emergency contact, which I am making her change tomorrow. And there is only one phone at the commune, it took them a while to call the hospital back and then me."

"Yeah we are changing that ASAP." I can't believe that she sat in the hospital all by herself for three hours, hurting and alone.

I pull the other chair to Lucy's side and sit, cradling her hand in mine. "Tell me again what is wrong?"

"The other car hit her on the driver's side. She has four bruised ribs on that side, the bruise on her cheek, a small cut above it and a severe concussion. The nurse will be in within the next few minutes to wake her again."

"Where is her car?" I can't take my eyes off of her. I could have lost her.

"I don't know. I'm sorry."

I turn to Callie, she is starting to get upset. "Callie, you have nothing to be sorry about." I stand and pull her in for a hug. "Why don't you and Craig go home? Get some rest and come back first thing in the morning."

She is actively crying now. I hug her a little tighter, knowing the fear she is feeling.

"Are you sure? Will you call me with any updates?"

"Of course."

We exchange numbers and I send her off to rest. I take my seat back to Lucy's side, staring at the poor, hurt woman who holds my heart. A nurse comes in a few minutes after Callie has left.

"Hello, I'm sorry but visiting hours are over."

"I'm not leaving her."

She smiles knowingly. "Are you Mason?" I nod. "I'm glad you are here. She was asking for you. She was very upset she didn't have your phone number memorized."

I chuckle with little humor. My poor love, she must have been so upset. Sitting here alone, needing someone and no one was here.

"I need to wake her up to check on the concussion."

"Can I stay? I want to see her when she wakes up."

She smiles that knowing smile at me again and moves to opposite side of the bed.

"Lucy, I'm going to need you to wake up for me. I have a couple of questions you need to answer."

Lucy slowly opens her eyes, and goes to turn on to her side, like she does in the mornings when I try to wake her up early. But her breath catches and then she cries out in pain from her bruised ribs.

"Oh, be careful, baby. Don't move too much."

"Mason, you're here." Her eyes fly open and she turns her head to me. I can see the tears in her eyes.

"Don't cry." I hold on to hand and give it a squeeze.

"I'm so glad you are here," she says in a tone filled with emotions.

"OK, Lucy. I have given you some more pain stuff, but I have a couple of questions. Can you tell me what day it is?" nurse Patty asks.

"Monday, unless it is after midnight. Then it would be Tuesday." Lucy closes her eyes as she quietly answers the questions.

The nurse laughs at her sass. "Very good. Keep those open for me. Can you tell me your address?"

Lucy easily rattles off her address. "Great, I'm going to let you rest now. I will be back in about two hours to check on you again. Hit your call light if you need anything."

The nurse leaves and Lucy turns her head to me. "Hi."

"Hi baby. How are you? Do you need anything?"

"Just you. I'm so glad you are here." She sighs.

I bring her hand to my lips and place a kiss there.

"Oh no, my car. My poor baby is completely destroyed." The tears are freely flowing down her cheeks and I can tell she is starting to get very upset.

I stand and move to sit next to her on the small hospital bed. She looks so small and helpless. And it is tearing me apart. "It's all going to be OK. We will get the car fixed or I will buy you a new one."

"But I have only had her for a little more than a year. And I haven't gotten to take her on a big road trip." Lucy is only taking short breaths in between each word.

"Baby, take a deep breath. You are getting upset."

"It hurts."

"What hurts?" I run my fingers down her cheeks wiping away the tears.

"It hurts to breathe."

I feel so awful for her. "I'm sorry, my love. I need you to calm down. You are getting worked up. This will not help you get better if you are all worked up and upset. Get some rest and I will figure out everything in the morning."

She gives me a watery smile and pulls my arm to her chest, hugging it close. I lay my head on her right shoulder and wrap my arm around her waist, being very careful to not hurt her ribs.

"I love you, Lucy. I was so worried about you and I am so glad that you are OK. I wouldn't be able to handle it if you weren't OK," I whisper to her. She is my life and my heart.

A few minutes later Lucy is finally calmed down and back to sleep. I leave Lucy for a minute to check in with the nurse and get some information about her going home tomorrow. I walk to the nurses' station not too far from her room. I see Lucy's nurse sitting by a computer.

"Excuse me, Patty?"

She looks up from her computer and gives me her warm smile. "What can I do for you?"

I need to update some paperwork for Lucy."

"Sure, let me get her chart for you."

She brings me a large green binder with Lucy's name and birthday printed on the side. I open up the front and find her emergency contact section. I take note of her parent's number and then scribble it out and replace their information with mine.

I close the binder and leave it at the nurses' station. I pick up my phone and call my dad. He should probably know what happened to Lucy. I won't be at work tomorrow and neither will she.

I hear his groggy, rough voice after a couple of rings. "MJ? What's wrong?"

"Hi Dad, I'm sorry to call you so late."

"There is no need to apologize. What is it?"

"Lucy was in a car accident tonight."

Before I could get out the rest of the sentence he interrupts me. "Is she OK?"

"She has a concussion and some bruised ribs. They are keeping her over night at KMC to make sure she is OK."

"What do you need?" I can hear him rustling around and my mom's voice in the background.

"We are OK for now. I'm going to stay with her overnight. Can you let Luke know Lucy won't be in?"

"Of course. I will take care of everything at work. You stay and take care of our girl. Call me tomorrow with an update when she is leaving."

I say a thank you and hang up from Dad. Our girl. My heart beat a little harder when I heard him say that. She is our girl.

I take my seat next to Lucy and lean over to lay my head on her lap. It is the closest I can be without crawling into the bed along with her. It is not the most comfortable position in the world but I can't think of leaving her side.

CHAPTER THIRTY-SIX
Lucy

I hate hospitals. As a child we never went to doctors, we had a medicine man at the commune who would treat us for the scrapes and bruises that would happen. Whenever someone would leave for the hospital, most of the time they wouldn't come back. The hospital was this big scary place that people went away to and never returned.

I open my eyes to see the sterile white room of my hospital room. My ribs are on fire, my head is pounding, and I have to pee. I stare at the ceiling for a long minute, thinking again of the events of the last 12 hours. My car is gone. All that work it took to afford my little car and in a split second it is gone. It all changed because of some black ice.

Don't get me wrong I have car insurance and they will replace it or have it fixed but it won't be the original. Plus, the cost of a night in the hospital and missed work. It feels like things are falling apart. I need to get out of here and get everything back to normal.

I slowly lift my head and start to sit up. Mason is sleeping and has his head in my lap. He must have slept like this all night. His poor back and neck are going to be so sore today. I comb my hands through his soft brown hair, scraping my nails on his scalp the way he likes, hoping to wake him.

His eyes flutter open and he turns his eyes toward me. "Good morning," I greet him in a small whisper.

He sits up and stretches his shoulders. I can see by his movements his back is tight. "Hi baby. How are you?" he asks with concern in his voice.

"My head and ribs hurt. And I really have to pee." I say matter of factly, I don't feel like sugar coating how I feel right now.

He jumps right up and is out the door, looking for my nurse. He is so caring and kind. Mason is always taking care of me. He comes back a minute later with the morning shift nurse.

"Good morning Lucy, I hear you are in some pain." She comes to my side and looks at the vitals machine.

"Yes, and I need to use the restroom." The need is starting to get urgent and uncomfortable.

"OK, let's do that first. Then we will get you settled back in for some pain meds. We are taking out your IV and switching you to pills. We are getting you ready for the transition home this morning."

The nurse spends a few minutes giving me the ability to leave my bed. Once she gives me the OK, I move slowly. I would never have thought that my ribs have any part of me being able to make the littlest movements, but I guess they do. And with each of those little movements, it brings on a pain that almost takes my breath away. I stand with Mason at my side, holding me close as I move toward the small bathroom. He steps out for me to relieve myself but stays close in case I need him.

I look into the mirror for the first time and see the large bruise that it is forming there. I look like a Bugs Bunny cartoon after he has been in a fight, all that is missing is the loose tooth. I look just awful.

I don't stay in the bathroom long, I want to get back in bed as soon as fast as I can and try to find a comfortable position. This little bit of effort has made me even more exhausted.

Mason helps me back into bed and the lovely nurse gives me a big pain pill. I settle back in, but try not go back to sleep. She is hoping to let me go home soon and I can't leave if I am asleep.

"Can you get me something to eat?" I ask Mason.

"Of course, baby. What would you like?"

"I would love some waffles." They sound delicious. I'm sure I shouldn't have anything so heavy but that is what I want.

"OK, baby. I think Callie was going to come by this morning. I will call her and have her bring it." He stands and pulls out his phone. He gives Callie an update on my condition and I can hear her sweet voice coming from his phone. He gets everything settled with Callie to bring me waffles from Le Pepe.

"Thank you," I say and close my eyes enjoying the darkness behind my eyelids. The overhead lights are so bright, they make the throbbing in my temples worse.

Mason leans over and kisses my forehead with his soft lips. "Don't go back to sleep, baby. We need to get you home this morning."

I sigh and slowly open my eyes to my handsome man. I'm so glad he is here. I wish he had been here the whole time. The paramedics had woken me after they pulled me from the car, it felt like hours before anyone was there with me. I felt so helpless and alone.

"Don't cry. What's wrong? What can I do?"

I shake my head. "Nothing. I'm just glad you are here. I need to change my emergency contact."

He runs his hand down my hair and cups my uninjured cheek. "I wouldn't be anywhere else. Not when the woman I love is hurt and in pain. And I already changed your emergency information. I will be the first call from now on."

He leans in and softly kisses my lips. I reach up and grasp his neck, bring his lips more fully on mine, and closer to me. He moves to sit on the side of the bed and continues to kiss me. He shifts his arms behind me to pull me closer but it upsets my ribs and I cry out in pain, pulling my lips away from him.

"Oh baby, I'm sorry. You made me forget how hurt you are." He sets his forehead on mine, and stares into my eyes. I move in and leave another small kiss on his lips.

"Your kisses are worth the pain," I say in a small voice.

He sits back and gives me a loving smile. "Your kisses are worth everything, but no more pain for you today."

"But staying away from you is so much worse than the pain in my ribs." I can feel tears forming in my eyes again. I don't want him to stay away. I need his strength.

"I need your strength too, baby. And I'm not staying away. You will have to deal with me for a very long time." My heart skips a beat at his sweet words. "Let's get you home and then I will be your personal pillow for as long as you need me."

He grips my hand and sits in the chair where he slept all night.

"Where is your purse?"

"It is over there, I think. Callie had it last night." I point to the small amour near the window. "Why?"

As he goes to reply, Callie rushes through the door carrying several bags of food. Craig is right behind her with another bag and a drink carrier filled with coffees.

"Hi sugar. Breakfast is here." She sets the food down, then rushes to my side and kisses my cheek. "How are you? You look better today, but still tired. Did they keep you up all night?"

I tell her about the hospital's routine of waking up patients with head injuries as she and Craig unpack the food. It smells wonderful, my stomach growls loudly in need of food. She brought me the waffle I requested with fried eggs cooked just the way I like them, sausage, hash browns and hot cocoa. She did the same for Mason, her, and Craig.

"And you will get to go home today?"

"I hope so. My bed sounds so nice right about now." I sigh at the idea of getting to be home, in my own bed.

I'm enjoying my delicious breakfast when there is a knock at the door. Mason's parents enter after the OK.

"Lucy, how are you?" Christine asks as she walks straight to my bedside.

"Hi Christine. I'm OK. Sore but the headache is getting better after some food. Thank you for coming by."

"Oh of course dear. When Mason called us last night that you were in the hospital, I wanted to come then but Richard talked me in to coming first thing this morning." I smile at this sweet woman.

"Lucy, my dad and I are going to step into the hallway for just a minute. Have someone come and get me if you need anything."

"OK."

"Keep eating, sugar. You need your strength," Callie encourages.

I'm exhausted and the thought of eating anymore sounds like a lot of work. "Callie I don't know if I can. I'm so tired."

"OK, sugar. I'm Callie by the way." She extends her hand to Christine.

"I'm sorry, yes Christine. This is my best friend Callie and her fiancé Craig. Guys this is Christine, Mason's mom."

Christine pulls them both in for a hug like they have known each other for years. She has such a sweet heart. "It is so wonderful to meet you both. So tell me, how is our Lucy really doing?"

"She has a couple of bruised ribs that I can tell hurt each time she moves. The bruise on her cheek is starting to fade already. I think she will be OK, but the pain in her ribs will be around for a few weeks." Callie gives Christine a full report, making me laugh.

"Yes, bruised ribs can be awful."

Another knock sounds at the door and we are joined by my nurse and a woman in a long white lab coat.

"Good morning, Lucy. I'm Dr. Adams, we have a full house in here."

Callie takes the hint and ushers her and Craig out the door, promising to be back in a few minutes. Christine stays and takes the spot next to me, holding my hand and smiling kindly at me.

"I'm going to give you a quick once over and make sure you are OK to go home. Is there someone who can stay with you for the next few days?"

"Yes, my boyfriend, Mason, will be with me."

"Good, now let's take a look."

CHAPTER THIRTY-SEVEN
MASON

I was surprised to see my parents arrive at the hospital but so glad to have them here. I love that they care so much about Lucy; she will be around for a very long time. I need my dad's help. I want to get all of Lucy's car stuff taken care of today but I don't want to leave her once I get her home.

I easily found Lucy's insurance information. That girl is so organized, she had copies of her insurance and registration information in her wallet.

"Dad, can you do me a favor today?"

"Sure, what do you need?"

I tell him my plan and he immediately agrees to help take care of everything. He picks up his phone and in less than a minute, he has found Lucy's car. I look over to her door and see Callie and Craig leaving. I walk to them, wanting to take the time to thank them for bringing breakfast.

"Mason, the doctor is in with Lucy, she is giving her the final OK to go home."

"Great, thank you guys for coming and bringing breakfast."

Callie hugs me close and I shake Craig's hand. "You are welcome. We are going to go. Please let us know if you need anything."

"I will stop by later tonight and visit her if that is OK?" Callie asks, but I'm pretty sure she would come even if I said no.

"Of course, you are welcome."

We say our goodbyes and I open the door to Lucy's room. The doctor is shining a light into Lucy's eyes, checking her pupils. The nurse is standing near the window chatting with my mother.

"This must be the boyfriend, I'm Dr. Adams. I was just telling Lucy, I think she is ready to go home, but I don't want her to sleep more than four hours at a time. And if her headache worsens or she has any changes in her eye sight like blurry vision, she must come back immediately."

"Thank you, Doctor."

"You are welcome. I will send in your prescriptions and discharge orders in a few minutes."

I follow the doctor out the door, wanting to ask her another question but out of earshot of my mother. "Dr. Adams, can I ask you one more question?"

She nods her head. "Yes."

"How long should be wait before getting physical?" I wanna just ask when I can make love to the woman I love, but I'm trying to have a little more tact.

"Because of her concussion, I would say at least a week. But with the bruised ribs, it might not be comfortable for her for several weeks or a month. Take it slow after a week and be very careful."

I take a deep breath and let it out on a low groan. I don't know if I can go that long without her, but her safety is way more important than my dick. "Thank you."

"I know it sounds like a long time when you love someone the way I can see in your eyes that you love Lucy, but I'm sure you don't want her hurting."

"No, of course not. Thank you again."

"Here is my card. Lucy mentioned she didn't have a primary care physician. I'm currently accepting new patients and I would be happy to have her as a patient."

"I will let her know."

I leave her and go back into Lucy's room. She is sitting up a little more now and I can see on her, the headache has eased. The pain behind her eyes has disappeared and I'm so thankful for that.

"Mason, are you taking Lucy back to your place or hers?" my mom asks from the chair I vacated earlier.

"I think she will be more comfortable at her place. Does that sound about right?" I direct the second part of the question to Lucy.

"Yes, please."

"Great, what do you need? Do you have enough food? Do you want anything?"

Nurse Sara walks in before Lucy can answer followed by my dad. "Alright, Lucy. I have your paperwork for you, discharge orders and prescription."

My mom grabs the paper from the nurse. "I will take those. We will stop and get you some items, then over to your place. We will meet you there in about an hour."

She hugs me goodbye and leaves with my dad while the nurse is telling Lucy some more instructions on her concussion. The nurse leaves and Lucy moves to stand. "Wow, baby. We don't have to leave right this second."

She looks so small in that oversized hospital gown. "But I want to. Please take me home, Mason."

I pull her close and give her a light squeeze. "Alright, let's get you dressed. Do you have your clothes from yesterday?" I walk to the amour where I find her purse.

"Yes, they are in a bag but Callie brought me some of my sweat pants." I find the tote bag and bring it to her.

"How did she get them?" I question as I help her dress.

"She has a key. She thought I would want some clean, comfortable clothes to go home in."

I didn't realize she had a key but that makes sense. "That was thoughtful of her." She lifts her arms and she winces at the pain of having them in the air. "Let me do the hard work, baby."

She accepts my helps and we get her dressed in her sweats and boots. We gather her things and head for home. I want to take her into my arms and carry her to the car but I have a feeling the hospital would frown on me doing that, they would prefer I use the wheelchair they have provided.

Our drive home is short and I settle Lucy in bed as soon as we get there. I leave her to sleep and set my alarm to wake her in four hours like the doctor said. I settle on the couch with my laptop and try to get some work done.

My parents arrive, and my mom has gone a little crazy. She asked earlier what some of Lucy's favorite foods are and she got them all. We are set for food for the whole week and then some.

"What time is Lucy set to wake up next?"

"A little over three hours."

"OK, I will be back then. I'm going to pick up a few more things for her."

"Mom, you got almost the whole grocery store. What else can we need?"

She comes and cups my face in her hands. "From what you have told me that girl in there has no family nearby besides her best friend Callie. And now that she is yours, I am now her family and I will take care of her as my own. She is in pain and I will do everything in my power to make sure it stops. I love you MJ and since you love that girl in there, I do too."

I hug my mom close and hold her tight for several long moments. "Thank you, Mommy." I kiss her cheek and she lets go of me, pats my arm and leaves.

True to her word she is back an hour later. She brings new pillows, new mattress pad, a new thick comforter and even some new flannel sheets. She is pampering my Lucy and my heart swells at her kindness. I show mom where Lucy's washer and dryer are and we get everything ready for the great switch when Lucy wakes.

Mom and I make some lunch, waiting for the alarm to go off. As we sit and eat, talking about everything and nothing all at once.

"MJ, can I ask you a question? What are your intentions with Lucy?"

I laugh, "I plan on making a life with her."

My mom smiles big and throws her arms around me. "That is the best news I have ever heard, do you have a plan? When will you ask her to marry you?"

Before I can answer, Lucy comes walking out of her room. She looks rumpled from sleep and a little green. I jump up and hurry to her. "Baby, are you OK?"

"No, I'm not feeling so good. Can I have some water?"

I settle her on the couch and she snuggles into my chest, resting on me for comfort. Mom hands me a glass of water and I instruct Lucy to take small sips, but she gulps it down quickly. "Can I have some more?" she requests.

We get her another glass and that seems to help. Mom comes over with some crackers too and Lucy takes one with her thanks.

"Lucy, I got you some new things for your bed. Do you mind if I go and put them on?"

Lucy nods and leans more closely into me. I hate seeing her this weak. "What else do you want, baby?"

"Nothing, just you. You help a lot." She wraps her arms around my middle. I gently pick her up and settle her in my lap. I looked online and they say that the first 24 hours after a car accident are the most painful. Her muscles are healing from the trauma of the impact.

"We are all set," Mom says from the door of the bedroom.

I lift Lucy in my arms as I had wanted to at the hospital and carry her toward our room. Mom went all out. There must be ten new pillows covering the bed. Body pillows, regular pillows and even one of those reading pillows that help people sit up in bed. The new flannel sheets are a beautiful light blue that I know Lucy will love. Mom got enough pillowcases for everything to match and a new dark blue cover for the comforter.

I can hear Lucy take in a gasp as she sees her bed. I set her on her feet just inside the door. "Oh Christine, thank you." Tears are flowing freely down her cheeks.

"You are welcome my dear." My mom pulls Lucy in for a hug and brushes the tears away. "I also brought you a big flannel shirt to get comfortable in. It should keep anything tight away from your ribs."

Lucy holds my mom close for a long time. You can tell there are a lot of emotions going through her right now. She is completely raw.

"Let's get you settled and back to sleep. MJ, will you help her change and I will get her something to eat and her pain pills."

Mom leaves the room and I help Lucy change. The flannel shirt was a great idea. It buttons up the front so Lucy doesn't have to lift her arms. I take a second and study her torso. She has some bruises on her ribs, on top of those injured ribs. There is a darker line that runs from her left hip to right beneath her right breast. That must be from the seat belt.

She is standing in front of me only wearing a simple pair of cotton panties. Even with the angry purple marks, she is so beautiful.

"Would you like to take a shower before you go back to bed?"

She just shakes her head.

"Still sleepy?"

This time, all I get is a nod.

"OK, baby. Let's get you settled back in bed so you can sleep."

"I need my favorite pillow."

"You need more pillows than what you have now?" I say with a laugh.

She gives me a questioning look and replies in a small uncertain voice. "You said you would be my human pillow. I need you."

Those are words that tug straight at my heart. I kiss her lips and help her to sit up with the pillow. Mom brings in some of the soup she and I had earlier with a small sandwich along with it. She even thought to buy Lucy a tray for eating in bed, we get her set up and Mom says her goodbyes. I walk her to the door and hug my dear mother close. She is a saint and I couldn't go without her.

"Your mom is the best," Lucy says as I return to the bedroom.

"Yes, she is. She thinks of you as hers now." I tell her, recalling the conversation her and I had earlier.

Lucy's head snaps up and her eyes find mine. "What do you mean?"

I find a spot in bed next to her and wrap an arm around her shoulder. She instantly melts into me. "She said that because I love you, she loves you too and sees you as part of the family. All of this stuff was her idea. She wanted to do everything she could to make sure you were comfortable."

Lucy takes a long minute processing my words. Her tears come fast and hard. She sobs into my shoulder. "Baby, I didn't tell you this for you to cry."

She takes a deep breath and winces a little less than she did earlier from the pain, then hiccups before speaking. "I know. No one has ever loved me like that before. My parents were a unit and I was the outcast. I was always a second thought."

I pull her closer and hold her tight. "You will never be a second thought again. You are my number one thought, Lucy. All day long, you are running through my head driving me crazy. It is going to be torture to not make love to you for the next few weeks."

"I'm sorry."

"You have nothing to be sorry about, baby. I would rather wait on you then have sex with anyone else. You are the only woman I want."

Tears are still flowing from her cheeks and I wish I could get them to stop. "You have so many sweet words today."

"And every one of them is true and straight from the heart. Is that the only reason you are crying?"

"No, I'm so exhausted and every move I make hurts. Everything seems to make me cry today. I'm surprised I didn't cry when Callie brought breakfast or when the doctor said I could go home."

"Then let's get you laid down so you can get a few more hours of sleep."

"You will stay with me, right?"

"Absolutely, just try and get rid of me."

"I don't want to." She hugs me tight and I let her hold me as long as she needs.

Her breathing evens out and she falls asleep holding me closer to her. I move slowly, doing my best not to hurt her ribs or wake me. I get her down and covered in the new soft sheets and comforter. I take the untouched lunch dishes back to the kitchen and leave them for later and hurry back to Lucy. I take my spot next to her. As soon as she feels me near she turns and snuggles into me. I kiss her hair, breathing in her sweet scent. I close my eyes and join her in an afternoon nap.

CHAPTER THIRTY-EIGHT
Lucy

I stir a few hours later, finally feeling like my head won't explode. Mason is lying next to me and I am wrapped around him like a vine, stealing as much comfort from him as I can.

I slowly sit up, making sure my head doesn't spin. I step into the bathroom to relieve myself. I catch my reflection in the mirror and wince. I am a total mess. My hair is greasy and knotted. There is a little dried blood in it too.

I turn on the shower and remove the soft flannel night-shirt. As the water heats, I take my time working my brush through my hair. It hurts to reach up and bring the comb through my knotted locks, so it takes a lot longer than normal.

I step under the hot spray, loving the heat on my sore muscles. I stand for a while under the water, letting it run over me and cleaning me of the memories from the last two days.

As I lean down for my shampoo, the shower curtain opens and Mason joins me. "How are you feeling, baby?" I wrap my arms around his naked torso and lean my head on his chest.

"Better."

"Can I help you wash?"

I nod and step back from him. I stand still as Mason takes the time to wash every inch of me. He even washes my hair twice, insisting the repeat part of the instructions are a must. My shower is big enough that Mason moves around me easily and there is no clumsiness from a lack of space.

Once we are both clean, he shuts off the water and he wraps me in a big towel. He dries me and sits me on the closed toilet seat. He dries himself and gets back in the clothes he had on.

"You should go get some clean clothes," I suggest.

"I will, once I get your hair dried and you back in bed." He takes out my hair dryer and takes the time to dry my hair. He takes great care in the job, making sure I am left with no tangles and soft hair.

He carries me back to bed and settles me in under the blanket. I take a second to marvel again at the kindness his mother showed me with this new bedding.

"Would you like something to eat?"

"Yes, please. I can make something." I move to leave the bed, but he stops me.

"No, you stay here. My mom brought us a bunch of food even I can't ruin."

He leaves, and I reach for my phone on the nightstand. There are several texts from people with well wishes and an email from my insurance company telling me my claim is being processed.

Mason comes back in the room with a bowl of something that smells like stew. "Here, baby."

"Thank you. Did you happen to call my insurance company?"

"No, but I asked my dad to take care of it for you."

"Oh, thank you." I'm grateful for the help but I want to know for myself what is going on. My self-reliant side wants those details for herself.

"Would you like me to call him and find out the status?"

I nod and show him the email. "I'm glad it is being dealt with."

Mason's dad was able to find my car and get it already appraised this morning by a representative from the insurance company. They had to total it and the insurance will be replacing it at the full amount. Mason thinks it would be best to wait till after the New Year before I buy a new one. He said I would be able to get more for my money in the New Year. And for the time being he said he would gladly be my chauffeur.

With my mind at ease and now showered with a full belly, sleep pulls at me again. Mason snuggles me in close and promises to wake me in another four hours to check on me. I nod my head and after a few deep breaths fall into a restful sleep. I am hoping the next time I wake I will be feeling better.

CHAPTER THIRTY-NINE
MASON

Tonight is the company holiday party and the night I have decided I'm going to ask Lucy to move in with me. The company rented a hall at the Coeur d'Alene resort. My dad booked the best event planner in the city and they will have the place completely decked out.

I rented a room in the south tower of the hotel so we would have a view of the lake to spend the night in. I want to make things as perfect as I can for tonight. We have finally gotten a good snowfall and everything surrounding the lake is white. The roads are a mess, and don't even get me started on the idiot drivers out there.

Lucy has been off all week, resting at home since the accident. I left work around lunchtime, so I could bring her here for a little pampering before the party. At my insistence, Lucy is getting the works done from the resort Spa. A manicure, pedicure, and a facial are all for her. The ladies are also doing her hair and make-up. Since it is only four days since the accident, lifting her arms to fuss with her hair and make-up is still very painful. She swears she doesn't need any help but I think she does and I am getting my way today.

"Mason, you don't have to do this."

"Of course, I do. My woman deserves pampering."

"Did you just say pampering?" she says in a bit of fake shock.

I chuckle. "Yes, pampering." I kiss her sweet lips, then send her off to the spa.

We are meeting in the lobby before heading into the party together. My dad and I decided that Lucy's and my personal lives did not need to be announced to the staff. She and I were going to spend the evening together at the party and let the staff come to their own conclusions.

After the issues with Mrs. Bell, Dad felt it was best that the company not be in the business of staff members' personal lives.

I check my watch and Lucy should be down any second. I checked us in early so she would be able to get ready in the room and not have to leave the resort after leaving the spa.

A flash of red catches my eye. I turn and lose my breath. All those silly cliches about everyone else in the world disappearing are completely true. Right now, she is all I can see. Everyone else just stopped existing. I can feel myself harden the longer I look at her. The whole place is about to see me rock hard and I don't give a flying fuck.

Lucy is walking from the elevators in a bright red, full-skirted dress. It ends a little bit below her knee and she is wearing sexy as fuck black high heels. Her hair is softly curled and is framing her beautiful face. Her make-up is thicker than I normally see on her to help cover the bruise on her cheek but it is done in a way that makes her eyes look so bright.

She walks toward me with a big smile on her face. "Hello there, handsome. Any chance you are looking for a date?"

"As a matter of fact, I am." I pull her into my arms and can't wait another second to kiss her. "You look so beautiful Lucy. God, I love you so much."

She gives me another big sweet smile. "I love you too. And you don't look so bad yourself. I love you in a suit. There is nothing sexier than a big strong man in a three-piece suit." She runs her hands up my lapels, feeling the soft material. I cover her hands with mine and bring them to my lips, placing a kiss on her palms.

"Let's head to the party. The quicker we get there, the quicker we can leave."

"Oh no, we are staying till the bitter end. We got all dressed up and we are going to stay the whole time. Oh, and we are going to take several pictures. I want to remember this night for a long time." She links her arm with mine and we head toward the ballrooms.

She is wearing a new perfume and it smells wonderful on her. I can't wait to bury my nose in her neck while I hold her close to me later.

We walk into the room and Lucy lets out a sigh. "Wow, this is amazing."

The party planner totally nailed it. She went with a white wonderland theme. Everything is white but still festive looking. Six-foot Christmas trees with small white lights are surrounding the perimeter of the room. The tables are covered in white flowers and at least a hundred little candles. I'm sure it cost my dad a large fortune, but he always goes all out for his staff this time of the year.

I look over to Lucy and see tears shining in her eyes. I put my arm around her shoulder and pull her in to my side. "What's wrong, baby?"

"Nothing, it is so beautiful. I love Christmas time." She has a little bit of awe in her voice.

"You are the most beautiful thing in this room."

She turns in my arms, steps onto her tiptoes and kisses my check. "Thank you, Pac. Should we find something to drink?"

I nod and we walk around the room, looking at the decorations and searching for the bar. About half the staff and their significant others are dotting the room. I keep Lucy close with my arm around her waist. I proudly look around the room, wanting everyone to see the beautiful woman that I have on my arm.

Luke is standing near the bar as we approach. "Hey, Luke."

He turns and smiles at us. "Lucy, Mason, great to see you. Lucy you look very nice tonight."

She blushes at his praise. "Thank you, Luke, you look very nice too."

"What are you drinking, Luke? Can I get you another?"

"Scotch, please."

"Got it, and you Lucy?"

"I feel like I should get something fancy, but I really just want a sparkling water."

I laugh and kiss her cheek. "Sparkling water it is, baby."

I smile at Luke and turn to the bar. Lucy sees a friend and walks away to speak with her. Luke steps up next to me. "You are a very lucky man, Mason. Lucy is a great girl." He pats me on the shoulder and takes the second drink I offer him.

I look over to Lucy and again, like it was by the elevator, the rest of the world floats away. The longer I stare at her, the more certain I am of spending the rest of my life with her. I'm sure she isn't ready for that, we haven't talked about the future yet, but I know she is the one for me.

The rest of the party is great. We have a wonderful time and Lucy ends up winning an award. She is so cute when she went up to accept it, her cheeks become super red and she stammers as she says her thankyous. My girl is adorable when she is nervous. Everyone took the news of Lucy's and my relationship in stride. They all seemed to be happy for us.

After dinner, we get on the dance floor and I hold her close for several songs. My dad hired a great local five-piece band and I know Lucy loves to dance but to make sure she doesn't hurt herself, I force her to slow dance with me for all of them. She leans her head on my shoulder and we rock back and forth clinging to one another.

As she requested, we are some of the last to leave the party. It's time to start the second half of our night.

CHAPTER FORTY
Lucy

The party wraps up around 11 o'clock and we head upstairs. I reach into my purse for my cell phone. I have several missed calls from Callie and a couple of 'Call Me Now' texts.

"Callie called me a bunch. I wonder if anything is wrong."

"I'm sure everything is fine, baby."

I smile at my big sexy boyfriend and dial my best friend's number. She answers after one ring.

"Lucy, I have some news," Callie's voice sounds excited.

Mason opens the door to our suite, and as soon as we are inside I kick off my high heels, feeling the soft carpet beneath my sore feet. "What's up?"

"I'm getting married."

"I know silly." Duh! I was there when Craig proposed.

"No, sugar. Craig and I decided we are going to elope in Las Vegas!" I can hear the excitement in her voice, but I am completely flabbergasted.

"What?"

"We decided we don't want to wait anymore and Vegas sounds like the best idea."

"Oh. When?"

"New Year's Day!"

"Callie, that's in sixteen days!" My head is starting to spin with all the thoughts and planning that will need to be done.

"I know sugar, but we don't want to wait anymore. It seems like every time we make plans and try to set a date, things happen, and we have to change the date. And Lucy, I want to be married to Craig… like now!"

"OK, well then we will get you married on New Year's Day!"

"Yay!" She ends the call and I take a deep breath.

My best friend is getting married. My person is getting married. And for some reason I'm having mixed feelings. I want her to be happy but a little bit of jealousy is starting to trickle in.

"Hey, baby," Mason wraps his arms around me from behind, "What's going on?"

"Callie and Craig are eloping to Las Vegas on New Year's Day."

"Oh wow! That is sudden."

I move away and take a few steps. "Yeah, they decided that they didn't want to wait anymore and are heading to Vegas." I hate that my emotions are all over the place, I should be jumping on the bed and throwing confetti. But ever since the accident, I have been an emotional wreck.

"Hey, what's wrong?" He can tell something isn't right but I'm not sure I can tell him. It is such a silly thought … why am I jealous of my best friend?

"I'm not sure I want to say it out loud," I say in a small voice.

He wraps his arms around me and I burrow my head into his chest. "You know you can tell me anything, baby."

"My best friend is getting married and I'm feeling a little jealous."

He pulls me back and looks down at me. His eyes are soft and concerning. "Why are you jealous?"

I take a long deep breath and let it out slowly. My stupid eyes are starting to leak tears, dumb girly annoying tears. "Well, we have never talked about this and now it feels silly to bring it up."

"What haven't we talked about, cupcake?"

"The future." As soon as the words leave my lips, I want to

take them back. I'm going to scare him away if I start bringing up the future like this.

He wipes the tears from my cheeks and kisses each softly. "What about the future, baby?"

"If you see us having one?" I say it in a small voice, taking my eyes from his.

"Well we do have plans for Christmas, next week," he says in a joking tone.

I roll my eyes at him. He does make me laugh when he is being evasive. "You know what I meant."

He grabs my hand and leads us toward the bedroom of our suite. The doors are closed and when he opens them, it takes my breath away. Just like at the cabin, the room is filled with flowers and candles. The sheets have been turned back and flower petals are scattered around.

My heart starts to race, holy moly! Is he about to propose right now? Isn't this too soon?

He walks around me and faces me. His face is sweet and hopeful, with those little worry lines forming around his hairline. "Lucy, although we haven't talked about the future, I do see one with you. And I know the first step I want to take toward that. Will you move in with me?"

I throw my head back, laughing long and hard, I'm not sure what is happening. Part of me is completely excited, knowing that Mason wants to be with me and he sees that we have a future together. The other half is let down that he didn't ask me to marry him. It is something I want for sure and I want it soon now that I have the idea in my mind.

As my laughing fit subsides, I look to Mason's face. His brows are pulled down low and his lips are making a pucker. He looks both freaked and concerned.

"Yes, yes I would love to move in with you."

It takes him a second before a small smile starts to form at his lips.

"Why are you laughing?"

"Because my emotions seem to be all over the place lately."

He pulls me in close and kisses my lips softly. I step up on my tiptoes and wrap my arms around his strong shoulder. Just having him close does make me feel better. I can feel his hand slide up my back and unzip the hidden zipper on my dress. I smile and shake my head.

"You have a one-track mind tonight, don't you," I say with sarcasm.

"I always have a one-track mind with you, baby. But I was actually thinking we could get more comfortable and talk about the future."

"I would love to talk about a future with you." I sigh, loving the idea of getting to talk about this with him.

"OK, put on the sexy nightie I saw in your bag and join me on the bed." He wiggles his eyebrows at me.

"You went through my bag?" I hit his arm. "That was supposed to be a surprise." I turn from him and start to unpack my overnight case.

"It was a great surprise, but the doctor doesn't want you seducing me quite yet."

"Well then I think we will have to wait on that sexy nightie until I can seduce you." Teasing him.

He groans and buries his face in my neck from behind me. "Pretty please. At least let me look at you in it. Something to keep in my mind."

"OK, fine. But I might need some help. "

He takes the hint and starts to peel the dress from my shoulders. He places a kiss on the skin he finds there. He follows the dress down my back to right above the bright red panties. The dress had a built-in bra so once the dress is gone, I am left in just those red lacy panties. I can hear his intake of breath as he takes me in from behind. I look over my shoulder and I can see the lust in his eyes.

He shakes his head and leaves me turned around. "Nope this won't work. I take it back. I can't see you like this and not make love to you."

I giggle at the desperation in his voice. Poor baby. I want to make love to him too, but I'm still healing from the concussion. He unbuttons his shirt and lays the crisp fabric over my shoulders. I push my arms through the sleeves and turn to face him.

The lust is still in his eyes and I can see how hard he is from the tenting of his slacks. He reaches out and slowly helps button the shirt. Taking his time and touching the skin he sees as he goes.

"This might be worse than that nightie." He pulls me close and wraps me in his big strong arms.

"Why?" I ask, running my hands up and down those arms.

"Seeing you in my shirt and smelling like me, it's like I have marked you. You are even more mine like this."

Swoon!

I lift up on my tiptoes and take his lips in a sweet kiss. I want so badly to bury my fingers in his hair but because of his height I can't right now. So instead, I explore his chest and arms, the parts I can reach without pain. As we kiss, I pull the undershirt from his dress slacks. My hands roam the warm, golden skin I find there. He moans at my exploration and I can feel it all the way down to my toes. He reaches behind his back, grabs a hand full of the undershirt and pulls it over his head. Our lips part only for long enough for the shirt to be removed.

I take a step back toward the bed and Mason follows me, staying close and continuing to ravish my mouth. When my knees hit the bed, I sit and scoot back. Mason starts to follow but stops before he covers my body with his.

"Damn it, Lucy. You almost made me forget." We are both breathing hard and my heart is pounding, I can feel the moisture that has gathered between my legs. I want so badly for him to slip inside of me.

"Please, Pac. I need you." I know he can be gentle and not hurt me.

"Lucy, I need you too. But I won't risk you getting hurt any more than you already are." He kisses my forehead and steps back from the bed. "I'm not rejecting you. I want nothing more than to be with you. And as soon as I can, you and I will stay in bed for at least two days." I can tell from his eyes he is serious. They are a deep dark blue, the color they always get when he is very turned on and ready to push inside me.

I nod and move to sit with my back to the headboard. There are several extra pillows on the bed and I quickly make myself comfortable. Mason changes into a pair of flannel sweat pants and I stare as he does. The muscles in his back flex and stretch with the movement. I marvel at his body and the things he makes me feel with that body.

"I can feel you staring at me," Mason says with his back to me. He turns around and smiles widely at me.

"Sorry, I can't help it. You are so hot."

He laughs and takes a spot next to me on the bed. He wraps his arm around my shoulder and pulls me to his chest.

"Now, let's talk about the future. I was thinking that after me move in together, we could get one of those flying cars."

I laugh at his wit and silly comments. "I was hoping we could get a place near the second moon of Jupiter."

"Lucy, don't be silly. Jupiter doesn't have two moons." We both laugh. He is so easy to be around. "But in all seriousness. What kind of future do you want? Where do you see yourself in five years?"

"I want to still be at Murphy and Glass, working my way toward being the president of accounting. Married, and maybe with some kids."

"How many kids do you want?"

I turn so I can look at him in the face. "Let's play a game. We take turns asking questions and answer together on the count of three."

"OK." He leans forward and gives me a chaste kiss. "How many kids do you want? One, two, three."

At the same time, we reply. "A million," I answer, while he answers with "Four."

We both laugh. "A million?" he asks with a little shock in his voice.

"OK, maybe not a million but as many as I can. I hated being an only child and don't want that for mine. Why four?"

"It's a good even number. More than two, less than six."

"OK, my turn. Where do you want to live with in the future? One, two, three."

"Here," we say at the same time.

"When do you want to get married? One, two, three." He keeps his eyes trained on me while he waits for my answer.

I respond with a quiet, "As soon as you ask me." He answers, "Soon." He smiles widely, matching mine.

We spend the next hour asking random silly questions, learning more and more about each other. We tell stories of good memories and things we want from our lives. We both want to travel and see the world, and to show our children the world. But we both want to stay and live near those we call family.

We fall asleep holding each other tight and I have a clear view of the future I want and who I want it with. For the first time in my life I have no worries for what is to come.

CHAPTER FORTY-ONE
Lucy

The week before Christmas turned into wedding craziness. When I wasn't at work or sleeping I was helping Callie plan her wedding. The wedding went from a small elopement to a quickly planned destination wedding. Callie being Callie is not doing the drive through Vegas chapel. She found a small church in North Las Vegas that was willing to have a wedding on New Year's Day.

Fifty of Callie's family members are flying in from Georgia to be there for the wedding, and a caravan of Craig's family are making the drive down. So my best friend's quickie Vegas wedding is now a full scale southern wedding but that is Callie, she does everything her way.

After my initial weirdness and feelings of jealousy, everything is back to normal and my excitement reaches a new height with each detail that is put into place. My talk with Mason really helped and having him around for support has been great. We, or should I say he, decided we would fly down a couple days before when Callie and Craig go down to help them do whatever it is that they need, and have a mini vacation together. Not our sex-filled vacation quite yet but a vacation together none the less.

Christmas Eve was much like Thanksgiving, with the two of us running from family to family but Christmas day was just him and me. I made us a large breakfast of French toast, bacon, sausage, hash browns and eggs. And just to make it a little more special, fresh squeezed orange juice and peppermint hot chocolate. We were both completely stuffed by the end.

As we sat at the table, Mason placed a large beautifully wrapped box on the table in front of me. "Merry Christmas, Lucy." I smile wide but before I open it, I run to the tree to get Mason's present too.

I practically skip back to the table with excitement as I place the box in front of him. "This one is for you. Merry Christmas, Pac."

He leans over the table and kisses me deeply. "You go first." He urges.

But I shake my head. "No, I'm too excited to see your face when you open it." I'm terrible at keeping secrets and I feel like I might bust if he doesn't open it soon.

"Lucy, what did you do?" He smiles and tears at the paper. He opens the box and his eyes go wide. "Holy crap, Lucy."

Mason pulls out the personalized Seattle Mariners' baseball jersey with his name on the back. Several of the players have signed it on the back over the number.

"How did you get this?" His voice is full of shock.

"I have my ways." I say in a sassy voice.

He picks me up from my chair and settles me on his lap. "Thank you, baby. I love it."

He kisses me long and passionately. I wrap my arms around him and thread my fingers into his hair. He leans back and pulls my present in front of us. "Your turn."

I kiss his cheek and rip at the wrapping. Under the paper is a large Coach box, my heart starts to pound with excitement. "Mason, is this what I think it is?"

"Open the box and find out."

I quickly pull the top off and almost drop the box in my haste. Inside I find a beautiful light blue coach purse with matching wallet and dust cover. The bottom has a wide squared base and moves delicately toward a rounded zippered top. The handles are short and set in the middle of the bag with an optional shoulder strap. It is the most beautiful and expensive thing I have ever owned.

Tears form in my eyes as I look into Mason's handsome face. "This is the most wonderful thing anyone has ever given me. Thank you so much."

"You are so welcome, love. Callie pointed me in the right direction, but as soon as I saw it I knew you needed it. But there is something inside."

I quickly unzip the bag, looking inside for the mentioned item. There is a small black velvet box. I give Mason a questioning glance as I open the box. Inside is a key fob for a BMW.

My eyes quickly move to Mason, searching for context.

"Put on your shoes. I have something you need to see," he prompts. I jump to my feet and run to the bedroom for the first pair of shoes I can find.

We head down stairs to our parking garage. There we find a dark blue BMW 3 series with a large red bow sitting on top. The exact car I had told Mason was a dream of mine to have.

I'm stunned silent for several seconds, trying to wrap my brain around this. He bought me a car?

"Well, what do you think?"

"You got me a car?"

"Yes, baby. Merry Christmas." He pulls me in and kisses me. I hold on tight and kiss him hungrily.

I pull away and stare at his handsome face. "Mason, I love it so, so much but it's too much." I push the key into his hand.

"Not at all, baby."

"This is a BMW."

"You deserve it, Lucy."

"You bought me a car."

"Here come and look." He pulls me to the car and unlocks the door. The first thing I notice is that amazing new car smell.

The seats are a fine, soft leather, I run my hands along the seats, scared that it is all a dream and it will all disappear when I wake up.

I slowly lower myself to the seat, and it fits me perfectly. Mason joins me in the passenger seat and begins to explain all the bells and whistles. I can hardly concentrate on his voice, I can hardly wrap my brain around this.

"Mason, I can't take this. It's too much. The purse was already pushing it."

He covers my hands and brings them to his lips. "No, it's not baby. You needed a new car and I wanted you to have your dream car."

"But Mason, this is a BMW. I had a Jetta."

"Would it make you feel better if your insurance money went toward the car?"

"Yes, but a BMW is like three times the cost of my Jetta." I leave the car and start to pace in the parking garage. "Mason this is too much."

He pulls me to him and stares into my eyes. "Lucy, stop. You needed a car and I got you one."

"But you didn't even check with me first. And you said it was best to wait until after the New Year."

"Yes because I wanted to be the one to get it for you. Lucy, stop. You deserve this, and I want you to have it. Please take it."

I take a breath, looking into his icy blue eyes. "You made this decision without me and I just feel a little railroaded." I head toward the elevator and away from the car and Mason.

"I'm sorry, baby. But you had a need and I took care of it."

"And I love you for that, but I need to run my own life." We walk from the elevator and back into my apartment.

"Your life is my life, Lucy. As soon as we made this commitment to be together your life became my life." He pulls me around, facing him. "You are my everything, baby. I love you. And I will do everything to make you happy, safe and get you what you need."

Tears form in my eyes as his words sink in. He frames my face and wipes the tears from my cheeks with his thumbs. "Baby, please take the car. If it makes you feel better, you can pay me back in sexual favors."

I chuckle a watery laugh and bury myself in Mason's chest, finding my favorite spot. He holds me tight and I feel all the love we have for each other. "You are my everything too," I confess, still pulled close to his chest.

He kisses me long and slow, removing all my uncertainty. We stand in each other's arms, soaking up each other's kisses.

"Wait, did we lock the car?" I run back down the hall to my new baby, followed by Mason's laugh. I think I might be camping out in my new car tonight.

Today we arrived in Las Vegas with Callie and Craig. She and I are both bouncing with excitement. We have everything arranged and the families aren't joining us till tomorrow, so tonight the four of us are going to enjoy a night out.

My life with Mason is starting to become more and more like a fairy tale with each passing day. Last night before I had started packing, he surprised me with a new luggage set. Blue of course, and very expensive. He has been showering me with gifts since Christmas. I try not to encourage him, but he says he loves seeing my face light up when I open his gifts. And how can I deny him that.

I experienced another first with Mason today; we flew first class. He insisted on us needing to fly first class and upgraded Callie and Craig's too, saying it was a part of his wedding present to them. Such a sweet boyfriend. He is always thinking of other people's comfort.

We are all staying in deluxe rooms in the Palazzo hotel and it is unlike any place I have ever stayed before. Mason laughed out loud at me as I ooh and awed through the lobby. Growing up a few hours from here, one would think I would have come here but just like with most things from my childhood, we never did it the normal way. Vegas is still this magical and mysterious place, covered in twinkling lights.

Our room is made up of a sitting room area with powder room and kitchenette. The bedroom is off to the side behind a set of double doors. There is a lavish en-suite bathroom, with a shower that could fit a football team, and a large jetted tub, which I plan to spend time in with Mason tonight.

The weather in Las Vegas is just beautiful, the sun is shining and there is a light breeze keeping the heat of the sun from becoming too much, a total 180° from the snow and freezing weather of northern Idaho. Callie and I convince the boys we need to spend the afternoon by the pool, since we won't get a chance for some sun for another six months in Idaho. They leave us to our sun and go to finish a few details for the wedding. Mason gives me a long and deep kiss that leaves my legs Jello.

"I can't believe you are getting married tomorrow," I muse as we soak up the rays on our comfortable pool chairs.

"I know, it is like a dream. Thank you for being here, Lucy. It means the world to me." She reaches over and squeezes my hand.

"You know there is no place else I would be on your wedding day."

She gives me a wide, happy smile. "Should we order some drinks? I think this pool party needs some rum."

I let out my best sorority girl wooh!, and call over the waitress for two very large, very fruity drinks.

Two hours and five drinks later, Callie and I are reddened from the sun and way closer to drunk than tipsy. We left tipsy long ago when Callie and I started our dance party with the music from her cell phone. It wasn't loud enough for anyone but us to hear so we looked totally crazy but we didn't care even a little bit. We never do. She is so carefree and when I'm with her I'm the same.

We stumble back to our rooms, laughing uncontrollably. It takes several tries for me to unlock my door, but thankfully Mason pulls the door open before I fully give up and fall to the floor laughing. Mason smiles down at me and pulls me up and into his arms. I yell my goodbye to Callie, whose room is right next door so there is no need to yell, but like I said, we were drunk.

Mason carries me inside and sets me down on the bed. "Did you have a good time, baby?" He asks as he helps me from my swimsuit cover-up.

"I did. Callie and I had an awesome drink called 'Sex on the Beach.' It was delicious."

He chuckles and kisses my nose. "You are yelling, Lucy."

"Oops, sorry. I might be a little drunk." I bring my right hand up in front of my face, showing him with my fingers the little bit I am drunk.

He throws his head back and laughs loudly at me. "Yeah I think you might be. Lets get you in the shower so we can nap for a little while before we meet Callie and Craig for dinner."

Mason pulls me from the bed and I follow along behind him to the bathroom. I chatter away about my time at the pool while Mason turns on the water for the shower and strips himself of his clothes.

My nipples pebble as I stare at the handsome naked man standing before me. Just being in his presence makes my blood heat and moisture gather on my pussy. His penis hardens at my gawking and I reach for him. It's been weeks since we have had sex or even just fooled around, and it is driving me crazy. I long to have him inside me.

He stalks toward me but stops my hands from touching his silky hard length, placing my hands on his strong shoulders. "Let's get you out of this swimsuit." I reach for the straps that are holding my bikini top to my breasts, quickly untying them and letting it fall to the bathroom floor. "Looks like you got a little sun today. Did you put sunscreen on?"

Words have escaped me from having him near to me. I nod my head and continue to stare at his structured chest and six pack abs. I pull him close and lean in for a kiss.

"Oh no, baby. No hanky-panky in the shower."

I reach between us and wrap my hand around his cock. "This guy doesn't seem to agree with that."

He growls and takes my lips in a hungry kiss, pulling me close and trapping my arms between us. I stroke him from root to tip, jacking him off as he frames my face and kisses me deeply, stealing my breath.

Mason's hands leave my face and reach under my arms moving them way from their mission to get him off and to his shoulders. I wrap them around his shoulder and bury my fingers in his hair. His hands move to my bikini-covered ass and pull the strings causing the fabric to fall to the floor with my top.

Once I'm free from the swimsuit, he lifts my legs and wraps them around his waist. His cock is resting against my pussy and I roll my hips, loving the feel of him. I need him now.

He walks us into the shower and under the hot spray. Mason leans me up against the shower wall. I pull my lips from his kiss and moan, "Mason, please get inside me."

He shakes his head. "Not yet. I need to clean you up a little before I get you dirty again."

I groan and lean my head against the wall, enjoying the feel of his lips on the skin of my neck.

He keeps me pressed to the wall with his pelvis and reaches for our body wash, lathering the soap in his hands and running it down my sides and over my stomach, up to my breasts. He rolls my nipples between his fingers making moisture surge to my pussy and making my eyes roll back in my head.

"Fuck, Mason. I need you now."

"And I need you to be ready for me, baby. You are still healing, and I can't take the chance on hurting you."

I shake my head, hoping to convince him. "No you could never hurt me."

"Of course not intentionally. Let me get you ready for me."

He moves my legs from his hips, setting one on the ground and the other on the built in bench seat. He reaches for the showerhead and washes the soap from my body. Once I am free of soap he returns the showerhead to the wall and turns his attention to me.

He gives me a hot and sexy smile, making my heart skip a beat. He steps between my spread thighs and runs his hands from my kneecaps toward their apex. The finger of his left hand finds my center and my breath catches.

"You are so wet." His voice is thick with lust.

"You turn me on, Pac. Please," I beg.

His large thumb circles around my clit and he inserts a long finger inside of me. His right hand finds my breast, squeezing and teasing the nipple. Mason works his finger in and out of me, setting a fast rhythm that soon has me seeing stars and crying out Mason's name with an intense orgasm.

My knees buckle from the pleasure but Mason is there to keep me from falling. He carries me from the shower, wraps me in a large fluffy towel and sets me on the edge of the tub. He returns to the shower to turn off the water.

I stand on my own and work the towel quickly over my body, needing to move on to the next phase of being with Mason. I drop the towel and when he turns to me, I am on my knees in front of him, eye level with his hard and impressive cock.

"Lucy, you don't have to." He places his hands on my shoulder, not encouraging but not pushing away either.

I look up at him and give him a sassy smile. I take him in my hand and lick from root to tip. "Oh yes I do." I get back to work, licking at him like the best ice cream cone I have ever eaten. His taste is heady and masculine, and so fucking sexy. The things this man can do with his cock, he deserves to come while I suck him off.

I take as much of him as I can into my mouth and hollow out my cheeks as I suck hard. He groans and throws his head back in pleasure. I look up and see his eyes are closed tight, and from the way his cock twitches in my hand and the big sack is pulled up tight, I can tell he is getting close to coming.

He reaches down and removes himself from my mouth before lifting me into his arms. "Hey! I wasn't done. I wanted to taste you come."

"Oh no, baby. We have talked about this before, I come in your pussy and nowhere else."

He lifts me on the edge of the bed but doesn't lie atop of me. I reach to pull him down but he stops me. "It will be more comfortable for you this way. Less pressure on your rubs."

I have almost forgotten about my bruised ribs. "Fuck that. I need you near me."

Mason retrieves a condom and is inside me in one quick thrust. "This isn't close enough for you?" He sets a fast rhythm but doesn't go too hard.

I wrap my legs around his hips and circle mine, bringing more friction to the area I need it so badly. Mason knows what I crave and reaches down to circle and tease my clit.

It doesn't take long before I am coming hard again. Only a few more thrusts and Mason follows behind me, this time shouting my name as he falls over the edge.

He rolls us to our sides and pulls me close, burying his face in my neck. "I love you, Lucy. So much."

"I love you, too," I respond as drunkenness and two orgasms pull me toward sleep. I snuggle in close and smile with the contentment and love that fills my heart and soul.

CHAPTER FORTY-TWO
MASON

I lie awake as Lucy sleeps after our love making. She looks so adorable in her post sex sleep. Most of the time after I make her come, she falls almost instantly into sleep. I have found the only way to keep her awake is to give her another orgasm, and then the sleep comes on again. It's a vicious cycle but I will continue to give her as many orgasms as I can. I love having her in my arms, with her soft skin pressed up against me. In sleep, she always holds me close and wraps as much of herself around me as she can.

She has been sleeping for about three hours while I held her close. I should be waking her up soon to get ready for dinner. We are meeting Craig and Callie in a bit and I know she will want time to get dressed up.

I lean down and run my lips across her forehead, slowly waking her up. "Lucy, my love."

She stirs but like always, snuggles in closer and tries to stay asleep. "Come on, baby. We need to get up and get ready for dinner with Craig and Callie."

She rolls a little and reaches down in between us, taking my semi-hard penis in her hand and I instantly harden at her touch. She opens her eyes and I can see the lust in her eyes. Looks like she is making up for our lost time. I roll and take her with me, settling her atop me with her pussy resting above my dick.

I help her take me inside her and let me set the rhythm. I watch her move on top of me getting herself off while riding me hard. I sit up and take her lips in a hot and hungry kiss, holding her close while she moves her hips atop me. We move together and within minutes come together, both crying out our pleasure.

I fall back to the bed and she collapses on to my chest. We lie together as we come down and our breathing slows. I run my fingers through her soft hair and down her back. Her breathing slows and evens out. I can tell she has fallen back asleep.

I guess she is sleeping for a little while longer. I wrap my hands around her and close my eyes, joining her in sleep.

We end up being a little late for dinner with Craig and Callie. A call to Lucy's phone awakens us and spurs us into action. We shower together to save time but that too adds to our lateness. It must be something with the oxygen they pump into place, as to why I can't keep my hands off of Lucy.

Fuck, that's not true. I can hardly keep my hands off her in Idaho either. I'm constantly on the razor's edge while she is around.

We leave the strip for dinner and head to an Italian restaurant a few minutes away. It's delicious and the wine and conversation flow easily. We spend most of the time not talking about the up-coming wedding the day after tomorrow, but instead laughing and joking, there is no stress for the fiancés.

After dinner, we decide to head back to the hotel for an early evening. All of Callie's family arrives tomorrow and it will be a long day for the girls.

I take Lucy to bed, making love to her again, slowly and passionately. Bringing her slowly to the edge and falling over along with her.

CHAPTER FORTY-THREE
Lucy

The day of New Year's Eve is a complete whirlwind. As soon as I wake up, Callie is calling my phone asking questions and working out details for the wedding. Her family arrives from Georgia late this afternoon, so we spent the morning in an Uber with our driver Josiah running from place-to-place gathering last-minute things we need. It's amazing how many tiny little things come up at the last minute. Flowers, napkins, centerpieces, candles and something called a branch spray, whatever that is.

We are lucky enough that the church has a staff who helps decorate for events and they were willing to help out a ton with the decorating for us. But Ms. Perfect, Callie, still wanted to make sure everything is done to her exact instructions, so we spend almost two hours at the church, walking the staff through all the things she is hoping for. She is far from a bridezilla, but I have had to remind her to breathe a couple of times when things weren't turning out exactly how she expected.

Craig is in charge of the rehearsal dinner tonight. A few weeks ago I convinced Callie to stay out of it and let him run the show. It was a struggle and she kept asking for hints but Craig was a good sport and didn't let her intimidate him. He, of course, kept everything from me too. He knows I would spill my guts. Mason is helping and I think he has some surprises in store, but like Craig he is tight lipped, letting nothing slip. Even sexual favors didn't work.

Craig did tell us that it would be black tie and will include a celebration at midnight of New Year's. Other than that it is a mystery. Craig has told the rest of the guests the location but kept us in the dark. Callie is hating it but she does love surprises so she is secretly loving it.

I splurged and found an expensive dress online. It has a high neckline that covers me up to my collar bone, a plunging back and a full bell skirt that ends a little above my knees. The color is of course a deep dark blue, but the material is iridescent, giving the illusion it is changing from the deep blue to purple as I move. I feel fantastic in it and can't wait to stand next to Mason in it.

He is already dressed and is watching TV in the sitting room, waiting while I finish getting ready. I slip my feet into a pair of peep-toe red heels, that the ladies in my favorite books would call "Come Fuck Me" heels and take one last look at myself. I look pretty good, if I do say so myself.

I curled my hair in beachy waves and have a section pinned beneath my right ear, showing off the pearl ear rings Callie and Craig gave me for Christmas. The rest of my hair is resting over my left shoulder, showing off my neck. My make-up is smoky and sparkly, making my eyes appear mysterious and sexy. I feel confident and I am ready to show my man.

I open the door and see Mason standing with his back to me. He turns when he hears the door and my breath is sucked from my body. I see him almost every day in a suit at work but this one fits him like a glove. It is a dark navy suit with thin gray pin stripes. He is wearing a matching three-button vest, crisp white dress shirt and satiny silver tie.

He gives me a brilliant smile and slowly walks toward. I am rooted in my spot as he stalks closer.

When he is less than a foot away he leans down and softly kisses my lips. "You look so stunning tonight, Lucy."

I beam at him from the praise. "Thank you. You look very handsome yourself."

"I'm not sure I want to share you with anyone else."

I give him a small chuckle. He reaches from my left hand and kisses my knuckle. "I think you might be missing something."

"I am?" I ask, mesmerized by his handsome face.

"Yes, turn around please."

I take a step back and spin, I hear his breath catch as he sees the back of the dress. He mumbles a damn and my insides turn to jelly. I look back over my shoulder and see him remove a jewelry box from his coat pocket.

He brings his hand in front of me, showing me a beautiful pearl necklace lying between his strong fingers. This time it is my turn to lose my breath. Mason fastens the necklace and turns me to face him. Words escape me and I am grinning like a fool.

"There! Now you are perfect." He kisses my forehead and leads me to the door.

It takes me all the way to the elevator before I am able to speak again. "Mason, these are so beautiful. Thank you so much." I run my fingers along the strand, loving the feel of the smooth surface below my fingers.

"You are very welcome, baby. They were my grandma's," he says nonchalantly.

My eyes fly to his. "What?"

"They belonged to my dad's mom. After seeing the ear rings you got for Christmas, I asked for them for you."

My jaw drops to the floor and I feel like a light breeze could push me over. "You gave me your grandmother's pearls?" I ask again in a stunned voice.

He pulls me close to him and kisses the top of my head. "Yes, baby. And they look absolutely perfect on you."

The elevator arrives at the ground floor and I still have no words to tell him what his gift means to me. I have nothing like this from my own family. Love is bursting from my chest at this amazing gesture. As we walk, I am beaming with pride. I'm standing next to the love of my life and I am wearing his beautiful gift.

We are walking through the casino, I ask Mason where we are going, hoping he will finally spill some details.

"It's not very far."

The casino floor is crowded with visitors in town for the holiday. Mason stays close to my side and we move our way through toward the lobby area. As we grow near the lobby two faces in the distance catch my eye.

I stop on a dime.

CHAPTER FORTY-FOUR
Lucy

"Mason, why are my parents here?" I stare in horror at the two faces coming closer. They are both smiling from ear to ear and my mother is waving wildly at us. They are dressed nicer than anything I have ever seen them wear before, my father is even in a suit.

He wraps his arms around me, kissing my cheek. "I called them, baby. I wanted to meet them and spend some time together." His voice is confident and full of pride.

My breathing is starting to speed up and my emotions are choking me. I shake my head, hoping they will disappear, wishing this was all a bad dream. "No, I don't want them here."

"Lucy, this is a good thing. They were excited to see you." He squeezes me reassuringly, but I have to get away.

"Mason, no! I told you I don't want anything to do with them." I turn to leave his arms, turning my back to my parents. I move away from him and frantically search for an exit. Any exit will do, I have to get away from them. My mind is spinning as I search for a way out and my vision starts to blur. I can hear Mason's voice behind me.

I can't believe he did this. All the pain and neglect from my childhood comes flowing back in that first second of seeing them. My heart is pounding so hard and I can feel the pressure in my chest trying to suffocate me.

He stops me and pulls me around. "Lucy, where are you going? What's wrong?"

Tears are streaming down my face unchecked. "How could you? I don't want to see them." I say in a voice I almost don't recognize. It is shrill and comes out a lot louder then it should. I can see people around us have stopped and are staring at me, but I don't care about the scene I am making.

"But Lucy, it is important…"

He can't finish his sentence. I interrupt and am full on yelling now. "No Mason, I told you this. You never listen to me. I can't do this anymore."

I break from his hold and stomp away finding an elevator to take me back to our room.

"Lucy, no. I get you are pissed but you need to go talk to them." He continues to follow along after me. His voice is calm, but that makes me even madder.

"No, Mason." I pin him with a hard glare. "I said no. I don't want anything to do with them and right now I don't want anything to do with you either."

"That's not how this works, baby." His eyes flash with anger and his voice is rising to meet mine.

"Right now, it is. Leave me alone Mason." I step into the elevator as it arrives and watches as the door closes leaving him on the other side.

But Mason's hand reaches out stopping the door. He steps inside and moves into my space, leaving only inches between us. "You need to talk to me. You don't get to just walk away." His words are clipped.

My emotions take over and I sob. "No Mason I don't. I tell you no, you should respect that." I take a shuddering breath and square my shoulders, stepping back putting space in between us. "I can't do this, Mason. I can't be with someone who won't listen to me."

His head snaps back as if I had slapped him. I close my eyes, trying to block out the hurt I see in his eyes. I hear the ding of the car arriving, and move out of it without meeting Mason eyes again. He doesn't follow me.

My heart is crushed. I can't believe he would just ignore me and invite my parents here. He knows what they did to me and how they ruined my childhood. I grew up neglected and made to feel like a second-class citizen. They showed me every day that they didn't love me as much as they loved each other.

My phone rings in my clutch but I ignore it. My heart is broken and I feel so betrayed. I don't want to be with a man who won't listen to me, who thinks he knows better. I need to be my own woman and to be able to make my own decisions.

I am weeping uncontrollably when I arrive at our room, sucking in breaths of air making my lungs burn. I throw myself onto the bed, wishing I could forget the last 20 minutes.

I spend the rest of the night in the room alone, I can't bring myself to leave and join Callie's rehearsal dinner. At midnight I can hear the celebration with the start of the New Year, but I stay huddled under the covers.

I heard Mason come in a little after I did but doesn't enter the bedroom area where I have locked myself. I'm not sure how I would handle seeing him.

The next morning, I wake up slowly, feeling the effects of a long night of crying. I leave the bed, heading to the bathroom. My eyes are red and puffy, and my skin looks paler than normal, almost sickly. I'll need a lot of help before Callie's wedding.

After leaving the bathroom, I finally check my phone to find several texts and missed calls from Callie. Her last texted instructs me to meet her down stairs in the spa at 9 a.m. I check the clock and jump in the shower, having just enough time for a quick one before I need to meet her.

Twenty minutes later I am ready to leave the room for the spa. I stand at the door and take a deep breath, finding the courage to face Mason. I slowly crack open the door and peek out. Mason is sitting on the couch, still wearing his suit from yesterday. His heads lifts and his eyes find mine when he hears the door open.

Emotions choke me as soon as I look at him. He turns up a half smile and I remove my gaze from his and quickly moving to the door before any words are spoken.

Callie is standing at the spa entrance holding iced coffees when I arrive. As soon as I see her, the flood gates open and the tears begin to flow again.

"Sugar, don't cry. It's my wedding day." She pulls me in for a hug and holds me while I cry. I try to explain to her what happened last night but my words are covered my sobs. We move over to a bench across from entrance, where she lets me cry through my story.

"Oh Lucy, I'm sorry." She says in a sweet voice, and rubs circles on my back. She doesn't offer any advice, just listens.

"No, I'm sorry. I missed your rehearsal dinner and now I am making your day about me." My tears start a new and I think of what I missed last night.

"You are a big part of my day so some of it can be a little about you. Take a deep breath." I follow her instructions, working on calming myself down. "There now dry your eyes, sugar. Let's go get pampered. It will make you feel better, I promise."

I nod, smile and we head for the spa.

The next few hours are filled with facials, pedicures, manicures, hair and makeup. Every girls' dream day. Several of Callie's cousins, her mom and Craig's aunt join us and bring the excitement back. Food is brought in at noon but I can't bring myself to touch any of it, my stomach is still in knots.

As they are putting the finishing touches on my hair, my phone buzzes with an incoming text.

Mason: *Hi, do you girls need anything?*

My eyes start to fill with tears but I hold them back, not wanting to have mascara running down my face. I meet Callie's eyes and she gives me a reassuring smile.

Me: *No, we are OK for right now.*
His response comes back quickly.
Mason: *OK, Lucy. I'm here when you need me.*
When you need me. Not if, but when.

I run back to the room to grab my dress and shoes before we head to the church and find the room empty. Housekeeping has come by to clean the room and I see Mason's suitcase sitting near the door, packed. My heart again aches at the sight. I move quickly through the room, gathering what I need, trying to spend as little time in here as I can.

Our relationship is over, and I hate that.

CHAPTER FORTY-FIVE
MASON

Lucy makes a beautiful bridesmaid. The dark purple dress looks stunning on her pale delicate skin. They say a bride is the center of attention of a wedding but I can't keep my eyes off of Lucy. She is so beautiful.

She wouldn't meet my eyes as she walked down the aisle, still clearly upset with me for the events of last night. I thought I was doing what was best for her, but she did not agree with me. She was hurt and needs space right now. She needs to understand that sometimes I am right and will do what I need to do.

I'm staying through the wedding but changed my ticket to head home tonight. If she wants space, I will give her space. But now seeing her smiling happily at her best friend, my plans seems to have some flaws. I want to run to the front of the small church, pull her into my arms and kiss the hurt away.

The wedding is quick but still heartfelt. You can tell Callie and Craig really love each other. He pulls her in for a long hungry kiss after the pastor names them husband and wife, to cheers and shout from the crowd. Lucy and I will be doing this soon.

The reception is taking place in the gym of the church, so we don't have far to travel. I wait by the door for Lucy, while the rest of the guests mingle and settle at their assigned seats. I grab a beer and camp out just inside the door and wait.

She enters with the rest of the wedding party about a half an hour later and I pull her to back into the entryway.

"You look so beautiful, Lucy."

She blushes but won't meet my gaze. "Thank you."

We stand in silence for a long moment, so I break the tension with, "I'm gonna head back to Idaho tonight."

Her eyes widen and fly to mine, but OK is all she says.

Anger surges through me. "That's all you have to say?"

"I'm not sure what you want me to say, Mason." She is starting to tremble, and emotions are heavy in her eyes.

"Maybe tell me not to leave."

She shakes her head and moves away from me. "Mason, I don't know what you want from me. We broke up."

"What?!?" I almost yell. "No we didn't. You said you needed some space. I'm giving you that space."

She turns on me, hurt flashing in her eyes. "Yes, we did Mason. I said I can't do this anymore Mason and I meant it. You are trying to run my life and I don't want that."

"Damn it, Lucy. I'm not trying to run your life. I'm trying to help you. I'm trying to make a life with you."

"You aren't helping me Mason. You are making decisions and dictating to me how things will be. I don't need or want you to run my life."

"I'm not running your life. For fuck sake, Lucy. I want what is best for you." I pace away from her and run my fingers through my hair in frustration.

"Don't cuss at me, Mason. I told you how I feel and you can't tell me that my feelings are wrong."

"But they are, Lucy. I fucking love you. Why would I do anything that wouldn't be in your best interest? You need to forgive your parents. You will want them in our lives when we have kids." Why the fuck isn't she getting this?

"It's not as easy as being in the same room for five minutes and then saying I forgive you. This is twenty seven years of hurt."

I've had about enough of her childish behavior. "Oh, grow up Lucy. Your parents didn't beat you, they didn't lock you in a closet. Let it go and let's move on."

"Fuck off, Mason." She spits the words at me and turns away toward the reception.

I move quickly, grabbing her arm and spinning her back to face me. "Stop! We are not done."

"Let go of me, Mason." Her words are clipped and laced with distain.

"We are not done talking." I'm less than an inch from her face and I can smell her sweet perfume. I'm torn between shaking her and kissing the fuck out of her.

"Is everything OK here, Lucy?" Caleb walks up behind her, breaking the tension between us. He sends me a hard glare.

I remove my hand from her arm and notice I have left red fingerprints behind. Damn it. I didn't mean to leave a mark. "It's fine, Caleb. Take Lucy inside. I'm leaving."

Caleb nods to me, placing his hand on the small of her back and leads Lucy into the party and away from me. Seeing the marks I left on her takes most of the wind from my sails. I fucking over reacted again and this time I don't think she is going to forgive me easily.

I will her to look back at me as she walks away with Caleb. I need to see just a little bit of love in her eyes that tells me I haven't completely fucked this all up.

"Look back at me. Look back at me, baby. Please turn around," I mumble to myself.

But she doesn't.

My future just walks away from me and it is my fault. Fuck!

This has been a shit couple of days. I'm sitting on my couch hating my fucking life. I miss Lucy like crazy and I hate that I left her in Las Vegas. I heard her come home a couple days later and it took everything in me not to run across the hall and pull her into my arms.

My phone rings as I open another beer.

"Hey Checks. What's up?"

"Hey Mas. Got some bad news. Jeff died last night."

"Fuck, man. I'm so sorry. What can I do?"

"Nothing man. The funeral will be in a couple of days."

"I will be there for sure."

"Thanks man. Actually, I will need some help with the shop. We had always talked about me buying the shop, but we never did anything with it. Can you help me?"

"Of course. We will talk later this week. And if you need anything, please let me know."

"Thanks, man."

I hang up and stare at my down at my phone. In an instant Check's life just completely changed. Jeff was like a father to him, and now he is gone. Life fucking changes in a blink of an eye. Check's just lost someone who meant the world to him.

My mind goes to Lucy. Fuck, someone has to tell her. They were one of her clients. She is going to take this so hard. She cares a lot about all of her clients and this will devastate her.

But she isn't ready to see me yet. I decide to have my dad tell her. It is a total cop out and I'm a fucking pussy for it. I just can't ruin this with her, I need to give her the space she asked for and let her come back down to me.

CHAPTER FORTY-SIX
Lucy

It's been six weeks since Mason and I broke up in Las Vegas, almost the same amount of time we were together. It's been completely awful.

The first week back was the worst. When I arrived home from Vegas, I expected Mason to be at my door with flowers and a lavish over the top apology, but there was nothing.

In my heart of hearts, I did want the big romantic gesture. The falling to his knees and begging me to forgive him, the 10,000 yellow daisies lining the streets of Stars Hallow, the quitting his job and leaving everything behind just so he can be with me, the forsaking the life he has always known and changing to be the man I need him to be. The way guys do it in romance novels and fairy tales. But real life isn't a fairy tale or a romance novel. I wasn't ready for us to be over, but I was justified in my actions or at least that's what I keep telling myself.

We have hardly seen each other in the past few weeks. He has kept his distance at work, being professional in all our interactions and going out of his way to ensure we aren't alone together. Mason's dad has also kept his distance and even Luke assured me that if I needed any time away from the office I was welcome to do whatever I needed.

Even when Jeff Miller passed away, Luke was the one that told me. I thought it would have been Mason, I hoped news like that would have come from him. He and Rob are such good friends, I would have thought he would want to be the one to tell me. But I guess I can understand why he didn't.

The funeral was not what I was expecting. The church service was sober and quick, but the reception was a wild party that I didn't see coming. Those diesel boys know how to party. But I didn't stay long. I wasn't able to stay there knowing Mason was there too. He had given me a small smile and curt nod when he saw me, and that small interaction was almost too much. I fled as soon as I said my goodbyes. I added it to the list of hard days I went through since Las Vegas.

Tonight is the first time I have been to bowling or even left my apartment for something other than work or runs to the store for more cookie dough icecream. It's three weeks until my birthday and two days since Valentine's Day, or I just broke up with the man I thought I would marry but let's pretend everything is fine, day. Not really a fine moment in my life.

"Have you seen Mason this week?" Callie asks, sitting beside me waiting for our turn to bowl.

"Yes, I saw him at a meeting on Tuesday." I admit in a small voice.

"Did you talk to him?"

"No, we still haven't spoken."

"Lucy, can I say something?" She waits for my approval and then continues. "Is spending an hour with your parents really worth losing the love of your life?"

Her question is one I have asked myself over and over.

I look down to the bowling alley floor, shaking my head in frustration. "Callie, I think that at least a million times a day. But …" The tears start to form in the corners of my eyes, I have cried more tears in the last month and a half then I have in my whole life. "But Callie what if I see them and nothing changes. What if all that pain comes back and Mason doesn't. What do I do then?"

Callie smiles softly at me and pulls me in close to her side, kissing my forehead. "Sugar, don't you think he is worth taking that chance for?"

I nod. Of course he is. He has my heart.

When I get home, I muster up my courage and dial my parent's number. It's late on Friday but knowing the schedule at the commune, they would just have gotten home from the "family" dinner.

My mom's voice answers after a couple rings. "Hello?"

"Mom, it's Lucy."

She pauses, before going on, "Hi Flower Bud. Let me get your father." She pulls the phone from her ear and I can hear her yell for my father to pick up the second phone.

"Hi Lucy," my dad says happily.

"Hi Dad. How are you guys?"

"We are good. We were hoping to spend some time with you while you were in Las Vegas. Mason said you weren't feeling well. He seems like a wonderful boyfriend," my mom comments.

"He is very nice but we actually aren't together anymore."

"Oh, I'm so sorry to hear that. What happened?"

"It actually had something to do with him inviting you to Las Vegas. He didn't tell me and I got upset."

"That makes sense. You haven't been very open to allowing us into your life since you left for college."

"No and we miss you Lucy." My dad chimes in.

I start to tear up thinking back on leaving for college. "Yeah, I'm sorry but I'm not sure I believe that Dad."

"Now why do you say that?" He sounds as if he is a little offended.

"Well, let me ask you a question? What is your favorite memory of me as a child?"

"Oh I know," my mom starts. "When we went to the Monterey Aquarium. That was a wonderful day."

Perfect example. "You mean the trip where I was left at the hotel while you and dad went sightseeing. You told me you would be right back but you were gone the whole day."

There is silence on the other end, so I press on with another example. "Or maybe you remember fondly the time we went to Sedona and you left me with that family I didn't know. You were supposed to be gone two days but didn't come back for more than a week." I am beginning to pace, my emotions building.

"Lucy, we did our best." My dad's voice is small.

"I'm sorry Dad, but the fact that you think that makes the pain so much worse for me. I was an afterthought," I reply immediately.

I can hear my mom is crying which brings the tears to my eyes too.

"I always thought you were just an independent child," Mom confirms.

"I had to learn to be independent, since I was always alone. I never wanted to be alone. Do you guys know that you never took me to school? Never picked me up either.

I wanted more than anything to be a part of your two-some. But I was always kept on the outside."

There is silence again and I wait, hoping they will have some magic words that will fix this all. Fix our relationship and fix my relationship with Mason.

"Lucy, my darling. Your mother and I love you very much. If we ever made you feel like you were not loved or not good enough, we are so sorry." My dad's voice is sincere.

"Is this why you have pushed us away?" she asks.

"Yes, I pushed you into the past and I went in search of a family I could make myself. You took away the opportunity I had to have a real family. I get that you wanted nothing to do with your parents, but I desired to know my grandparents. I desired the chance to make that choice for myself."

"We thought we were doing what was best for you. Our parents were toxic to the life we wanted to bring you into. We thought having them out of it, you would have a better chance." My mom explains, her voice is thick with emotion.

I can't speak for minute or two. I want to scream, I want to yell, I want to tell them how much I hate them, but none of that will fix anything. I have spent too much time letting my anger toward them hold me back. And it ruined the one relationship that should have been forever.

"Lucy, we love you. We want to be a part of your life, will you let us?"

As soon as I hear the question, I know the answer in my heart. "Yes, I would like that. But I think we should go slowly. Learn how to communicate with each other."

"That sounds perfect, we would love that. Call us next week and you can tell us all about Idaho."

We say our goodbyes and I hang up the phone. As soon as I put down the phone, I want to run across the hall and tell Mason all about it. I throw my arms around him and apologize for everything I said and did and for our lost time. I beg him to forgive me and perform as many sexual favors as I need to.

I step out of the door and as I do, there is movement from Mason's doorway, drawing my eye. The door opens and a tall blonde woman wearing thigh high stiletto and a short skirt walks out, closing the door behind her. She smiles at me as she walks by, she is stunning.

Who the fuck is that?

Should I follow her? I decide that's a little too weird and let her walk down the hall.

I still want to talk to Mason, so I square my shoulders and knock. I'm surprised to find Rob is the one who opens the door.

"Hey, Lucy." Rob greets me and opens the door wide and invites me in.

"Hey, is Mason here?" I look around his place, and I'm surprised to find the state it is in. He is not a messy person but his place is trashed. There are bowls, plates and cups everywhere. A large stack of pizza boxes are building toward the ceiling on his kitchen table.

"He is sleeping. He was super drunk when we got here."

"We?" The woman from earlier?

"Yeah it's a long story," He goes to continue but is interrupted by a loud drunk yell coming from Mason's bedroom. "Sorry, Lucy. I gotta take care of him."

He leaves me standing in Mason's living room. I really want to stay, to go and help. He is not a great drunk and he doesn't take being sick well, but I leave and head back to my place. I need to come up with a plan. I need to get my man back.

My whole plan is worked out by Saturday night, but I woke up with a terrible head cold the next morning. I spent my whole Sunday sleeping or sneezing, but I had a big meeting with a potential new client this morning, so I am putting on a brave face and head in to work.

"Good Morning, Lucy." Candice greets me as I arrive. "Oh, no. Are you feeling OK?" She comes around the desk and pulls me in for a hug. Her attitude toward me has completely changed since our confrontation back in December. It turns out that Clay told her all sorts of lies about me. Once she saw for herself that I was nothing like that, we have a whole new relationship.

"No," I say. "I have a cold."

"Would you like me to reschedule your meeting this morning?" She offers.

"No, that's alright. I'll be OK." I give her the best smile I can muster and head down to my office.

The potential clients coming in today are from the largest manufacturer of hand-made wooden cabinets in North America. They will be a huge account for our company. They were given my name by another of my clients and told I was the one they needed to meet. Luke was practically salivating when I told him they had approached me. He and Mason will be in the meeting to ensure it all goes smoothly.

The morning goes by painfully slow before the start of the meeting. I go through almost a whole box of tissues. I've basically become a walking snot factory. My throat is raw and drinking anything is agonizing. My chest burns each time I cough, and I go from freezing cold to a thousand degrees in a second.

After one of my major coughing fits, Candice informs me that they have arrived. I gather my things, steal my emotions for being in the same room as Mason and head toward the conference room.

Several men in suits are standing with Mason and Luke just inside the door. Luke turns to me and announces my entrance, proclaiming me as the woman of the hour. Introductions are made; they have brought their owner, vice president and head of manufacturing.

"Hello, everyone." I work to sound like I'm not about to die. I meet everyone's gaze and smile at them. But Mason's face looks concerned when I get to his, I promise I tried to avoid him, I really did.

"Shall we sit down?" Luke invites, but Mason interrupts.

"Do you mind if I steal Lucy for just a second?"

Both dread and excitement settle in my chest. I shake my head, but he guides me out of the room with his hand on the small of my back. I feel electricity at that simple touch.

He leans down, bringing his face near to mine and stares into my eyes with concern. "Are you OK?" He asks, his voice soft.

"Yes, it's just a little cold. I will be fine for the meeting." I'm not convincing, especially when I launch into a coughing fit before I can finish my sentence, which leaves my throat raw and chest aching.

"No, I think we will have to do this one without you."

"No, we can't. They're here to meet me. I can't screw that up. They're a huge, potential client for this company."

He takes a deep breath and squares his shoulders answering me with a simple, "OK."

He leads me back into the room and I take my spot at the head of the table. Mason places a cup of water in front of me before taking his own seat. I'm so grateful and take large drink, but cringe at the pain of it going down my sore throat.

I take a steadying breath and begin my presentation.

CHAPTER FORTY-SEVEN
MASON

Watching Lucy stand at the front of the room, giving this presentation makes me miss her all the more. She is kicking ass, but I can tell she feels like crap.

I have stayed away from her since we broke up and I have hated every minute of it. I do my best to leave her alone, but I have found myself watching her when she isn't looking. Even to go as far as running to the door to look out the peephole when I hear movement at her door. It's pathetic, I know. But I can't help myself. I miss that woman so fucking much.

She finishes her presentation and opens the floor to any questions. She knocked it out of the park.

"Thank you so much Lucy. You did a very wonderful job. And I'm sorry to say, you look miserable." The room chuckles. "Which is even more impressive. For us this is more of a chance to meet you. From the reputation this company has and the rave reviews we have heard about you, we were sold before we even walked in the door."

The owner stands and reaches out to shake Lucy's hand. She smiles, and I can see she wants to jump up and down, like she does when she is really excited.

Lucy goes to shake his hand but stops herself. "That might not be such a good idea. Germs." The rest of us all laugh, stand and shake hands, finalizing the deal with that handshake.

Luke walks the men out and I'm left in the room with Lucy. She has a dreamy smile on her face and she sits in the closest chair, flopping back. You can tell all her stress has left, replaced with the joy of landing a big client.

I sit near her and hold her small delicate hand in mine. "You did so good, baby." I bring her hand to my lips.

She turns her head toward me and gives me a breath-taking smile. But all too soon, it is replaced with sadness. She pulls her hand away and stares at the top where my lips just were.

"Lucy, listen I think…" Before I can finish my statement, Luke walks in and interrupts us.

"Lucy, you were amazing. Congratulations! Wonderful job! But you need to go home, now. You need to get some rest and get better." Luke pulls her from the chair and directs her toward her office.

She goes along willingly but looks over her shoulder at me as she crosses the threshold of the conference room. Hope blooms in my chest. It's the most promising thing I have seen from her in weeks. I follow along after them, that small look hooking me like a fish and dragging me with her.

Luke stays in the room as Lucy gathers her things, chatting and making small talk. I don't hear any of it, I just simply stare at Lucy, waiting for the opportunity to talk to her alone.

"I'll drive you home." I say and take the keys from her hand.

"Thank you, Mason. We will see you when you are better and not a minute before that." Luke hugs Lucy goodbye and points her toward the elevator doors.

I get her settled in the car and we drive the five miles to her apartment.

"Do you need anything before we get home?"

"No, I just want to go home." She says quietly.

I find myself wanting to drive 5 mph, just to prolong the time I have with her.

All too soon we are at her door and she is leaving me behind in the hall. I'm searching for anything to stay with her. I have been mumbling gibberish, but she isn't really listening to me.

"I hope you feel better," I say still searching for something, anything.

"Thanks." She whispers and closes the door.

I stare at the door for a long second bracing my hands on the jam. I let out a long groan before turning away and going to my own. I hate what has happened. That woman behind that door is the love of my life and I need her back in my life.

My phone beeps as I enter my apartment, but I ignore it while I take off my jacket and my tie. I can't deal with the world right now. I feel like a caged tiger, ready to snap at the next zoo keeper who brings me food.

I need my girl back. I have given her space and I have let her be on her own but my life without her is just fucking awful. My family only looks at me with pity right now, Michelle keeps calling me a pussy and Checkers will hardly take my calls anymore. He came over last weekend to hang out and brought some girl with him. But by the time he arrived I was fucking wasted and don't remember shit. According to him I was blubbering like a baby and talking about how the world stopped being round when she broke up with me. Who the fuck knows what that was about?

My phone reminds me of the awaiting text. I run my hands through my hair and decide to check it before turning it off for the night. Tonight, it will be just me and a bottle of Jim Beam.

Holy fuck, it's from Lucy.

Lucy: Come back, please?

I drop my phone and rush through the door toward her. She asked me back, and now I will never ever leave her side again.

She opens the door before I can knock and I pull her straight into my arms, holding her close to me. I slam the door and pin her up against the door, her legs are wrapped around my hips and her fingers are buried in my hair. My lips find hers in a heated and passionate kiss, pouring all my feelings into it. The world is finally right again. Or like the world is round again, according to my drunk self.

I pepper her face, hair and everything I can reach with kisses. I can hear her soft giggles as I do.

"Hi," I pull back to look at her sweet smile. Her eyes are watery and happy.

"Hi. Thank you for coming back to me," she says in a small sweet whisper.

"Anything for you, baby." I carry her over to the couch and settle her on my lap.

She leans her head on my chest, snuggling close to me. And for the first time since Vegas, the 600-pound elephant that has taken up residence on my chest, is finally gone. She is back and I am never letting her go again.

"Talk to me, baby. How are you?"

"Well, not so good. I've missed you. And I'm very, very sorry for everything that happened in Vegas." Her tears are forming, and I wipe them away from the apples of her cheeks.

"Don't cry baby. It kills me to see you cry." I kiss each of her eyelids.

"But I'm sad." Her voice is sad and low.

I kiss her forehead and ask, "Why are you sad?"

"Because I missed out on six weeks with you. I want to spend forever with you, and now I get six weeks less. And I had a whole plan to win you back but then I got sick and I didn't get to do any of it." She buries her face in my neck and her body is racked with sobs.

Her words sink in and my heart feels like it might burst from my chest. "Lucy, my love. Please don't cry. I love you so much, baby. We will have forever together. It's OK. Tell me about this plan of yours."

She doesn't lift her head from my shoulder but tries to snuggle in closer. "I love you too," she mumbles into my chest.

"Can you say that again, please?" I rub my hands down her back.

Lucy sits up and turns her beautiful face to me. "I love you."

I crush my lips to hers, showing her my love and holding her close. We stay pressed together for a long time, holding each other tight. We finally pull apart, we are breathing hard and the tears on her cheeks have dried. She starts to cough, and I remember how sick she is. It takes a few moments before she stops and her breathing calms.

"Baby, we need to get you into bed."

She nods her head but doesn't move from her spot on my lap with her arms clutching me close. I chuckle and do the hard work for her, lifting her in my arms and carrying her to the bedroom.

Lucy fell asleep within seconds of getting her settled into bed and under the covers. She held me close while she slept, snaking around me like a vine. In my excitement to have her back, I forgot how sick she was and was ready to take her there on the couch. But now that she is back, I can't ever let her go again. I need to bind her to me forever.

CHAPTER FORTY-EIGHT
Lucy

It's my birthday! I love birthdays. They have been one of the best memories from my childhood. The people at the commune made a big deal about the day mother earth allowed you to exist. There was always special food and homemade presents.

Mason has some big plans for it, but it's a total surprise. I love that he likes to surprise me. We have had the greatest three weeks since being back together. He flew us down to Nevada and we spent a weekend with my parents. The first day was awkward but having Mason with me helped a lot. I was able to open up and really communicate with my parents for the first time.

"Are you ready, baby?" Mason walks into the bedroom behind me, startling me and pulling me from my thoughts.

"You scared me. I didn't hear you come in." I add the last finishing touches to my make-up.

"Once we move in together, I'll try not to do that."

"Why do we have to wait?"

"Because you don't want to break your lease yet."

I chuckle, "No! Why do we have to wait for you to stop scaring me."

He wraps his arms around my waist and pulls me close, "I'm just adding a little excitement to our relationship."

I throw my head back and let out a belly laugh, "Thank you for that."

He smiles and places his lips on mine for a long and sexy kiss. God, this man can make my toes curl.

"I'm almost ready to go, can you give me five more minutes?" I turn in his arms and he doesn't let go. We move together toward the vanity and I do my best to finish my make-up with a very sexy man attached to my back, doing everything he can to distract me. I can feel his hard erection and I wiggle just a little against him, earning a groan.

"Are you teasing me, baby?"

"Who, me?" I say in my best innocent voice.

In the next second, I am turned around and hoisted on to the counter. Mason pushes my legs wide and steps in between them. He steals my breath with a quick and fast kiss. His hands are in my hair and all the work I did to pull it up into a sexy up-do is ruined. He is holding me at just the right angle he prefers as he ravishes my mouth with his kisses.

I reach between us and work to unbutton his pant, hoping to reach inside and feel his hard length.

"Are you ready to come, birthday girl?" He asks as he reaches under the skirt of my dress, pulling my panties to the side and pushes himself inside of me.

"Yes, Mason. I need you." He lifts me from the counter and takes me to my bed, never leaving his spot buried inside me.

"You know we are going to be late now," he says moving in and out of me.

How can he even think right now? "I don't care. Harder Mason."

He chuckles and quickens his pace. "Like this?"

I throw my head back and cry out as the orgasm moves through me. He pumps three more times and follows me behind me.

"I can't wait to do that with you for the rest of our lives." I muse as I come down from my high.

He pushes back and stares into my face. "I love you, Lucy!"

"I love you, too."

"OK, time to get ready, lazy." He pulls me from the bed.

"What? I'm not lazy. We were in bed because you couldn't keep your hands off me!" I laugh.

"I can't help that I want you all the time." We walk to the bathroom, I push him out the door and close it in his face. I can hear him laugh on the other side, I rush to clean myself up and fix what he has messed up.

"Where are we going?" I ask after we are in the car.

"To dinner," he says but with no more detail.

"And where will we be having this dinner?"

He laughs at me and kisses our intertwined hands. "You will see soon, baby."

I let out a sigh and sit back, watching the road go by. We are heading toward downtown, and my mind is racing thinking of the places we could be going.

He pulls in to the parking lot at city beach and park in the mostly empty lot. The weather has still been pretty cold, but the snow is mostly gone. Mason reaches behind me and grabs two large coats from the back seat and exits the car. He walks over and opens the door for me.

"Here. You are going to need this coat." He wraps the long puffy coat that reaches down to my knees around my shoulders. He gives me a quick kiss and puts on his own coat.

He walks us down toward the pier where a large party boat is parked. Strings of lights are lining the sides of the boat.

I stop Mason before we get on the boat, "Are we going on a boat?"

He pulls me into his arms and holds me close, "Don't worry, baby. You won't fall off."

I don't believe him, and I know it shows on my face. He kisses me again and soon all the thoughts in my head are gone, only Mason and his kisses remain.

"Better?" He asks as he pulls back, we are both breathing a little heavy.

I nod my head and we get on to the large party boat. I know these boats do tours of the lake during the summer, but I didn't think they ran in the winter.

We are greeted by a man wearing a captain's hat. "Hello, Mr. Glass and Happy Birthday Ms. Harvey. Welcome aboard."

"Thank you. Is everything ready to go?"

"Yes, sir. Your guests are waiting upstairs."

Guests? OK, what is he up to!

"Great." He nods his head to the captain and guides me toward the stairs.

"Mason, what are you up to?"

He ignores my question, but I can see the smirk that forms on his lips.

We arrive at the top of the stairs and my breath leaves me. The top deck of the boat is filled with my friends and family. They yell surprise and tears cloud my vision.

Everyone I love and care about is standing on the top deck of the boat. My smile grows as I look around, seeing the happy face of my still newlywed best friend, Mason's parents who you can tell are so proud of him. And for the first time ever, I'm excited to see my parents. My second family is now mixed with my real family.

I look over to the man who has made all this happen and find Mason on his knee kneeling next to me.

My hands fly to my face and I am completely in shock.

"Lucy, I love you so much. The day you walked in to my life was the best day of my life and now I can't imagine a life without you.

"Will you marry me, Lucy?"

It takes me a second before I throw myself into Mason arms and pepper his face with kisses. He lifts me into the air spins me around to the hoots and hollers of the crowd. Our lips meet, and

I kiss him with everything I have in me. Mason has changed everything about me in the seven months we have known each other. He helped me to be more confident and be sure of myself. He has shown what real love in a relationship really means.

He pulls back and leans his forehead onto mine. "Is that a yes?"

I simply nod my head, my throat to thick with emotion.

"Sorry, baby. I have to hear you say it out loud."

I chuckle, clear my throat, and yell out the biggest YES I can muster.

He smiles the widest and most handsome smile I have ever seen.

CHAPTER FORTY-NINE
Lucy

Three months later.

"Are you sure you want to do this?"

"Yes, Callie. I'm sure that I want the hydrangeas in the centerpieces and the cream table linens. "

Callie has been trying to get me to have an all glitter wedding but that is not our style at all.

"Fine, have a wedding with no bling. But just know it is all on you." She gives me her best pout and walks down the next aisle of Hobby Lobby.

We are three weeks until the wedding and the whole planning experience has been amazing. Between Callie, Christine and even my mom, I have had more help than I could have ever hoped for. Even Mason has been a complete dream. He is involved and makes the decisions when I ask but he has let me make it into my dream wedding.

I have a little surprise for him on our wedding night. In six short months we are going to be parents. I haven't told anyone yet and it's killing me. Every time Mason walks into the room, I have to stop myself from screaming out my news at the top of my lungs.

My phone rings as I stare longing at the online baby shower decorations. "Hey Pac."

"Hi baby," Oh how fitting a nickname of this very moment. "How is shopping going."

"It's good. Callie is still trying to talk me into glitter but I'm holding strong. How is the moving going?"

"Good, Check and the boys have everything out of the apartments and we are heading over to the new house. Want to order pizza for dinner?"

"That sounds perfect! I'll order it for everyone and have there in an hour. Do you need beer too?"

"Beer sounds good for us boys, but what is my pregnant fiancé going to drink?"

I stop in my tracks and stare down at my phone. "What? How did you figure it out?"

"Baby, I can read your mind. Plus, you have been crying at everything, your boobs are way more sensitive than before and your Amazon viewing history is pages and pages of baby stuff instead of wedding items."

"Oh, are you mad I haven't told you yet?"

"No, baby. I have a feeling you were planning a big surprise for me."

"Yeah, I guess I'm not so good at the surprise."

"Leave the surprises up to me, little momma. I'll see you at the new house in a little bit."

"I love you, Daddy!" It's hard to keep the excitement out of my voice. This little peanut might not have been planned but it is still a miracle. Mason is going to be the most amazing dad and I can't wait to be a mom.

"I love you too, Momma!" I can hear the smile in his voice.

I hang up with Mason and smile down at my phone. He is my perfect match, my happily ever after.

"Did you just call Mason, Daddy? Are you pregnant?" I hear the squeal from behind me.

Oops! I guess Callie knows now, too.

About the Author

Growing up, S.R. Mullins was always told to "Write what you know about." So, living in Coeur d'Alene, Idaho, this beautiful backdrop was inspiration for this book.

A phenomenal baker, S.R. is also a particular foodie. If you ever find yourself in Coeur d'Alene, visit the restaurants Lucy and Mason frequented, you might just fall in love with their offerings as well.

S. R. is an avid romance fan herself and loves the opportunity to create and share with the world stories of love.

Facebook
www.facebook.com/srmullinsauthor
Twitter
www.twitter.com/srmullinsauthor
Instagram
@srmullinsauthor
Goodreads
www.goodreads.com/author/show/18165435.S_R_Mullins